MW01670755

HARBINGER

HARBINGER

DAVID JAMES BRIGHT

Hobbes End Publishing, LLC

Harbinger
by David James Bright
Published by Hobbes End Publishing, LLC, a division of Hobbes End Entertainment, LLC

Harbinger
All rights reserved.
Copyright 2014, David James Bright

ISBN: 978-0-9859110-6-5

Produced by Vincent Hobbes
Cover and internal design: Jordan Benoit

The sale of this book without its cover is unauthorized. If you purchased this book without a cover, you should be aware that it was reported to the publisher as "unsold and destroyed." Neither the author nor the publisher has received payment for the sale of the "stripped book."

This product is a work of fiction. Names, characters, places and incidents are either the product of the authors' imagination or used fictitiously. Any resemblance to actual events or locales or persons, living or dead, is entirely coincidental.

Without limiting the rights under copyright reserved above, no part of this publication may be reproduced, stored in or introduced into a retrieval system, or transmitted, in any form, or by any means (electronic, mechanical, photocopying, recording, or otherwise), without written, express permission from Hobbes End Entertainment, LLC. The scanning, uploading, and distribution of this book via the Internet or via any other means without the permission of the publisher is illegal and punishable by law. Please purchase only authorized electronic editions, and do not participate in or encourage electronic piracy of copyrighted materials. Your support of the authors' rights is appreciated.

Harbinger is the sole property of Hobbes End. All artwork, cover, and characters are exclusively owned and licensed by Hobbes End Entertainment, LLC and Hobbes End Publishing, LLC accordingly. All rights reserved to Hobbes End Entertainment, LLC. This includes the right to reproduce this book or portions thereof in any form whatsoever.

For information, contact:
Hobbes End Entertainment, LLC
PO Box 193
Aubrey, TX 76227
www.hobbesendpublishing.com

For Mom and Dad.
Without your love and support
I wouldn't have made it this far.
Rest in peace, Father.

SPECIAL THANKS

Harmony Schmitt
AJ Llaneza
Adrienne Lombardo
Evan West

HARBINGER

One

Mitch Joiner was the first in town to realize something was wrong. He realized it only a brief moment after stepping out from his gated yard onto the worn, cracked sidewalk running alongside Bell Street.

Whenever he noticed the sign or was reminded of his address, Mitch would internally scoff the name of the street on which he lived. He knew the man for which Bell Street had been named, Jimmy Bell, and that man had been nothing but a two timing shyster. His living relatives were no different. It was hard to imagine, when one looked at the white trash the Bell family had become, that they used to be one of the most prominent families in Rowley, highlighted by the boisterous and portly mayor, Jimmy Bell.

That job should have been mine, Mitch would think with a pent up bitterness that only grew uglier over the years.

It was ironic Mitch had ended up living on the street bearing the name of his past rival. Jimmy Bell was the one man Mitch could never settle his grudge with and living on the street was a constant reminder of a personal failure he'd never been able to get over.

That day however, when Mitch Joiner stepped onto Bell Street, he didn't think about the festering hatred he harbored for the late Jimmy Bell, or any of his wretched spawn who still populated the town. That day, Mitch could only notice one thing; and that thing was a peculiar absence.

Where the hell are all the birds?

Mitch Joiner had gone for a morning jog every day of his life since he was twenty, and the streak was still well alive fifty-one years later. It was a habit he prided himself on, and he made sure to bring the fact up every time he encountered a new acquaintance.

Regardless of the circumstances, Mitch had never missed a single day of his routine. If he was out of town he made sure to get up at the crack of dawn and take a jog. If he had early responsibilities to attend to on the upcoming day he would get up even earlier. Jogging was Mitch's way of getting away from the past and assuring himself he would never suffer the same fate as his parents.

Mitch Joiner had watched two parents die in their early fifties—his father's heart no longer able to supply blood to the bloated body years of unchecked gluttony had given him, and his mother a victim of lung cancer due to thirty years of smoking.

Because of those events, Mitch had decided he would not follow in the habits of his parents. He would be fit and trim, and live a long healthy life, free of concern from matters of health and longevity.

Even at seventy-one he could run two miles without stopping, and a third if he was feeling particularly limber and energetic. He had always taken pride in the fact he was in better shape than most of the lazy children of the town. The old man had some step, and he figured with how well he had treated himself over the years he would live to be one hundred.

He was wrong.

The birds weren't chirping that day. Not a single peep could be heard from either side of the eerily silent Bell Street. This struck Mitch as strange; almost every time he had gone to take his daily jogs (save for the times it was down-pouring, times which he stilled trucked through the weather for his run) the birds were singing happily all up and down the street. There were sparrows and blue-jays and cardinals, all delightful little beings gracing the morning with their song.

For a man who was so bitter toward his past and people in the present, the carefree innocent sound of the birds always provided him a moment of peace and relaxation. It was like experiencing the wonderful feelings of the birds he had never been able to attain on his own.

But today there was nothing.

Just dead silence.

Not only did he not hear any birds, Mitch didn't hear any resonance of sound at all. There were no birds, there was no sound of distant cars, no sound of a loose piece of trash scraping across the street.

Just dead silence.

This shouldn't have been all that unusual. Rowley was a sleepy town of two thousand residents, with one traffic light and no bustling nightlife or packed morning commutes. At ten before six it wasn't a shocker to have the streets barren of people and vehicles, but Mitch still couldn't shake the suspicion something wasn't right.

Then Mitch saw the fog creeping in, moving from the intersection of Bell and River Street, gravitating toward him with a speed fog shouldn't possess. At first he couldn't put his finger on exactly why it disturbed him—it wasn't like hadn't jogged in inclement weather other the years. Rain, sleet, snow, or hail, Mitch had gone right on jogging.

But there was something wrong with this mist, the way it seemed to be moving, gravitating, and creeping toward where he stood. It almost moved like it was *alive,* which Mitch knew was ridiculous.

Even still, something inside him was screaming to run far, far away. *There's bad news coming your way, Mitch. Bad, bad news. We're not talking about those Bunzler boys who used to beat you up in the schoolyard back in your old days. Oh no, we're talking about the real bad stuff, the type of stuff that puts you in the ground. We're talking about a one way trip to hell coming right at you, Mitch!*

As Mitch looked at the fog he noticed it morphing and changing. Questions flew through his mind at a rapid pace and he barely had the wherewithal to process them.

Has it grown thicker? Was Mitch's mind deceiving him? *And is it moving faster?* Mitch felt his heart kick-start and pump adrenaline through his veins, his instincts telling him something his rational mind could not quite understand: *run for your life.*

The glow of the rising sun had faded, and was now completely consumed by the thick, billowing fog. In fact, everything it seemed to creep by disappeared within it, becoming consumed and lost within a void. Mitch shuddered involuntarily and for just a moment, for the first time in his life, he felt old.

You're old, feeble, and scared. You're scared of the past, you're scared of the present, and you're scared of your future where you're bound to end up in a casket. No one is going to attend your funeral, Mitch Joiner, because you're a crotchety old geezer that rubs everyone the wrong way! The thoughts in his head were stinging, they were thoughts he did not want to confront, and they were thoughts that even seemed foreign.

Mitch snapped out of it, shaking his head back and forth. The thought of going into his home and back to bed was fleeting and not given fair consideration. He was far too proud to give up the routine which was a staple of his identity. Still, he didn't want to jog into the fog and his usual route would have to be diverted. He couldn't risk injury due to low visibility after all.

Is that really the reason you're avoiding it? The thought that flashed through his mind was alienating. *You're scared and you should be. Run away, old man! Run as fast as those feeble little legs can carry you!*

Mitch shook it off and began jogging down Bell, going the opposite way of the bizarre fog and toward Washington Street. He could take a left there and make a little route by going onto Smith and then Overlook. There was a bit of a hill there but the route was shorter so the harder work would make up for it.

Mitch jogged, sporadically looking back over his shoulder to check if the fog was gaining on him. It was an irrational fear, and he hated himself for having it, but the paranoid sensation building up within him just refused to be quelled.

Run, you old coot! Get those creaky knees going! Don't slip up now!

As his jog progressed and he made his way onto Washington, he began to relax and rid himself of the lingering feelings of paranoia. There couldn't be anything wrong, nothing was unnatural about the morning—it was just some fog the weatherman had overlooked. The weather reports weren't all that reliable anyway. Maybe the birds had sensed the approaching bad weather and flew off; nothing which had happened that morning was concrete evidence of anything unusual.

Can't rely on the news station, the papers, or anyone in or around this little dirt-hole of a town, Mitch thought bitterly. Despite living all of his seventy-one years in Rowley, his harsh feelings toward the town had never subsided. His criticisms ran deep, however none of those thoughts or feelings ever compelled Mitch to leave.

Mitch was a small town man used to small town living,

and unbeknownst to him he never truly knew anything but a deep seated hatred toward everyone and everything not quite like himself.

Sure, Mitch Joiner would give you a handshake, give you some pleasant small talk and a pat on the back if you had good news, but under the facade was a man who wanted nothing to do with you or your way of life. Mitch Joiner wanted his own realm, his daily jog, his comfortable house, and people who were like him. Mitch couldn't relate to the residents of Rowley; they were out of shape, ignorant, and petulant in all matters. Though truly almost every citizen in Rowley harbored the same viewpoint and resentment toward the town as he did, and though he never knew it, Mitch Joiner was perfectly suited for the town of Rowley, Pennsylvania.

As his jog went on, he couldn't help but find his thoughts shifting back to Jimmy Bell, and how that "fat lug" had stolen the mayoral election away from him some forty years earlier. It was true that Jimmy Bell had won the popular vote but he had deceived the population into voting for him by making crooked deals and slandering Mitch behind his back.

It never occurred to Mitch that he only wanted the job to have the authority to boss others around and make them see his point of view. His intolerance toward other opinions would certainly have created great conflict. He wanted to make others think like him, to mimic him and his way of life so Rowley could reach all of its potential.

And why shouldn't everyone think like him? Mitch Joiner was an America-loving, God-fearing man, who was bound to live to the ripe old age of one hundred and five, and—

Lost in feelings and memories of the past, Mitch Joiner

failed to keep track of his stride as he began to jog up the incline of Overlook Street. His foot struck the sidewalk, toe hitting the concrete before the sole of his shoe, and he lost his balance, sprawling on the ground.

Mitch didn't have time to brace himself as he fell, only managing to wiggle his body to the side in mid-air in order to avoid a nasty face-plant. He felt a hot, sharp dagger of pain slice into his side as two of his brittle ribs cracked. Despite the ability to run every day, avoiding arthritis, obesity, and heart conditions, Mitch Joiner could not outrun Father Time completely.

"Oof! Owww!" He wheezed as he lay on the unforgiving concrete writhing in pain. He felt a searing agony setting his rib-cage on fire, but the physical pain was only the initial sting—on top of it all he felt insulted.

Mitch didn't view himself as a decrepit old man; he had experienced countless falls in his life and gotten up just fine. He had taken perfect care of his body and one stumble had led to this? How could this happen to him? How could a simple fall break *his* ribs? Mitch Joiner was not helpless and he didn't need doctors advising him not to run or to take it easy at his age. He could outperform almost all of them in a fitness test and he would be damned to believe they would age as well as he had. But as he helplessly laid on the sidewalk, he realized none of that actually mattered.

Mitch was faced with the reality of aging as he dealt with his wounds, breathing heavily with his hands clenched tightly to his side. Every breath was painful, but the hurtful sensations only seemed to increase his breathing and make it more laborious, contributing to a vicious cycle of pain.

"You're breaking down! Time to put you out to pasture, you old fuck!" The voice he heard in his head oddly was not his own, but was one from the past. The scalding insults came to him in the voice of Jimmy Bell, the fat old bastard taunting him from beyond the grave.

"I'm . . . not . . . old," he huffed to no one as he used his last bit of pride to push himself to a seated position. Then he managed to climb to his feet. He refused to be found lying pathetically on the side of the road. Oh what noise that would make throughout the gossip-ridden town.

Just as his frustration was rising to a peak, it suddenly dropped off and disappeared, replaced by a powerful sense of trepidation.

The fog was back.

How had he not noticed it? Wasn't it just clear a moment ago? There might have been a little mist but this was much more than that. It had overtaken him so quickly, he hadn't even the time to realize it.

It was the same fog, the exact same batch of fog from before. Mitch just knew it, and the fact he instinctively did know it frightened him badly. It had rapidly crept over him and consumed him while he was focusing on his throbbing ribs. The pain and humiliation from his injuries was now eons away as he dealt with the return of his frantic paranoia.

It wasn't normal fog, it almost seemed to be constantly moving, constantly *consuming*. It was unnaturally thick, to the point where visibility was instantaneously cut off. In a matter of moments, Mitch had gone from jogging up the hill under clear conditions to being unable to see across the street. He had been pulled into some strange gray void, and as it continued enveloping him, he began to notice it was even difficult to see houses on the same side of the street. They were becoming shadows and fading away before his eyes. Soon even the fence five feet from where he stood would become a shadow, and then a gray nothingness within the fog.

His heart race increased. His breathing followed suit with his heart, his lungs working fast despite the pain it caused his ribs. The pain was too far away to recognize now, and all thoughts of it faded entirely when he noticed the smell.

It was acrid, the smell of death mixed in with some type of burning smell—no, the smell of something that *had* been burnt and now was smoldering. It was arid and dead, the air suddenly thin and devoid of moisture and life, filled only with this strange, terrible essence.

It was the essence Mitch imagined floated around crematoriums, only this had to be thicker. This was stronger. This was death. It wasn't even something that could be described as the smell of death but the actual *essence* of death, the very emotion and energy that came with it.

This isn't real, this can't be real. You can't smell death! It's some garbage on the side of someone's house, or some road-kill. People can't sense death! Mitch's thoughts ran rampant as fear took rule of his conscience.

"Don't run, Mitch. Stay and chat. Come catch up with your old pal Jimmy! We can talk about that election I kicked your sorry ass in!" Every hair on Mitch's body stood on end. Had he heard those words or simply thought them? He wasn't sure his ears had picked up anything but he could have sworn he truly *heard* Jimmy Bell's voice from somewhere in the fog.

No, no I didn't. That's crazy talk! I'm just freaking out a little.

Everything is fine.

But still, despite his rational protest, Mitch knew something was wrong.

He had to run.

It was then his other senses kicked in even further, spurred by his flight or fight style reaction. His ears physically heard nothing, but there was something he could detect, something he could hear in his mind.

It was like white noise all around him, an odd silent static in the air penetrating its way into his head. Mitch wasn't exactly sure what it was or how to describe it, but he did know he hated it.

Then he heard something more.

Jimmy Bell's laughter, as clear as day. It mixed in with the static—no, it was *a part* of the static. Mitch couldn't tell but as the noises filled up his head he was able to discern one thing: the sounds were evil. Its existence was wrong, its makeup was wicked, and he wanted to get as far away from the white noise as possible.

But he's dead! Jimmy's dead! And—

"AHAHAHAHAHA! I'm right here, Mitch! I never left you, you old sack of shit!"

His eyes began scanning all around him and, to his dismay, he realized visibility had become limited to a mere arm's length. He stuck his arm out into the fog and barely could make out the shape of his hand in front of his face.

His breathing now came at a furious pace as panicked fear held the reigns, and suddenly he could taste it. He could taste the fog, he could taste the death. It was all around him, it was taking him in, and he was becoming a part of it.

He wanted to run, but knew this would be a near impossible task. He turned with haste and began walking down the incline of Overlook Street at a brisk pace, grinding his teeth together as the reality of his cracked ribs found its way back into his head in the form of sharp, stabbing pains to his side. He was breaking free from the terrible white noise, and now he could only hear the dull thud of his own footsteps. They would echo off into the fog then stop abruptly, as if some invisible wall was containing the sound around him.

Mitch walked faster and faster with a desperate need to get off Overlook Street and escape the all-consuming fog. But why wasn't he already at Washington? He was barely up the incline when he fell onto the sidewalk, so he should have been only a few paces away from the intersection. How far had he gone, fifteen steps, twenty? Where was Washington Street? Why was he still walking down the small slope of an incline? The hill shouldn't have gone on that long—it wasn't right. At that moment nothing was right.

Mitch stopped, attempting to survey his surroundings. The effort was in vain, for he could only see the small patch of cracked sidewalk directly below his feet, and everywhere else was just a blanket of gray. It was impossible to see anything at all, and besides the sidewalk below him there was no detectable evidence Mitch was even in a town.

There was no sight, no sound—just nothing.

Nothing but the fog.

Fog and Death. He shuddered and made the motions to keep walking when the sudden noise froze him in his tracks.

On a normal day such a small sound would have gone unnoticed to Mitch who, although he would not admit it, had a waning sense of hearing. Today was different; today the place he found himself in was free of all sounds to the point where even the slightest noise would jump out as a bellowing sound. This is why the slight *whoosh* caught his attention and had him standing straight and erect, on guard for whatever was near.

Was that wind, or maybe a piece of clothing? His mind searched for plausible answers with a frenzied desperation. Mitch's mind tried to associate the noise he heard—sheets blowing and whipping in the wind was the closest comparison he could find. Was he near someone's home?

No, there was no wind; the air was stagnant. Something had moved, and whatever it was had moved not far from where he was standing, just off to his right. How far he couldn't tell, he was becoming disoriented due to his sensory perceptions being rendered useless.

Whoosh. It happened again, this time closer, and this time behind him. Had it been behind him before? Mitch wasn't sure but he didn't think so. Whatever was moving was moving around him.

Circling me, entrapping me, just like the fog. His thoughts were tormenting.

Then he heard it, a sound that was simple and not overly loud, but for some reason it was the most terrible sound Mitch had ever heard in his life. It came from behind him, and although it was low, Mitch could tell the sound was closer than the whoosh preceding it.

Tssskkktcchhnntcch. Tsskkchnnnkkchtth. It was like the air was being let out of a balloon, yet the sound also had a strained quality, a grinding, gurgling quality. It was barely a whisper but to Mitch it was powerful. It was an evil growl, the type of noise some nightmarish cockroach would make.

Tsskkcchhshhhnssncchk. It hissed again, this time much closer, and although the whisper-like hiss was the same tone as before, Mitch could sense something new: hunger.

Mitch ran. There was no consideration for the glaring pain in his side, or worry he may fall and injury himself again—this was life or death. Whatever made that noise was something awful, something Mitch could only imagine in his worst nightmares.

And it wanted him, it *craved* him.

Where the hell is Washington Street? I should be close to home by now with the way I'm running! How the hell am I still on Overlook?

Suddenly the voice of Jimmy Bell jumped into his head to answer his question.

"Oh, you're not on Overlook, Mitch! You're in the fog! Come join me and my buddies out here in it. Stay for a while, heck, stay forever! You and I will have plenty of time to settle our differences. Just fall on the ground and accept it! Give in and take the reaper's hand!"

Mitch wasn't sure he was still on Overlook, or even if he was still in Rowley. He saw no signs of life, no signs of a town, no way to discern where he was or what in the world was going on. The thing that made the least amount of sense, on top of everything else, was he still seemed to be on the exact same patch of sidewalk where he had fallen. It was as if he had kept running and come back to the same place, but that was absurd.

Wasn't it?

Tssskkkknnnnncchhhttt. The hiss seemed more desperate now. Mitch abandoned the sidewalk, running off the pavement and into the grass toward whatever house was next to this particular bit of sidewalk. Was it the Martins who lived at the beginning of Overlook, or that bachelor John Wisham? It didn't matter. Mitch would be overjoyed to get into any house—to get inside and away from the terrible fog and whatever lurked behind it.

He stumbled, gasping as he nearly fell again, but waved his arms and was somehow able to maintain his balance. He continued running across the patch of grass, surely heading toward a home and guaranteed safety.

Why is it taking so long? I should be at a house by now! He panted and his mind ran wild. *There's no patch of grass this big near Overlook, only a few small lawns! I should have hit someone's house already! I should be safe! What in God's name is going on?*

Tsskkknnnnnntchhkknntch.

"You can't run, Mitch! You can't beat me, you never could!" Mitch wasn't sure whether he truly heard Jimmy's voice again or whether he had deciphered the words from the hiss.

Finally, he emerged from the grass, but was near no home. He felt his shoes walking on pavement, as if he was walking across an angle, a slope.

Horrified, Mitch Joiner looked down and realized he was on the same patch of Overlook Street he had started on. He had run into the grass and come out on the same street. It was impossible, it was absolutely impossible. He hadn't got turned around, and hadn't retraced his own steps. He had run in a straight line and ended up in the exact same place in which he started. This certainly was Overlook—it was the only road with a hill like this in the entire town. It was unmistakable.

Complete madness trapped Mitch. The pain in his side was now becoming intolerable. He wanted to fall down, to lie on the street pathetically and wait for someone to help him. Any semblance of pride was now long gone; Mitch would swallow his ego to get out of this terrible dreamscape in which he was trapped.

Whoosh. He saw a dark shape streak across the fog in front of him, only feet from where he stood. Was it flying? *No, more like gliding, but how . . . what? What could move like that?*

Whoosh. This time it came from beside him—he could feel the air around him move and that's when the sensation hit him.

Mitch felt the air be sucked from his lungs, something yanking the wind right out of him. He lost his breath, and felt both cold and hopeless.

It wasn't the type of cold that came on a snowy winter day; Mitch had weathered his fair share of those over his years. This type of cold was different, the type of cold that radiated in the bones, refusing to go away. Mitch was chilled to the core, his was frozen and he felt any trace of warmth or happiness fade from his body.

He tried to breathe to bring life back into his being, but received nothing. The air had lost the quality making it air; no life could be supported by the cold aura surrounding him. There wasn't anything that could live amongst this dead, unforgiving fog, yet something was moving amongst it. Something was coming.

It was a Harbinger of Death. It was the bringing of what was to come.

Mitch stood mouth agape, shaking uncontrollably and ignoring the piss running down his leg, visible as a long dark stain in his blue running shorts.

Whoosh. Whoosh. Whoosh. The dark figure moved with dizzying speed as it circled him, drawing closer and closer with each pass. Mitch felt himself pushed to the brink of madness by the inability to discover exactly what it was.

Then it stopped, closer than ever. He saw its tall elongated outline, its shadowy form barely five feet from where he stood, still mostly obscured by the thick fog. It moved unnaturally, jerking in ways Mitch had never even imagined. It also moved slowly, as if it was calculating its motion, sizing him up.

Or just playing with me, he thought, panicked.

Tcchhnnnkkkktssssshhttttch. Mitch took a step backward.

Tssschchkknnnntchhhhnnntth.

Whoosh. He spun around and there it was, barely three feet in front of him now. He whipped around to run again.

Whoosh. It stood before him. The assailant was dark and concealed by the fog—no *blended in* with the fog. It was as if the massive figure was a dark, wispy part of the mist itself.

"What are you? What the fuck are you? Jesus save me oh please Lord save me!" Mitch, who claimed to be a follower but only attended service once a year, fell to his knees and begged, the tears trailing from his face now gushing out at a faster rate than the urine that formed a puddle around him.

"Get the hell away from me!" There was no authoritative tone to his voice. Whatever this thing was, Mitch could do nothing but beg for its mercy—if it was even capable of grasping the concept.

And for a moment it did stop. Barely an arm's length away from Mitch it stopped, and for an instant Mitch almost mustered the courage to look directly at it, but no—that was something he dared not do. This thing was something his mind did not want to see; eyes trained on the ground, he began reciting the Lord's Prayer.

Then with impossible speed, it jumped the few feet between itself and Mitch in less time than Mitch's mind could perceive.

He felt a sick, wet ripping sensation as the creature effortlessly dug into his midsection and tore a chunk out of his stomach, nearly ripping out his entrails in the process. Mitch could hear the sound of his blood pouring out of his body and splashing onto the street below.

Mitch fell without struggle or sound. His body approached a state of shock as it struggled to deal with the massive damage done in less than a second. Without any strain the thing had dug into his body and nearly ripped him in half.Mitch reached down to assess the damage. He felt a wet, pulpy mess. There was drippy, torn meat and slippery tubes amongst the mix he realized once had been his intestines. He grasped them and they moved along as easily as silly string. Vomit, combined with thick clumps of blood, shot up his throat and spurted out his lips. The spray came back down and splattered Mitch's face, burning his eyes. Mitch moaned with agony, and the world started to become fuzzy.

His entrails now decorated the sidewalk and death would come soon—death would be a welcomed escape from the choking fear, the suffocating fog, and the evil, demented creature.

As Mitch Joiner was approaching his exit from this world, he felt the blood pooled around his body cool, he felt his lungs stop working, and he felt his heart skip a beat as the beast moved over him.

Then he saw it; the culmination of every nightmare Mitch had ever had was staring him in the face, and countless more he never imagined grinned down at him. His mind couldn't comprehend it, he was driven over the edge of insanity in one brief, awful moment seeming to span into eternity.

Jimmy Bell started laughing again and it was the last sound Mitch Joiner ever heard. Then came the teeth. Countless teeth. Ripping. Tearing. Consuming.

Mitch left the world with his body convulsing in the purest form of agony, his conscience petrified by the sight of Hell itself.

Two

It was chasing him, and it was gaining fast. The darkness, the creature, the ungodly horror was coming for him and at this rate it was going to catch him. He cried out, reaching blindly for anyone or anything that could help him.

But he was alone.

Isolated.

Stranded.

Oh how it wanted him, it wanted to have him, to *consume* him, to make him part of the never ending darkness. It could have whatever it wanted, there was no way he could stop it.

Would he die? Or would he suffer a soulless eternity?

Swipe. It reached, almost grabbing him, and he shouted out as he felt the back of his shirt ripping, beads of sweat nearly blinding him as he ran down the empty street.

Where was anyone? Where was anything? No one could help him, no one could save him. It was getting dark, it was getting cold, and the consumer was here.

No one could stop its hunger.

Nearly running into the brick wall in front of him, he saw it spread out as far as the eye could see in either direction. He was trapped.

A rat in a maze.

The test was over.

Termination.

There it was, approaching slowly, methodically. Approaching as slow as it possibly could, exasperating his fear to its highest peak before it would move in and torture him, playing with its meal before taking him in forever.

Eternity.

He opened his mouth to scream and the darkness came closer—the consumer of man and soul, that's what it was. The reality was dawning upon him as it crept nearer. He could almost see it coming into shape.

And he could hold his scream no longer.

Ben Dowling shot up out of bed mid-scream, unaware of how loud his bellows were or how long they had been going on. A thick coat of sweat soaked him, his t-shirt and boxer shorts sticking to his body, but he didn't notice this, he was still screaming.

His bedroom door burst open and in rushed Laura Dowling, spurred by a mother's instinct still, despite the fact Ben was twenty years old.

Her blue eyes were frantic, alive with a fire burning furiously with a passion to protect her son. "Ben! What's wrong?"

Ben's scream was cut short as he turned and saw his mother. Her eyes were wild, the same light, icy blue eyes he had himself. Her hair color was passed on to him as well, a deep reddish brown, although the rest of his physical looks bore a closer resemblance to his father.

The sight of his mother calmed him. He wasn't alone; he wasn't stuck with that *thing*.

There was an awkward moment of silence as they stared at each other, the only noise their individual panting breaths.

"B-bad dream. That's . . . that's all." Ben finally sputtered.

Ben saw the motherly instinct fade from Laura Dowling's face, replaced by frustration laced with a fair amount of disappointment.

"Come on, Ben, you're twenty years old. You're going to wake up the whole neighborhood just because of a bad dream? You almost gave me a heart attack." Her tone was light, but the words held a critical sting.

Ben was still gaining his composure after jumping out of such a nightmare. "I know, Mom. I'm sorry, it just was such an awful dream. Never had one that bad." His shaken tone seemed to convince his mother, and her loving instincts kicked back in.

"Well, don't worry about it. I guess you never outgrow bad dreams, huh? I know what will make it better. How about some of my famous chocolate chip pancakes?" She looked hopeful that her mother's touch could quickly douse any remaining disturbed feelings.

Ben did his best to act excited for the sake of his mother—he certainly did love her pancakes, they were the best he ever had—but pancakes wouldn't remedy the haunting memories of that dream.

It just seemed so real.

"Pancakes sound great, Mom. Just what I need."

"Wonderful. I'll have 'em ready in a jiffy." With that she exited, leaving Ben to his thoughts.

His recollection of what happened in the dream was becoming hazy now, *foggy*. Whatever had tormented him didn't seem to be a product of his imagination; it seemed far too real, far too close.

Ben sighed and got out of bed, hoping maybe the pancakes would take his mind off the nightmare. He doubted anything could take his mind off it, but pancakes were certainly worth a try.

He walked over a stray shirt on the floor and made his way over to his closet, directly opposite his bed. Greeting him on the closet door was a poster of Spiderman, spinning a web upward and swinging through the cityscape. Ben often got flak from friends, and even his parents, about how he kept his room decorated with things from his childhood—he was a man now, shouldn't his room reflect that?

Ben opened his closet door and rummaged through his shirts, finding his work shirt, blue with the words "Braylon's

Market" stitched in small red letters on the front right. Glancing back at his bedside clock, he saw it was only fifteen past eight. He didn't have to be into work for another three hours, but he needed out of his soaking clothes and it wouldn't do any harm to be ready early.

He moved to his dresser, not bothering to close the closet door, and opened the top drawer to fetch a pair of boxers and a pair of socks, then the second drawer to get his jeans. He changed in front of the mirror hanging on the wall over his squat dresser, not paying too much attention to his lean body.

Why should my room have to reflect that I'm older? Ben thought. Looking at the top of his dresser he noticed some of the treasured possessions of his youth: a Gameboy, trading cards, and a Street Shark action figure. *Aren't we supposed to celebrate getting older? Why do so many people hate it then? Just because you enjoy your childhood memories doesn't mean you can't be an adult. People only want to forget the past if they regret it.*

Ben didn't regret his past, nor was he regretting his present, but his parents seemed to think he did. He was on summer break after his sophomore year at Allegheny State University, but that was a place he didn't want to be—it was a place he had never wanted to be.

Ben had only one career path in mind. Ben had a boundless imagination, part of him felt it was why he held onto the imaginative characters of his childhood. He wanted to be a writer. He wanted to captivate people and spur their thoughts and imagination.

Why did he have to go to a university for that? Why should

he have to pay money for four years, and take two years of classes having absolutely nothing to do with his dream of being a writer? What would a piece of paper say about the quality of his ideas or the craft of his storytelling?

Ben had tried to express this to his parents over two years ago, but they would have nothing of it. It didn't matter that Ben had already finished a novel by the age of eighteen, or that the novel drew the attention of several literary agents who took long, long looks at it before eventually turning it down. It didn't matter that he already had four short stories published in some well-known literary magazines, or that he had made himself a handsome profit (at least for someone his age) off of them. His potential wasn't a concern to his parents, Bill and Laura Dowling only wanted their son to be a success *in a conventional way.*

In a small town like Rowley, kids had two options. One was stay and do nothing with their lives, becoming a part of the ever growing white trash population putting a dent into the welfare system. Two was get the hell out. There were no jobs in Rowley and certainly no opportunities for college graduates. A sign of success in the small town was getting away from it and moving onto bigger, better ventures. That's what Ben's parents envisioned for him; that was exactly what they wanted to show the community.

But Ben didn't want to leave. *How is that a bad thing*? Ben wanted to accomplish, Ben wanted to work, Ben wanted to fulfill his dreams—but that didn't mean he had to leave Rowley. In many ways he thought he was the only person who even liked the town. It had a quaint, small town charm, and was surrounded by some of the most beautiful rolling hills and forests in Pennsylvania. It was a far cry from the chaotic hustle and bustle of any city life. Sure, some of the people were a bit bitter, but the area itself was gorgeous and peaceful. It was what Ben wanted.

But that doesn't matter, Ben lamented. He didn't want to disappoint or upset his parents, he loved them both dearly. He had agreed to go on scholarship to Allegheny State University, across the state just north of Pittsburgh. It was a prestigious school with a golden track record. His parents were overjoyed when he finally agreed to go, but his experience there had been fairly miserable.

Whereas he was criticized for at times being too child-like, he found people at college more child-like than he could ever be.

They drank to get shit-faced, banged for the sake of banging, and ran around doing anything wild just to keep their attention. It was fast paced, like a bunch of children being set free on the world and now living out their most immature fantasies. It wasn't about making real friends or accomplishing real goals. The kids there wanted to party and enjoy the moment, while setting themselves up for a mediocre job that would put food on the table. Ben couldn't relate to anyone there.

The people were not the only problem; Ben quickly found that his writing classes, taught by so called "professionals," were nothing but a joke. Each professor taught "their" way of writing and interpreting, and each claimed to have a monopoly on the knowledge of what made a good story. Ben thought this was their own way of justifying their own styles—and perhaps on many levels their own failures, but he had never brought it up. He remembered one particular encounter:

"And you have to figure out just what is the PURPOSE of your story. You have to know right away what MESSAGE and what MEANING you are trying to convey." Professor Kennison flailed his scrawny arms with each emphasis.

Ben decided to play devil's advocate. He raised his hand.

"Yes, Benjamin?" Kennison was not fond of shortened versions of students' names.

"What if your purpose is simply to write a good story? Isn't that meaning in itself?"

Kennison chuckled. "That's naivety. Anyone can write a story that is interesting, but only the talented authors can write something that is MEANINGFUL."

"But how is something that is interesting not meaningful? Interest has to mean something if people choose to read it. Who is to say what is more meaningful to whom? The story might MEAN a lot of different things to a lot of different people."

"That is a post-modernist stance, Benjamin. You have to take into account what you as the WRITER intend, not what a hodge-podge of people will make of it."

"Both are what matter." Ben was more serious now. "Isn't creativity meaningful, and isn't sharing a vision and a whole world with someone meaningful? I mean, I'm not saying it's wrong to have a moral message or meaning to your story, but that doesn't mean it's the only thing that's right. Creativity is an extension of the human soul, of what makes people beautiful, and I think we can all find different ways of appreciating that." For added effect Ben put the professor on the spot. "Don't you?"

His speech was met by a steady rise of applause and the reddened embarrassed face of his professor. For Ben it was a temporary moment of triumph, but he would never receive a grade above a B in Kennison's course for the rest of the semester, despite the fact he was easily the most talented writer in the class. It was the way of the game—and Ben didn't want to play it anymore.

He sighed as he adjusted his shirt, tugging and pulling until it fit just right. He didn't bother with the tufts of his hair, poking out wildly in all directions, waves and curls going here and there. His hair wasn't that long, but it was long enough to give him a shaggy dog appearance when unkempt.

"Ben, the first batch is coming up!" he heard his mother's voice call. This put a smile on his face, which seemed to brighten up entirely. The memories of the terrible dream had now all but faded.

Then Ben glanced out of his window.

Fog.

Ben didn't like fog, and he especially didn't like this fog. It was light and not yet overly dense, but there was something odd about it, something off.

His fear returned.

"Damn these are too good, Laura. They'll make me pack on the pounds," Bill Dowling said as he took another hearty mouthful of gooey, syrupy pancake. Truth of the matter was Bill Dowling had already packed on the pounds, a good ninety since his marriage. Laura wasn't particularly the greatest chef in the world, but if there was one thing she knew how to make it was the sweets.

"Mmmnomnom. S-so good," he said mid-chew. Ben couldn't stand to watch his father wolf down food the way he did, it was crushing his own appetite. His slow moving, small forkfuls were nothing in comparison to the fully-loaded, rapidly moving ones of his father.

Bill Dowling had once been a handsome man, the looks he had passed onto Ben were evidence of that, but years of eating without a care and disregarding his health had him looking nothing like the gent he used to be. His once prominent cheek bones, chin, and nose had now become round and doughy with excess weight, and the lower portion of his face was constantly obscured by a perpetual five o'clock shadow. His form was once stocky, but in a powerful, strong way. Now it was pudgy and rotund, with a gut that refused to wait behind his belt. His hair had been dark, and for a man's particularly silky; now it hung listlessly, wispy, and balding in a horseshoe pattern. His eyes were still as deep and brown as they had always been, but they lacked the wisdom and vigor of his younger years. Bill Dowling had not aged well for a man of forty-five, but he was also the type of man who was successful and comfortable enough not to care.

Pictures had shown Ben that he was the spitting image of his father, back when his father had been vivacious and handsome. His face held a hidden wisdom his father's once shared, but after that the similarities ended. Ben had the eyes and hair of his mother, along with her elongated skinny form. He liked to think he more closely resembled his mother in personality as well; his father was far too bullheaded to truly be considered affable.

"So, son," his father said, for the first time in the meal setting the fork down. "Do you still got that nonsense in your head about not wanting to go back to college?" His tone was light but condescending. Ben often had the feeling his father thought he would always be superior to Ben.

Ben took a bite of pancake before he answered, and enjoyed the chocolaty goodness for the brief moment he could. "I don't want to talk about it, Dad." He looked away, not wanting to start the morning off in that manner.

"You gotta talk about it. I'm your father and I worry about your future. You always have your head in the clouds, Ben. You have to be practical. You have some good ideas in that head of yours but good ideas don't always put pancakes on the table. Ya gotta have initiative. Ya gotta have a plan." He picked his fork up and stuck it into the lone remaining pancake on his plate, as added emphasis, though the gesture almost made Ben laugh at the absurdity.

"If I work hard enough at what I love, I can succeed. I know it."

"You're young and foolish. I don't want you stuck in this town forever."

"I thought you liked it here, Dad."

"This is the type of place you go once you have money, not to make money. This place has nothing here for you, son."

Ben pushed half of his pancake around in the syrup ocean created around it. He didn't want to have this discussion; it was one they had been having often for the last few weeks.

"Honor thy father, right? Don't worry I'm going back."

If his father was enthralled by this news, he had a solid enough poker face to hide it. "Consider changing your major too. If you want to be a writer you don't have to major in writing, you can major in something practical and get a real job while doing your hobby on the side. You can do both. Don't be thick, Ben."

A real job. The words stung. Ben knew the viewpoint was naive, but he wondered why anyone would want to take classes, or get a job, in an area that did not interest them. Money wasn't everything, and no matter what argument was thrown his way he would stick to his guns on that one.

"I'll think about it, Dad. Maybe I can switch to political science, or history, or philosophy."

"Oh that crap ain't good unless you're going to law school. Right there, that is something you should consider. Law school." His dad began more bites of his delicious breakfast.

"I'll talk to my counselor about it, see what room I have and what I can work out." His voice was far away and listless. "Yeah, you're right, I can write on the side."

"Hmmhmm." His father's response may have been approval over his answer or simply ecstasy over the pancakes—to Ben it didn't matter.

"TV's on the fritz," his mother said as she entered the kitchen. "Static on every channel, I could barely get the weather report."

"What did it have to say, anything about when this fog will clear up?" his father asked.

"You know, funny thing, it didn't say anything at all about fog, at least from what I could see. No mention at all, it's supposed to be a sunny day out there."

“Fucking weathermen, can’t trust ‘em as far as you can throw ‘em.”

Ben felt a chill as he looked out the kitchen window into the fog.

Had it grown thicker?

Three

Ben went trudging along the sidewalk on the way to his job at Braylon's Market. It was less than a mile and he never minded the walk, but now as he trekked through the fog he began wondering if he should have taken the car instead. There was something so bizarre about this particular haze, it almost seemed like it wasn't real fog at all.

His eyes couldn't prove it, but Ben knew there was more to it than met the eye. He had a gut feeling, one of those feelings where one just knows something without having to see it. It had never failed him in his life and Ben wasn't going to start ignoring it now.

As he continued walking at a lull of a pace, his senses did manage to pick out something peculiar about the setting. *Why can't I hear anything?*

Ben stopped for a moment and took a long listen. His ears searched and found nothing, not a single sound at all. This struck Ben as unsettling, even though Rowley was a sleepy town it wasn't a ghost town. There were cars and people and stray cats and—

And life.

Now there was only complete silence, and that, combined with the visual effect of the fog, made for an eerie scene. The road ahead of Ben seemed to disappear, like the road itself would drop off into nowhere. The houses on either side of the street were barely visible, and it appeared that they too were being swallowed up by the fog. This wasn't just a visual effect either, it really seemed like the haze was consuming the town, moving with a purpose to cover everything up and hide it all away.

The thought was paranoid, but Ben couldn't shake the notion that the fog was moving in over his town and blanketing it, taking away all sight and sound and leaving it isolated from the world.

He felt an odd chill, and wondered if he was dreaming again.

Stop it, he told himself. *You're just dealing with an overacting imagination spurred by that bad dream. Sit down and write a story about it, don't let it make you late for work.*

Ben increased his pace, wanting to outrun the irrational fears beginning to grip him. He was relieved when he saw a car pull by him on the street. There were still cars, people, and life in the town—no strange isolation.

"You're wasting your life. You're more of a disappointment than a son." Ben stopped as he heard the voice of his father. Voice? Or what is a thought? He was slightly unnerved to find he couldn't immediately tell. It was faint and faraway, but it couldn't have been his father's voice. The man was gruff but not outright cruel.

Now I'm making myself hear things. Not the way to start the day, Ben thought glumly.

He surveyed the area around him before continuing to walk, dismissing the noise as a lingering thought about his college situation.

Convinced he was buying too far into paranoia, Ben chose to ignore the slight decaying smell the air held, like the smell of burning, decomposing leaves. As he got onto Main Street, the fog let up slightly, still noticeable in the air but giving way to mild visibility. Two more cars cruised by and Ben's tensions were quickly fading away.

Ben got to the intersection of Church and Main, the first intersection once one got into town from 6 West, and because of that fact the location of most of the restaurants and businesses the town harbored. There were a few gems. Rollie's Cafe looked like a tiny hole in the wall with the way it was wedged between the liquor store and John's Pizzeria, but it had the best sandwiches in town. Despite the fact all of the little restaurants in town were competitors for the tourists' business, none of them had really gone over the top to make their buildings look aesthetically pleasing. Like most of the town, each place was small and forgettable, but maybe that was because there were such few options the customers were plenty for each. The only way the businesses would really compete with each other would be through the method of spreading slander; trying to convince tourists that one place had bugs or used expired food. It was petty enough, though Ben always had the feeling John Brusciante would bury Rollie Peterson if he had the chance.

Ben walked down Main toward the supermarket, taking in the rest of the scenery of Main Street as he walked away from what the locals referred to as town's square. After the slew of businesses there wasn't much to see on Main Street. The diner was a little farther down from the rest, then the music shop, two antique places right next to each other, and then only houses.

Rowley claimed to be a Victorian town, and there may have been a time when Rowley had been a Victorian town, but in its current stage of existence Ben could only consider Rowley Victorian if by Victorian someone meant filled with big, old houses.

Most of the homes in Rowley were bordering on ancient. The town essentially stopped expanding in the late 1800s when the trains stopped passing through. The homes were old and most certainly had once been beautiful, but as so happens when affluent property falls down into the hands of pauper's, the state of the homes had declined greatly since their heyday, victims of neglect and general apathy.

Main Street was the closest exception to this rule, with most of the large homes having retained some of their unique charm, but generally it was a shame to see how run down some of the beautiful works of architecture had become. Despite this, Ben still thought Rowley had some nice areas to look at, and that sufficed for him. It was no Victorian paradise, but it still held a charm to it. The label Victorian Paradise had been slapped on the town by a local newspaper, and subsequently had ended up on the burgundy banners decorating every light-post on Main Street. *Rowley Pennsylvania: A Victorian Paradise. Come to get away, plan to stay!*

Rowley was a tourist town through and through. Without tourists the lifeblood of the already dying economy would stop flowing and Rowley would eventually cease to be. The only reason Rowley even had a piece of the tourist pie was Lake Wiladongun, a popular tourist lake that sat only four miles beyond Rowley's limits. The lake was manmade nearly a century earlier in order to harness hydroelectric power for the whole area, but its immense size (sixty miles of shoreline) and unquestionable beauty had lent it to become the economic backbone of the rural area as a whole. Wayne County bordered New York, and only a sliver of Pike County separated it from New Jersey. The lake's central location, only two hours from New York City, had made it a prime getaway for city dwellers.

In the summer this meant big money. In fact, many of the businesses in communities around Rowley existed solely off their summer earnings alone. It wasn't uncommon for the locals to be grossly outnumbered by New Yorkers and New Jerseyans during the summer months, especially the weekends, and this was exactly the plan for the local entrepreneurs. In order to keep the steady flow of tourism running every year, the Rowley News made sure to very selectively choose what image and what information about the town would be portrayed. Due to this, the newspaper could only be partially trusted, anything that would be seen as a threat to the sanctity of the "private Victorian paradise" image would be omitted from its pages.

It bothered Ben that so many people in the town attempted to make it out to be something it was not. Crime was never spoken about or reported in the paper, no burglaries or drug busts would be mentioned. These crimes were not as prevalent as they would be in a city area, but by no means were they non-existent. A facade was maintained so Rowley and the surrounding area could keep up their pristine, private retreat image.

What particularly agitated Ben was how even the locals bought into this idea, seeming to highlight all of the good things about the town while ignoring the problems. There were drug deals being done in the park downtown at night, there were occasional break-ins, and a sizable portion of the residents were welfare abusers, drug addicts, or a combination of both.

But these weren't the types of things you heard about. Everyone knew that Jack Handlan beat the shit out of his wife every day, and people saw the bruises that jumped out as truth, but would anyone do anything about it? Would anyone talk about it in public?

No. Instead you would hear about this festival, or this farmer's market, or that fundraiser. You'd hear it in a conversation between two people, who you knew for a fact hated each other—but there they would be standing with painted smiles and fake demeanors.

This didn't suit Ben, the petty dancing around truths and

attempts to keep up an image for others. Wasn't Rowley okay for what it was? It was small, private, aesthetically beautiful, why not talk about the problems? Why not fix them? If you truly love something you don't unconditionally support it; you work to make it the best it can be—you attempt to do the BEST for it.

Maybe Ben was the only person in the town that truly loved it; maybe he was the only person who truly wanted to be there. Maybe he wanted to stay to fix it, to make it more genuine.

Money isn't the only thing in the world.

Past the row of nice homes that decorated Main Street, across from Rowley Public Park, Ben could see the brown, unimpressive building with the big blue sign reading, *"Braylon's Market."* It was a squat cube with large sections of windows slapped onto the front. It was ultimately forgettable but it had done well for itself and its owner over the years.

Charlie Braylon was the owner of supermarket and he was a man Ben had only met on a handful of occasions. Charlie mainly left the job of running the market to his managers. Mr. Braylon was a known alcoholic, and it was rumored he had cheated on his wife with half a dozen women over the years. However, this was often left out of the papers when he donated two hundred dollars every three years toward a scholarship fund for local high school students. He was painted as a kind-hearted soul and a true philanthropist.

Ben walked through the mostly empty parking lot to the automatic entrance door at the front of the building. He let out a belabored sigh. He didn't feel like working that day, although he supposed every day he worked at the supermarket deli was a day he didn't want to work. On the list of best summer jobs, deli worker at Braylon's was certainly a position near the bottom.

He had the job running on three years, and whenever he was back from break they gave him solid hours so he couldn't complain. But every day he greeted his customers with genuine friendliness and a happy smile, and often he was met by plastic expressions with eyes that showed blaring distrust and a great deal of wear.

Maybe I'm just being cynical myself.

The day had been going uneventfully enough for Ben two hours into his shift. There wasn't a steady rush of customers so it had been relaxing enough; albeit a little boring. That was until he waited on Mrs. Pelland, an elderly woman who had been a friend of his grandmother's. She looked like a bird with a posture problem, with a big beak of a nose sticking out from behind a pair of overly thick glasses. Her hair was gray, short, and curly, a typical elderly woman's hair style, and despite initial views of her as awkward looking, her demeanor was always bright enough to make her look cute—in the way a sweet old woman could be.

"Did you hear the news, Ben?" she asked as he handed her the half pound of liverwurst she had ordered.

"What news, Mrs. Pelland?"

"Oh it's horrible, absolutely horrible!" She said horrible in a way that almost sounded like a squawk. Ben felt awful at his mental conceptions of the dear old woman as a giant turkey.

"What's horrible?" He expected some of her normal gossip, perhaps someone had ruined her lawn decorations again, or maybe she would divulge something real juicy like how she was POSITIVE that girl Lucy Jenkins was pregnant and had gotten an abortion. Rich Miller may have wrecked his car again while he was drunk, or maybe Mr. Dillard, the town pharmacist, was finally proven to be selling pills on the side. Whatever it was Ben didn't care much; this was just the type of gossip he always got when Mrs. Pelland graced his presence.

"Mitch Joiner is dead! He was murdered!" She threw her arms up with emphasis, almost as if she was reenacting an overly dramatic scene from a B movie.

Ben's heart sank; this was not the normal bullshit that came with talking to the townsfolk. No, this was serious.

"Dead? Murdered? Mr. Joiner, who owns the hardware store? How do you know?"

There was an odd type of joy about Mrs. Pelland, despite the awful news she conveyed she seemed overjoyed to be conveying it, as if the weight of the news she was telegraphing made it that much more important.

"Oh yes, that Mitch Joiner. Dead as a doorknob. They found him on the sidewalk on Overlook Street this morning. Paul Roberts was delivering the papers, you know to the subscribers, and there Mitch was right on the street. He was taking his morning jog, you know like he always does, and someone got him!" The chatter had become more excited at the end, and for a moment the bird-like Mrs. Pelland appeared to be a giddy school girl.

"That's horrible." Ben was genuinely upset. Mr. Joiner had

always been a grumpy old man, but he was a staple in the town, his hardware store the only one Ben had ever known. Somewhere he always felt the grumpy old man exterior was just a front. He was a grouch sure, but murdered? Why would anyone do something so terrible to an old man?

"How do they know it's murder?" Ben blurted out.

"Well, no one knows for sure yet, that's the police's job. But according to Milly Reiter, who is good friends with Paul's wife," she looked at Ben like this was a particular bit of inside information, "Paul found his body torn apart, an absolute gory mess."

Ben's blood chilled. He thought of his dream, he thought of the awful creature that wanted to eat him. Out of fear, more so than curiosity, he asked, "Couldn't it have been . . . an animal, a dog or a bear?"

Mrs. Pelland tilted her head. "Yes, I suppose it could have been a dog. I doubt anyone really owns a big one in town, well besides the Shultz's and Bubba is a gentle giant of a Doberman. We really don't have any wild one's roaming around here either. Could be a bear, it's been a couple years since we had one roaming the town, but Mitch could have gotten unlucky." She paused for a moment, then added with a salacious tone, "But the way I hear it, Paul didn't think any animal did that. Said it was too savage, you hear that, too savage even for a bear." She leaned over the counter nearly whispering the last bit into Ben's ear, and he wished he were far away from her.

Mrs. Pelland noticed the color draining from his face.

"Sorry for startling you, my dear. Just thought everyone should know. Want to keep our little town safe after all. You watch out for yourself and tell your mother I send my best." With that she scooped up her liverwurst, heading off with her cart toward the bread aisle.

Ben watched her go, and by the time he was able to pull himself back to his duties, his hands were shaking.

The rest of Ben's shift could have been considered typical, but a few more occurrences throughout the day made him unable to relax and breathe easy. First was a guy who came in, a New Yorker (his Long Island accent was unmistakable), and he made small talk about how the fog was only situated around Rowley.

"Funny, I was just up at the lake house with my family, ran down to town here to get some sandwich supplies for our get together later, and I'm driving down 6 in the most beautiful weather you can imagine then BOOM, I hit this cloud. It's like the fog is hovering around Rowley and nowhere else. Let me tell you, buddy, absolutely gorgeous by the lake, feel bad for you folks down here."

"That's pretty odd. It's probably setting down in the little valley around the town." Ben's voice sounded fearful even to himself and he saw the tourist's eye narrow as he spoke. He couldn't shake the feeling that something was wrong—not wrong in the sense of inconvenient weather, in a sense that was all too serious.

Ben thought he was feeling some type of survival instinct, the type humans had left behind thousands of years ago. It was the type of reaction animals have when they know a natural disaster is coming, the kind of knowledge that sends them far from the trouble area. Nowadays it would be called a gut feeling, and Ben could not deny he was having one and it was telling him danger was on the horizon.

"Well you have a good day then, pal. Hope this weather gets better for ya." The man threw his supplies into his cart and made his way off, leaving Ben only able to nod in response.

Then the lights started flickering.

FOUR

Rowley Sheriff Tom Williams paced around the scene of the crime, still in disbelief at what laid before him on the sidewalk.

In this town, in our town.

Tom had dealt with his fair share of problems over the past fifteen years. Seven years ago, a tourist had one too many drinks at Mac's Bar, and got into a scuff with Steve Byson—which was a poor decision since Steve stood six foot four and weighed nearly three-hundred pounds. The fool lost nearly all of his teeth and had to have his jaw wired shut. There also was that time ten years ago where Billy Johnson stabbed Phil Djurek over a botched drug deal, luckily for Djurek and the town he lived.

Tom had dealt with small drug busts, car accidents, assaults and even a firebug—but a murderer? In his town? The reality was dizzying and Tom was quickly hit with a head rush as he realized maybe this type of case was too big for him and his force. The streets of Rowley were quiet day in and day out; there were your everyday problems yes, but nothing near this magnitude. Could his men deal with it? Could he deal with it?

Tom took in a long breath and decided he didn't have a choice. This was his job, his duty, and even though he had taken it with the assurance he would earn a fine living without really ever having to do anything at all, he still had enough of a sense of responsibility to consider this his commitment.

That didn't mean he had to enjoy it though, oh no, he stopped enjoying being a sheriff as soon as he had seen that body.

Tom wasn't a particularly squeamish man; he had the body of a bear and the face of a grizzled war veteran. Truth of the matter was however, Tom had a problem when it came to dead bodies; he never really had to deal with them in his life. Sure, he took a few reports at homes of residents with family members who had heart attacks, strokes, and other natural deaths. He had seen the bodies being removed, but in his combined thirty years of police work in Rowley he had never dealt with a single murder, in fact he only knew of two that had ever occurred in his life, and the last had been twenty years earlier.

What Tom Williams had failed to consider in his review of the town's history, were the numerous "accidents" reported in and around Rowley that had not been sufficiently investigated. Just last year, Williams himself had declared the incident with Shelly Benning an accident, coinciding with the report provided by the only other occupant of the boat she had been on in Lake Wiladongun. The story was that they had been drinking, and Shelly had fallen overboard and was unable to swim due to her inebriation. Most citizens of Rowley had considered the strong possibility that Teddy Rowlings had killed her, he wasn't known as the kindest soul when he had a few beers in him, but no one made a big deal about it. It was easier to believe it had been an accident—it was a notion everyone came to believe and accept out of convenience. An accident wouldn't tarnish the town's reputation or crush its spirit for years to come, an accident would fade away with time and life would go on as normal. No one could believe the Benning incident had been anything but an accident. Violence and murders just didn't happen in a place as quiet and beautiful as Rowley.

The papers usually agreed with this sentiment, murder was bad for tourism, so although there had in fact been a handful of suspicious "accidents" throughout Tom Williams' reign as sheriff, a murder had not been officially recognized.

But in this particular case, Tom was having a difficult time forcing himself to accept the notion that this could be an accident.

He glanced down at what once had been Mitch Joiner, grimacing at the grizzly sight.

Whatever attacked him had torn him up real good. His rib cage had been ripped open, broken down the middle and seemingly pried apart. The broken ends of his ribs jutted up through his ripped, red muscle, and held within the bowl his rib-cage had become was some grotesque organ stew.

His lungs had been yanked out of place. Tom was no doctor but he could tell they weren't where they were supposed to be. They had been forcefully moved and severely mutilated—badly bitten before being thrown on top of the horrible smorgasbord that had once been Mitch Joiner's functioning organs.

His heart was only half complete, the other half was ripped, cut, or eaten. It laid yanked away from its veins and arteries, which could be seen strewn as strands amongst the rest of the eviscerated organs.

His liver was cut into pieces and his intestines had been yanked up from his lower belly into his chest, capping the gruesome mess like they were a swirl of whipped cream topping off a nightmare sundae.

Not only had everything been pulled violently apart posthumously, each organ was missing large chunks, as if they had been removed in gashing cuts or bites.

Tom shuddered. Mitch also had slash wounds up and down his arms and legs; his left hand was missing completely, the victim of a knife or saw . . .

Or teeth.

His clothes were in complete tatters, the rips and tears correlating with the slash mark injuries all across his body. His neck was slashed as well, with a single long cut so deep it was a miracle Mitch hadn't been decapitated. His head barely hung on and slumped to the side in an unnatural position, giving the appearance that Mitch had the ability to turn his head only from the mid-neck up.

What perhaps startled Tom the most, however, were

Mitch's eyes. They were frozen open, pupils somehow still wide with fear of some unholy terror. Whatever killed him, he saw it, and he had been alive and awake for most of the damage.. His mouth was open in a terrible scream and his eyes looked ready to pop out of his head, as if they had seen something no eyes ever wanted to lay witness to.

Just looking at that face made Tom break out in goosebumps. He was pulled from his thoughts by a hand on his shoulder, nearly making him jump.

"Sheriff, you sure this wasn't an animal attack? Something looks like it ripped him up and ate him," his deputy, Dan McNair, asked with concern.

"I don't know if it was, Dan. Tell you the truth, I hope it was some type of animal attack, because I don't want to imagine there's a son of a bitch alive capable of doing something like this."

"A person wouldn't do this, not around here." McNair's tone seemed unconvinced, and he paused to contemplate. "I mean, who would eat his insides?"

"What could have happened," began Tom, taking particular note of the all too precise slash across his neck, "is some sicko could have killed him, and fed him to his dog or something like that for added effect."

Dan McNair's eyes were wide with disbelief. "You don't think some guy would really do that, do you?"

"I don't know." Tom let his frustration show. "I don't know what the hell is going on, Dan, but I'm putting ideas out there. Maybe Stuart will tell us the wounds are similar to that of a bear attack, maybe this is no criminal case, but . . ." he trailed off and Dan understood his meaning without having to hear anymore.

Dan McNair was no fool; he too could sense something was wrong. This wasn't the type of crime people heard about around Rowley, or anywhere for that matter. There had been so much hate put into the dismemberment of Mitch Joiner—the concept was blood-chilling. Dan had a sinking feeling this wasn't the end of the gore, and his peaceful little town was about to get rocked.

Then Dan McNair took a glance over at Tom Williams, and he was hit with a strong sense of doubt. Could Tom handle this situation? Could he keep order and safety if there really was some nut-case on the loose?

From working with the Sheriff for five years, he knew Tom was incapable of dealing with even a mildly stressful situation. Williams liked the expected, he liked the simple, and McNair knew this would be anything but.

Maybe you're the man for the job. The thought sliced through the rest, and was powerful enough to make Dan's body stiffen. It had popped into his head so forcefully it almost seemed alien.

Maybe I am the man for the job. At least I'm better suited to deal with a situation than Tom Williams is. He's only a sheriff in title, not in practice, that's for sure.

Dan began to seriously consider whether he was suited to be playing the role of sheriff in the tense production that had just concluded its opening act. The thought fled as quickly as it came—things would not have to come to anything like that. This was only one event, one isolated event.

Perhaps it was just one bizarre animal attack.

Just one odd occurrence

Perhaps.

Five

Around seven that evening, coincidentally at the same time Ben Dowling was getting out of work, Jack Handlan was getting done with a "responsibility" of his own.

He had gotten home from a hard day at work for the tree service, taking down three trees and trimming the branches of a few others, essentially all by himself since the other guy on the job, Billy Brissler, couldn't even tie his shoes correctly.

Jack had sweated, Jack had bled, but he had put in a solid day of work and had been paid accordingly. He busted his back and his ass to put food on the table when he got home, so when he walked in and found that particular night's meal to be cold and unsavory, he knew what had to be done.

Kelly was a sweet girl with an angelic face that could pass for eighteen even at age twenty-eight. Her eyes were deep, dark, and sensual, and her hair matched perfectly. Her face was a smooth, pale palate without a single natural flaw. She was a sweet dream of a woman.

The fact remained that she *was* a woman, and Jack Handlan was of the opinion that a strong man had to keep his woman in line.

With the new age feminism bullshit springing up left and right, it appeared to Jack that every woman got it in her head that it was okay to be a regular slut; to show her tits off and shake her ass toward any cock that came her way. Jack would have a woman who was proper like his mother had been—and Jack knew she was proper because his father had kept her in line.

Jack only hit Kelly because he loved her; he wanted her to be the very best wife and person she could be. Any little slip up could start a bad habit, and one bad habit left unchecked and festering could end up derailing someone's life. He didn't want that for Kelly, so he played the role of authority in her life, a role she desperately needed and one he was more than happy to fulfill.

It meant he loved her.

The moment he took a bite into the cold chicken and mashed potatoes, Jack Handlan lost any trace of love or happiness. His body ached from a hard day's work and his stomach craved nourishment. After all he had done to bring home some money, that ungrateful *bitch* couldn't even find the time to make him a proper meal. It wasn't like she had much else to do the rest of the day; Jack was the only one bringing home the bacon.

Kelly needed a lesson in appreciation. Kelly needed a lesson in manners.

"I'm sorry, I'm sorry!" She raised her hands in self-defense as she backed up toward the wall, her one hundred and twenty pound figure dwarfed by his two hundred and twenty pound frame.

"I was just catching up on the laundry. I didn't know when you would be in and—" Jack wouldn't let her spit excuses any longer.

POP! He hit her on the side of the face with a half closed fist and she stumbled backward, somehow maintaining her balance. *Years ago,* Jack thought mildly, *that would have dropped her without any resistance. I'm putting some piss and vinegar in her that's for sure.*

She held her face, and the excuses were gone. "I'll make it again. I'll make you a proper dinner." Her voice was now filled with shame. She knew she had done her man wrong, and if it hadn't been such a rough day, Jack would have considered letting her off with one good pop.

But he was in such a terrible mood.

BAM! Words weren't needed as he spoke with his fists, this time hitting her in the eye with a straight right. She let out a shriek and fell backward into the wall, sliding down and crumpling into a pathetic, weeping heap.

He heard the crying now as she held her face in her hands, both out of pain and shame. Jack had given her a black eye a few weeks earlier over the fact she had run up the phone bill and the swelling and discoloration had only just faded away.

Now her eye was swollen shut once more.

Jack had never gone too easy on his wife when he beat her—his father had always said if you hit like a woman, someone would mistake you for a woman. It was important to let Kelly know Jack was a man and she would get no slack if she did wrong.

"You just don't learn do you, you dumb bitch? I don't ask for too much and this is how you treat me?"

"I'm sorry, Jack! I'm sorry! Please . . ." Kelly pleaded, hiding her face, too ashamed to stare at the man she married and the life she had chosen for herself.

Jack kicked her in the side, specifically aiming for the ribs so she would feel it enough to never forget to serve him a real dinner. Kelly let out a short yelp, but besides the initial reaction did not make a sound. She knew at that point she would only make it worse for herself, so she did the only thing she could: accept her punishment and wait for it to be over.

He kept kicking, two in the gut, then a few more to her shins as she balled up and made a weak attempt at defending herself. He hated when she went silent like that. He never knew if he was doing a good enough job at hitting her unless he could hear its effect—no man wants his treatment to be ineffective after all. In order to assure she was getting the message clear as crystal, Jack aimed his last kick at her head, precisely connecting the toe of his work-boot to her forehead through the small opening her arms provided.

Kelly's head shot backward, the force from the kick soon matched as her head slammed off the wall behind her with a loud thud. From there she slid down and fell to the floor, lying as a limp form on the carpet, battered, bruised, and thoroughly beaten.

The pathetic sight convinced Jack that Kelly had learned her lesson.

"Now make me a real dinner. I'm going out to get a drink but by the time I get back there better be something mouth-watering on this fucking table. And wear something sexy too, I'm planning on plowing you later."

Her silence was acceptance. Jack knew she would listen, and by the off chance she didn't, she would get a rough beating again.

After he was done with his duty, Jack stood outside his small home, a rundown modular on a dirt road just off Washington Street, and considered what he had done.

I taught her good, I'm doing a good job keeping that bitch in line. Once she realizes how good she has it thanks to my work, I can be a little softer on her but 'til then I can't tolerate slip ups, no sir.

He stared off into the foggy evening, thinking of his father and all the beatings he had let loose on Jack and his mother. Kelly had it easy compared to what Jack's mom had to suffer through. If Jack's father was ever offered a cold dinner, that woman would lose a tooth, and if Jack ever had anything to say about it he would lose one too.

As he looked out into the fog, he could hear his father's voice telling him he would amount to nothing, he would never be half the man his father had been.

"You're soft, Jack, just a regular momma's boy. You wanna

keep suckling on her? You're never going to go anywhere in life, you soft little shit."

Jack took a somber moment to reflect on whether he was doing his father proud. As he took the first few steps away from his home, he noticed something odd.

Did the fog just get thicker, right in front of my eyes? The thought seemed absurd.

His pickup was only twenty feet away from him, and a moment earlier had been in perfect sight behind the light layer of mist. Now it was like a cloud had swept in and isolated him from his vehicle. He had just seen the truck but now it seemed like it was a football field away. It was only a small, dark outline behind the haze, and it seemed to be shrinking, disappearing.

What the fuck? he thought, straining his eyes in an attempt to best the optical illusion. Then he heard it.

Tssssshhhhkkkkssshhh.

The noise came from behind him, reminding him of the sound made when his father used to sharpen the ax before they went off to chop firewood back in his childhood, except this noise wasn't completely a metallic grind—it had a guttural sound to it. Jack spun around furiously, seeing nothing but smog.

"What the fuck was that?" His shout seemed to hit a wall only a few feet in front of him. There was no response and, to Jack's dismay, he could no longer see his home.

"*Going to give you a lickin', Jacky boy! Gonna get the belt out for this one, you little shit!*" Lawrence Handlan taunted his son from beyond the grave.

Whoosh. Whoosh. Something moved with amazing speed

in the fog, just off to his right. It moved so fast he could hear the air stir as the thing sliced through it, the sudden motion and noise causing him to jump back in shock.

"Hey, whoever the fuck you are get out of here before I break your fucking face!" Anger was Jack's initial reaction in most situations, but even he could not deny the creeping sensations of fear coming over him.

Whoosh. This time it passed close in front of him, and he could make out a dark blur. He stumbled back, nearly falling, but the close contact with the figure was not the only thing that startled him.

The smell, he thought. *What the fuck is that smell? It smells like a tower of burning tires, or some three week old road-kill, or maybe some mix of both.*

It was a pungent odor, the type that seemed to stick to him despite how quickly he recoiled from its source. It was vile, sickening, and so overwhelming. Jack had done enough physical labor and had ended up in enough dive bars to have experienced his fair share of foul odors—but none of them could compare with what he had taken a whiff of in that brief moment.

The noxious nature of the fumes bothered him, even frightened him. *What in God's name is that fucking smell*?

Whoosh. It was behind him.

"*Come get what you deserve, you little bastard,*" his father cackled at him.

Jack spun around but his eyes revealed nothing to console him, instead they only witnessed something senseless; something impossible.

The figure was coming out of the fog, yet he figured it was

a *part* of the fog. It seemed to be fading in and out of the haze, becoming more and less visible as it slowly drifted back and forth. Jack's mind couldn't immediately understand the physical nature of what was before him, and he didn't have the composure to settle down and truly take in the form of the beast.

He saw darkness, deep darkness, around a body vaguely resembling that of a human. It faded in and out of the gray fog, and Jack couldn't avoid the thought that shot through his head.

He's hiding in the fog. He's not revealing himself to me. There's more . . . there's a lot more.

"What the fuck do you want?" Jack did his best to maintain his tough guy edge, even though he was shaking so badly he couldn't have intimidated the most skittish five year old.

The figure did not respond. It moved through the mist with eerie grace, gliding through the noxious fog without effort. It stared at him with eyes Jack could not see, but eyes he could feel, gazing at him with the most malevolent form of desire. It circled around Jack, drawing closer and closer with each pass, and with each pass the creature's form started to solidify. Soon Jack's mind began to piece together and reveal the shape of the monster bearing down on him.

What the hell? That's not possible. This thing is not possible.

At first his eyes were captivated by the slow reveal of the beast, but now the nightmare they were perceiving was too much—Jack wanted out. Spinning away from his hunter, he made the first steps in what he thought would be an escape.

He was sorely mistaken.

Tssschnkkktchchhhnnktcchh, it screeched in protest and

halted its slow, graceful motions. With a *whoosh* its speed returned and the thing moved in front of Jack, cutting him off only a few steps into his run, making his escape attempt look like foolish child's play. It had been toying with him, however, it still would not tolerate the insult of Jack holding out hope for survival.

Jack had barely managed to turn and run when it blocked him off. *It's just that fast.* This was his first thought despite the face of the threat directly in front of him. In his bewilderment, his mind could come up with no other conclusion. Nothing could move *that* fast, but his eyes were telling him this thing did.

Fear and frustration filled Jack. He was on the wrong side of a cat and mouse game, and it didn't look like there was an escape. His terror began to climax as the shadow beast fully emerged from the fog, letting Jack distinguish its horrifying nature.

There was only one thing Jack could do in the face of such a tormentor. As a temperamental and violent man, Jack held esteem in his ability to solve problems with his fists. His next course of action was brought on by his panicked fear combined with raw survival instinct: *Fight.*

It towered above Jack, he now put the figure's height at around seven feet, but it had not been that large earlier—had it *grown*? It stood looking down at him, unmoving, gazing at him through infinite darkness. He could now make out nearly the whole form of the monster, but felt fortunate to see its face was still clouded amongst the foggy darkness. That face was something he didn't want to see—something he had to make go away.

Jack swung like he had never swung before, throwing his full body into the hay-maker aimed for the side of the thing's head. His furious hook was cut short by a vice with the stopping power of a brick wall.

With effortless precision, the creature grabbed a hold of Jack's arm halfway between his wrist and his elbow. Jack felt the most horrible sensation on his skin as the dead hand (*claw?*) held him tight.

His skin was on fire, or was it freezing? It was the worst of both worlds in the creature's grip. His skin was filled with awful sensations of discomfort, somehow too hot and too cold at the same time.

There was no dispute as to what was happening in the rest of his body however: he was becoming incredibly cold. He felt his warm blood moving up to his arm and stopping there. On the way back, everything was cold as ice and he felt a shock to his system as his heart attempted to process the too quickly chilled fluid.

It's draining me of heat, it's draining my blood of life.

Jack couldn't even offer a struggle in the being's mighty grasp. He was helpless to resist as the creature made its first devastating move.

SNAP! It sounded like the snapping of small tree branches, a sound Jack often encountered in his tree service job. He would habitually snap small bothersome branches out of the way so he wouldn't have to pull out the chainsaw to deal with them, only the big branches really required that baby anyway. But this wasn't a simple tree branch that had snapped.

It was his arm.

With the slightest turn of its wrist, the monstrosity had

snapped Jack's forearm in half. He felt a hot rush of pain and disorientation, his nerves screaming in protest as jagged ends of bone stabbed their way through his flesh.

He tried to fall but the monster held tight to his limb, now broken in two at the forearm. He was held up by his tearing muscle, tendons, and skin, only furthering the damage done as bone dug through them. Blood began squirting out of severed veins, spraying up and soon landing on Jack's arm, dripping down the rest of it and leaving deep stains on his shirt.

Jack Handlan screamed a wet, pitiful scream into the fog, but it traveled only a handful of feet, heard only by his own ears.

He was crying now. He hadn't cried since he was a child, he hadn't cried since his father had beaten him mercilessly for acting like a "goddamn sissy boy." He couldn't help it now as he felt the agony from his broken arm. Jack was a frightened child at the mercy of his father once more. The tears continued to pour as he glanced up and saw the dark figure leaning down, the terrible monster moving its face closer to him.

Jack turned his head away in fear, like Kelly had done so many times over the years when he was about to hit her. How things had come full circle.

He cried out in disgust and fear at what came next.

It felt like a tentacle, but Jack recognized it as the creature's tongue. It ran up and down his arm, near where it had been split in two, licking and lapping at his bloody wounds with long rough strokes which tasted his blood and essence.

Tsssskkknnnnnchhhttch. The cry had the same emotionless tone as it did before, but Jack could sense something more;

he sensed this utterance was one of *pleasure.*

Then the licking stopped. Jack held back the bile rising up in his throat, nearly choking on it with the effort. There was a silent moment, Jack's head was down and the creature held him in place by the arm. After a full minute of this, curiosity took over, and Jack timidly began to look up, finally gaining the courage to see what was happening.

SWIPE. It was the same motion Jack had used when he had given Kelly the black eye, but the results were much more severe.

Jack's head jolted backward as the monster's claws tore through the flesh of his face. One claw grazed his eye and sunk into it, popping it instantly. Blood and fluid spilled onto his cheek as his eye-socket suddenly became a gelatinous mess, his eye having the appearance of a half-eaten cherry.

The flesh on the left side of his face was almost torn away. Hot searing pain radiated throughout Jack as the claws tore off the side of his face like wrapping paper. Strips of skin and muscle were ripped away and Jack could feel the skin remaining on the left side of his face hanging and dangling while hot blood pushed past, gushing out at an exponential rate.

Muscle fiber was torn, skin hung lifelessly, and eyeball fluid poured down into the remains of his tattered cheek and into the hole where his left nostril had once been. Jack Handlan was the image of a living corpse.

He fell to his back and gurgled a low scream, choked and cut off as blood found its way into the giant slit that was the side of his mouth. He could feel the area flapping as he let air in and out, and spat the blood upward. The pain was excruciating, more pain than he could ever imagine. He wanted to lift his hand to his face to examine his wounds, but was too fearful to attempt the feat.

Then it was over him, and with his one remaining eye he could see it fully for the first time. He was too terrified to scream.

Jack felt a vice tightening around his heart, his sanity failing as he stared into the eyes of Death itself. He managed to move—somehow his survival instincts driving through the insanity, breaking through the paralysis caused by laying eyes upon something so perverted and inconceivable. He began to shuffle backward, throwing all his weight into the motions in an attempt to scuttle away from the beast.

Jack was barely able to move a half a foot before the teeth came. There was an ungodly amount of teeth that appeared out of nowhere, surrounding him like the fog itself. They ripped, tore, and tasted indiscriminately. Chunks of his chest were suddenly gone, his genitals were chomped off next, and finally his stomach was torn open, revealing his entrails.

Jack Handlan had no time to scream, but an eternity to suffer as his body was eaten and his soul consumed. All he could register were absolute pain and suffering before his world abruptly faded to black.

Six

The moment Jack Handlan died, Ben Dowling felt an icy shiver spread throughout his body, the source of which seemed to be his very core.

He had an unsettling feeling as he walked home from work. He felt the chill all over his skin, causing it to break out in gooseflesh.

Is it that cold out? he thought, while continuing to walk through the fog. The temperature was what you would expect on an August night, but the fog itself was cold. It wasn't cold in the physical sense, but in a mental way—an *emotional* way. The fog seemed to drain away happiness. Ben couldn't muster one warm thought or feeling while he was amongst it. It was chilling and desolate in a way he never imagined; it made the setting around him devoid of life.

What he had heard about Mr. Joiner hadn't helped either. He was simply jogging in the fog and someone—or something—got him. Something had been waiting out there and the old man could do nothing to stop it.

Ben hadn't been the only one to notice it either. Usually the townspeople were filled with gripes about this, that, and the other thing, ranging from a wasted opportunity to bitterness over a common family spat. Ben had become well-adjusted to the regular customers, who usually had a stick up their ass, wedged tightly there next to their own heads. But today there was something more. Not only did they seem especially bitter, they also seemed deeply troubled, some of them overtly frightened. As the day progressed, more and more people became fidgety, seeming desperate to grab their food and get home.

Was it the fog bothering them? Was it getting to their heads? Or was Ben losing it?

Shhhtch. The sound halted Ben's thoughts and froze him in his tracks. His eyes frantically sought answers to no avail and his ears compensated. He could hear a light scraping noise, inconsistent and a fair distance away, but it was approaching.

Ben's heart began beating out of control. He felt a bead of sweat well up on the side of his head and become engorged quickly, sliding down his head in a sloppy zigzagging pattern. *Shhhttch, crrtcchh!* The scraping noise continued, moving quickly, and Ben took a hard step backward, ready to take off and flee whatever unknown entity was coming his way.

It was the figure from his dream, rushing toward him to claim its meal. He had escaped it in the dream realm, but now this was the real world. Now Mommy couldn't save him from the big bad boogey man, he was coming and he was full of rage.

He was hungry.

Ben gasped as it descended on him, and his pupils blew up to the point where his blue eyes turned black.

Donnie Shultz nearly collided with Ben as he rode his skateboard through the blinding fog. The sixteen year old had enough experience under his belt to pull a smooth turn to the right just at the last moment, skillfully gliding past Ben with little effort. Donnie was a bit surprised at the sudden appearance of the wide-eyed obstacle in his path, but years of navigating the town on his trusty skateboard had left him more than capable of dealing with tricky situations.

Ben felt an instant rush of embarrassment, his face hot and turning beet red. He could not believe he had been terror-stricken by some teenager on a skateboard. As the boy flew by, Ben was able to shake off the shame along with the fear, telling himself all of it had to be his vivid imagination. There was no nightmare unfolding in his small, out of the way town—his creativity was just running rampant and out of control. He was imagining it all.

Wasn't he?

The first thing Ben heard as he opened the door to his home was a sound he had become all too familiar with over the years. It was typical for Ben to walk into the house and be greeted by the sound of his father engaging in one of his favorite pastimes: complaining. Ben couldn't immediately decipher the words, but the something-is-a-pain-in-my-ass tone that his father was speaking in was a dead giveaway something was bugging him.

"The fucking phones too! No one gets anything done in this damn town!" He was sitting at the dinner table expressing his frustrations in the direction of Ben's mother, who gazed at him sympathetically.

"What's the matter, Pops?" Ben asked as he stepped in, closing the door behind him.

"The TV's still getting static on every channel. So what do we do? We try to call the cable company of course. Well guess what? The phone's got static too!"

Ben felt a pang of fear dig sharply into his chest. "Static?"

"Yeah, static. All you hear is crackling static, can't even understand what the people on the other line are saying. Maybe it's this goddamn weather, interfering with signals or whatever the hell they use."

"What about your cell phone?" Ben asked with the slightest hint of trepidation.

"Same thing." His father's tone was flat and frustrated.

"It must be some type of interference with radio signals then, towers and that type of thing. Television and cell phones all work with towers now. Once the fog passes I'm sure everything will work just fine." Ben's mother did her best to provide a reasonable explanation, and placate her husband's mood.

Ben didn't want to point out that the hole in her theory was the house phone, which should only be affected by the condition of the lines connected to the house. It seemed too coincidental that the weather had crippled TV and cell phones, and at the same time the phone company was experiencing separately caused problems of their own. Normally he wouldn't point things out because he didn't want to distress his parents, but in this instance he wanted to avoid distressing himself.

An awkward silence hung over the kitchen, and Ben decided to break it.

"I b-better go change for dinner," he said, motioning down to his work clothes, which were now decorated with a mess of meat bits and chunks, remnants of a day's worth of slicing customer's orders.

"Yes, go clean up. We're having pot roast for dinner." His mother motioned to the table in front of her where a spread of pot roast and sides was already laid out in anticipation of his arrival.

"Looks good." Ben didn't even glance at the food as he walked past his parents and exited the room, taking a brief step into the living room before going up the staircase to enter his bedroom, the first door on the left.

He changed his clothes quickly, discarding his soiled ones into his laundry basket. Before he went to join his family for dinner, he couldn't help but glance out his window into the fog.

Something was out there. Waiting. Creeping. Watching.

Ben couldn't fool himself, none of this was his imagination. Some type of innate instinct was screaming at him, and it was telling him something was horribly wrong. There was no point in trying to put these worries on the back-burner, his feelings kept pulling them right to the forefront.

Ben let out a weary sigh and headed downstairs for dinner.

"Elise is coming over tonight," Ben stated, but with an upward inflection at the end of the statement, still respecting his parents authority over their home. He had planned the get together the day before, on account of the rare occasion when he wasn't working the closing shift.

Bill Dowling gobbled down his bite of pot roast before responding, "Yeah, and why is she coming over?"

"Just to hang out, play some video games, the usual." Ben poked at his mashed potatoes. He couldn't find the appetite to dive right in despite the fact they were unusually good that evening.

"Are you screwing around with her, Ben?" Bill Dowling was a man not known for his tact. Laura Dowling let out a gasp that turned into a choke as she coughed up her green beans.

Ben's eyes grew wide and his face felt warm once more. "No! What the hell are you talking about, Dad? We're just friends."

"Well," his father said before pausing to down another bite of pot roast, "When are you going to make a move, Ben? Playing video games with the girl? Why don't you take her out on a date? You haven't taken a girl out in years."

"We're *just* friends," Ben insisted, knuckles whitening around his fork.

His dad chuckled. "You guys aren't kids anymore, Ben. What, will you two be thirty, sitting in a small room playing Mario?"

"Maybe we will," Ben responded stubbornly.

"She is a good looking girl," his mother added, subtly supporting her husband's viewpoint. "And so sweet, so well-mannered for a girl your age."

"Take a whack at her," his father said.

"BILL!" Laura gasped. For a moment it looked like she was going to cough up some of her food.

"Dad!" Ben's tone was more annoyed than shocked.

His dad erupted in a fit of laughter. Bits of meat fell down his chin as his belly wobbled back and forth, striking the table and causing it to rock lightly.

"So crude," Ben's mother said, scooping herself another serving of potatoes.

"Don't say things like that, Dad. I wouldn't "take a whack at her" unless we were dating for a long time. You don't treat sweet girls like objects."

His father's hearty laugh downshifted into a chuckle. "Ben, sometimes you act like you're ten, other times you act like you're fifty. Lighten up, son, have some fun. I'm just messing with you."

Ben took a bite of pot roast and didn't answer. His father was a brash man who had his views on the world—the views he thought were the only ones suitable. What Ben and Elise had was a friendship, a long lasting friendship.

Does that mean you don't want to date her? His mind allowed his heart into the debate.

For the third time in a brief period, Ben felt himself blushing.

Donnie Shultz didn't share Ben's sentiments when it came

to women. Donnie was a hormonally driven sixteen year old boy who didn't grasp the concept of a moral compass. He would take a whack at whatever insecure, confused, hormonally driven sixteen year old girl that came his way.

This was the reason he had been skateboarding at such a fast rate down the sidewalk when he had nearly ran into Ben. Jess Ramos was planning to meet Donnie in the park around seven-thirty, and from the exchange of text messages between them earlier in the day, Donnie had been led to believe he was destined to receive a blowjob.

A blowjob *in the park,* he thought with glee.

For a sixteen year old, this was a revolutionary concept, and the promise of such an action would compel a boy with more hormones than brain cells to run to the ends of the Earth to receive his reward if need be.

Donnie had always thought fondly of Jess; she was pretty, funny, smart—well at least the smartest person Donnie had ever hung around. They had been in geometry class, and if it hadn't been for Jess letting Donnie cheat off her on every exam, he wouldn't have been able to pull out his D and pass the class.

None of that prevented Donnie from objectifying Jess and viewing her as the means to the end of his pleasure though. He was a teenage boy, what other concerns did he have in the world?

Donnie lived a responsibility free life, spending most of his days riding through Rowley on his trusty skateboard, grinding whatever rail he could find and kick-flipping over every set of steps in town. He was free as a bird when he cruised through town—skateboarding was his escape from a broken family life. When he was out there enjoying free air and mastering new tricks, he didn't have to think about the deteriorating state of his home or his parents.

Donnie's parents were both heroin junkies. It had become so bad that neither had held a job in over two years, and neither had the urge to find one since they had been getting by on unemployment benefits. The only thing Adam and Darlene Shultz cared about was getting high, and because of this Donnie had been neglected since childhood. He had learned from a young age not to love his parents because the emotion would only lead to disappointment and pain—but the sight of his parents slowly withering away and killing themselves was often too much to bear. Out on the streets there were no worries, just freedom, liberation, and the guiding spirit of adventure.

Often the spirit of adventure had told him to get the hell out of this dead end town. It told him to get away from the boredom, the lack of fun and culture that came with a place like Rowley. There was no night life, no attractions within a reasonable distance, no arcade, no movie theater, no mall, no fast food restaurant, no nothing. On top of that, when Donnie was out cruising the streets looking to have a good time he had to deal with the grouchy residents, who would keep a sharp eye on him and make sure he didn't come within an inch of their property. Rowley was a dive, the type of place that sucked the life out of people.

"Oh but it's so pretty here!" he would hear constantly.

Trees and a few old houses can only be exciting for so long.

As he rode down Main Street, Donnie couldn't see any of the houses or trees that gave the town its "charm." He could barely see the sidewalk in front of him as he cruised toward the park, still not bothering to slow his normal pace despite the poor visibility. He had almost collided with a wide-eyed kid, who had to be at least a few years older than him. From the shocked look on his face Donnie thought he had scared him good. Maybe the dude was weirded out because of all the fog.

Donnie wasn't particularly frightened of the unknown. The things he had known and become familiar with were frightening in their own right—what else was there to fear? He was a daredevil, someone constantly looking for something new and different. He didn't mind being far away and lost in the fog, in a way it was another escape for him.

He arrived at the park (he could only tell because he noticed the wooden fence surrounding the parking lot next to the sidewalk) and hopped off his skateboard. He walked into the gravel parking lot and headed toward the white wooden pavilion that sat at the end of it, at the beginning of the park itself. The park was nothing special; a basketball court, a tennis court, and one big green field—there was no skate park, and for this reason Donnie didn't find himself going there all too often.

This night was different though. This night Donnie was finally going to get blown by Jess Ramos, and he was going to get blown in the pavilion.

He casually strolled across the parking lot with his skateboard in hand, feeling warmth in his pants over the anticipation of what was to come.

Then suddenly something was wrong.

Donnie took a breath and almost gagged. The air was stagnant, and had a strange burnt odor to it. Donnie was all of a sudden hit by the urge to vomit.

The smell hadn't been detected by his nose initially; he only sensed it when he breathed in the air, when he tasted it.

"What the hell?" He spat a few times and swatted at the air to clear himself of the unpleasant sensation before continuing to walk toward his goal. No bad smell was going to stop him from getting a blowjob.

He nearly stopped again when he heard a distance voice, one that couldn't be calling out to him. It came from somewhere in the fog yet still seemed eons away. When he heard it, he knew it had to be coming from his thoughts.

"You're a waste of my money, kid," Donnie's father said. *"A waste of my time and money. If I didn't have to pay for you over the years I could have had a lot more fun, ya hear me? You shackled me down, you little ungrateful fuck."* Donnie felt glum as he heard the words, and figured they had to be a memory since they were verbatim what his father had once said to him while high.

He shook the thoughts from his head but couldn't rid himself of depression's cold touch. The memory had stripped him of all joy.

He kept walking however. Even if the strange sensation had robbed him of happiness it certainly hadn't rid him of *desire.* And after hearing it now, more than ever, Donnie wanted to use Jess for his own purposes.

The pavilion was a dark outline, and he couldn't distinguish if anyone was there waiting for him. He certainly hoped Jess was, he was too impatient to stand around and wait for *her* to show up.

He stepped on something and nearly tripped. Looking down, Donnie recognized the object that almost forced him to roll his ankle. He set his skateboard down as he used two hands to pick up the object and examine it.

Why is it just lying here?

It was Jess's purse. Donnie recognized it due to its small size and distinctive zebra print pattern. Had Jess dropped it?

Then, turning it over in his hands, Donnie noticed something more: dark, blotchy stains ruining the smooth curves of the zebra pattern. Blood.

Jess's blood.

Donnie heard it, and he froze. *Tsscchhnnntkcnnntchkkcchhhh.*

It was behind him.

Seven

"You cheap bastard!" Elise Sutter exclaimed, half angry, half laughing, as Ben blasted past in the last moment to win the race. She dropped the Nintendo 64 controller and slapped at his arms playfully. "Cheater, cheater, cheater! You're too proud to ever let me win aren't you?"

"It's not my fault you suck!" Ben exclaimed, doing his best to avoid the barrage of slaps that continued to come his way.

Both of them ended up bursting out laughing and falling backward, laying on his bed in a fit of laughter, leaving the game unattended.

Ben glanced over at Elise, at her wavy dark blonde hair and alluring emerald green eyes, her skin seemed to radiate a beautiful glow. Despite her many beautiful physical traits, Ben found himself appreciating the moment he was having with her. On an emotional level he was finding Elise absolutely stunning.

Elise was the type of girl Ben could have fun with, let loose with, and act like an idiot with. One of the reasons for this was her love of video games, especially old school video games—a passion Ben shared with her. Because of this they would spend hours competing on the Super Nintendo and Nintendo 64, the systems they grew up on. Their competition was playful, but each always tried their hardest to best the other—it was always good clean fun.

Ben had met Elise when they were ten years old. They had shared the same homeroom teacher and were in all of the same classes together. In English class one day, they had to give a presentation on something that inspired them to be creative—both Ben and Elise had chosen video games as their presentation and from that day on their friendship blossomed.

They would visit each other's houses and play video and board games, get together with other pals and play manhunt or pickup games of basketball. They were a picturesque pair of loyal, lifelong friends. Things had stayed that way even into high school, where Elise had developed a strong popularity and contingency of followers, while Ben, with his more introverted personality, kept to his small, tight knit group of pals. They had grown slightly more distant in that time, especially when Elise got distracted by a chain of relationships (all of which had gone sour, and all of which she had stuck with despite Ben's insistence to the contrary). They had still remained friends and had found time for each other.

Elise was the type of person one could share anything with; the type of person Ben could be himself around and feel one hundred percent comfortable. There was nothing taboo between the two of them.

Had things changed since they had gone separate ways, each attending different colleges? Ben didn't think so, every summer had been just the same, and although they weren't one another's shadow anymore, they still had a strong fondness for each other.

Lying on the bed, staring Elise in the eyes, Ben could not help wonder if that fondness was beginning to lean toward love.

"You're never going to be a gentleman and let the lady win, are you?" Elise asked with a smile, stretching her arms far back behind her head as she did.

"You'll earn it one day, I actually think you go easy on me—that's why I win."

"I've beaten you before, don't forget it," she said with a smirk.

"Those times are the exceptions, not the rule." Ben stuck his tongue out at her.

"Will this ever get old?" Elise's expression faded from playful to contemplative and the sudden seriousness took Ben aback.

"I don't think it has to—I mean we don't have to play video games forever, but this type of fun, these good times, there's no limit to them."

She tilted her head and stared into his eyes. He felt his heart flutter and inadvertently stared away. Elise didn't seem to notice.

"Life gets in the way though. These fun, carefree summers aren't going to last forever. In some ways this is one of the last true summers of our childhood." So quickly she had mentally gone from a kid to an adult, reminding Ben of the transitional stage of their lives they were in.

"We're at that strange crossroad, that's for sure. We're still ready to act like kids, make immature jokes, play video games, and yet we're on the threshold of having careers and responsibilities. It's kind of surreal."

Elise chuckled and Ben felt his face grow hot. "What's so funny?" The question had a sharper edge than he intended.

"You really are a writer, Ben. You talk just like one. Embellishing your thoughts and ideas like the world was a blank piece of paper."

"I think I'll get published, maybe not soon, but eventually," Ben mused, thoughts briefly abandoning the topic of Elise's beauty.

"Are you going back to Allegheny State? I know you don't want to."

"I don't know. I guess I'm committed at this point."

"Don't be foolish." She spoke with a tone of concern, the type of tone he would expect from his mother. "Your ideas and dreams are great, but going through college doesn't hurt your chances at all—in fact it probably helps them. You may not like it there, but I have a feeling the ends will justify the means."

The more she spoke, the more she articulated, the more

beautiful she became, and this was striking to Ben. He realized for the first time he was truly looking at Elise as more than just a friend, despite the fact his mind had contained him to only those thoughts for the previous ten years. Maybe it was because he didn't want to disrespect Elise by making her an object of his affection, maybe he wanted to appreciate her sans his desire to have her. Maybe that desire had been lurking all along, but only now was he brave enough to embrace it.

"You're right," Ben admitted, and Elise broke out in a grin.

"Admitting you were wrong? Ben Dowling, this is a momentous occasion. I have to say I'm quite flattered." Her sarcasm was charming, and Ben couldn't help but break out in a goofy grin of his own.

They laid on his bed, heads turned to each other gazing. As would any man his age, Ben wondered if there was something more to the stare, if there was reason for him to act on impulse. The warm moment was finally broken when Elise brought up something Ben wished no one would mention.

"Ben, can . . . I tell you something?" For the first time in years Ben thought Elise looked vulnerable, frightened to some degree.

"You can tell me anything, Elise, never hesitate, never bother to ask."

"Just don't think I'm out of my mind or anything like that." She seemed nervous and Ben was beginning to worry.

"I already think you're out of your mind, you have nothing to lose." Ben's comment was meant to ease the tension, but it seemed to have no effect.

Elise took a breath. "Have you ever had one of those bad

feelings, where you know something is wrong but don't know what it is?"

Ben *felt* his pupils widen as he pulled in a sharp intake of air. "I-I know exactly what you're talking about. Did, did you have one?"

Elise looked away for a moment, obviously troubled, and Ben understood.

"The fog, I don't know what it is, but something is not right with it. Mr. Joiner was murdered, and there's something awful about it. I know I'm not being paranoid, I just know it. Something is wrong and something about what's going on is unnatural." She seemed to cut herself short, looking to Ben with eager eyes, hoping rejection wasn't coming her way.

Ben didn't know what to say. On one hand he shared her fear, on the other he wanted to ease her concerns and rid her of tension. He wasn't sure he'd be able to do that; both knew something strange was happening in their town.

Their eyes locked again, and dubious feelings enveloped them.

"You too?" she asked quietly.

"Yeah, me too," Ben admitted after a pause. "Something is wrong. Something is up with this fog, and I think it may have something to do with Mitch Joiner's death."

Ben half expected to see a look of disbelief dawn upon Elise's face, but it didn't. They shared the same amount of conviction toward the belief that something was awry.

"We sound kind of nuts, don't we?" Elise seemed to be directing the question more toward herself.

"What's insanity in an insane world?"

That broke the tension, and Elise burst out giggling again,

"Way to go all philosophical on me, Ben, you're something else."

Ben's smile was a tentative one. Elise seemed happy to laugh and break the topic of the fog. Ben was as well, but he knew it would still be there the next day, and maybe even days after. If they mentioned it or not, it was going to be there, and something (the dark figure in his dream perhaps?) would be waiting outside for them.

"How about a few more games?" Elise asked, sharing in Ben's desire to temporarily forget the troubling feelings.

Ben forced a smiled. "You're just a sucker for punishment, aren't ya?"

"I'm going to knock your ass right off that high-horse, mister."

The rest of the night went smoothly enough for them. They played more Nintendo 64, talked about college experiences and people they had met. It was pleasant conversation but conversation that served to distract them from their lingering thoughts of the fog. They laughed and smiled, but both couldn't shake the unspoken tension beginning to fester. They had frightened each other by mentioning their own suspicions and despite the fun they were having, those feelings were becoming more and more powerful.

When he was walking Elise out of his house, Ben broke the unspoken agreement of silence on the issue.

"Do you want me to go with you, on your way home I mean?" It had come out more awkward than he intended, but with the nervous air about the both of them it went unnoticed.

"It's okay, I'm driving after all. I'll be fine. Thank you though." She gazed out of the door into the fog. In a strange way it was hypnotizing. The fog was a spectacle to behold, and Elise could have sworn she saw it moving and growing as she kept her eyes locked upon it.

"Okay then. Shoot me a call or text when you're back so I know you're safe. I mean, if you can."

Both had a feeling phones had been rendered useless, but both chose not to express it.

"I'll try. Don't worry about me, I'm a tough ol' broad." She grinned, and he grinned back.

"I know you are." They gave each other a strong hug, holding the embrace for a long moment before departing, Elise stepping out of Ben's home into the gray blanket of fog.

They exchanged goodnights as she turned and offered him a wave.

As Elise walked toward her car and was covered in a shroud, Ben had the urge to run after her, to protect her, to save her. Ben still didn't know exactly from what he would be saving her, but he knew there was something.

He took a deep breath and closed the door.

"I'll see her tomorrow. I gotta stop being so paranoid."

He prayed he was right.

Eight

The drive home was stressful. With zero visibility, Elise had to drive her SUV at a sluggish pace despite the fact there was no traffic.

At night, Rowley was absolutely dead.

She drove down Main Street, which was also a part of Pennsylvania State Route 6, passing the closed businesses, John's Pizza, Down in Chinatown, Rollie's Cafe, all restaurants that made a killing from the tourists who rolled down 6 looking for food or entertainment and were forced to settle for these local yokel establishments.

The business season would soon be ending, and this would be tough on the business owners, including Elise's own parents who owned a small antique shop on Willow Street. The fall and winter always brought rough financial times, and the stressful nature of business in a small rural town was what had urged her parents to invest all they could into a college fund for Elise, so she could get away and move onto bigger and better things.

Like Ben, Elise didn't particularly mind Rowley; it was cute in its own strange way. She had done paintings based off the old bridge over the stream near the edge of town, and of the old Aldon house that sat perched over the park. There was inspiration and creativity to be found there but it always seemed to go untapped by others.

Unlike Ben, Elise knew the practicality of setting herself up with a degree and broadening her future horizons. Ben was stubborn, obstinate in his ways and thoughts. Although he considered a great deal of things, he wasn't always as open minded toward the theories of others, as Elise herself was.

She considered herself the voice of reason for Ben. It was a role she had always undertaken and one she was happy to fulfill. She liked Ben, he was a good friend and a wonderful person, but even she was surprised at what she had felt when they had lied down on his bed.

For the first time, she really noticed that Ben was *handsome*. In one way she had always thought this, his facial features were cute and his hair was adorable, but he had always been just that: cute and adorable in the same way as a child. Now she realized Ben wasn't just cute, he was full-blown handsome.

She wasn't overwhelmed by this fact, simply amused. She had a strong feeling that Ben had a crush on her, a reality she was used to by this point; it was a situation she had encountered with most of her male friends. She wasn't distressed or worried over this, she knew no matter what she and Ben would be dear friends. And who knew, there was always the possibility for more.

A shadow.

Elise took her eyes off the road as she saw the outline of a figure, the only one on the barren street. Her visibility was obscured, she could barely see onto the sidewalk of Main Street, but there was something there, something moving. She slowed down to see if she could get a better look, and the figure froze and stood in place, motionless. Elise held her breath for a moment before hitting the accelerator and buzzing off. She didn't want to find out the identity of whatever it was, and that included the reasoning that she didn't want to look like a fool if it was just her imagination playing tricks on her.

Elise bit her lower lip as she continued her short drive home, but she was fidgety, she was worried, because, as Ben had said, something was wrong.

Something big is happening.

Phil Brooks looked at the car as it slowed to a near stop and paused a moment on Main Street, and wondered if the driver was looking his way. He stopped walking, glancing back at it, attempting to see who exactly was spying his way. Then, as if spooked, the SUV sped off, and Phil could do nothing but shrug his shoulders and continue on his merry way.

Phil was only merry because of the amount of whiskey in his system. Whiskey was the only medicine that made Phil smile at all, and Mac's Bar was his premiere watering-hole.

Mac's Bar would be considered a downer for anyone who didn't view themselves as a full-blown alcoholic. It was the type of place where locals would go to drown away their pains, the type of place went to in order to forget about real life and responsibilities.

Phil had hit it pretty hard that night, taking round after round and getting lost in the bliss of his drunken stupor. His straggly beard stunk of cheap whiskey, and his flannel sleeves were damp with the remnants of an unclean bar.

As Phil walked down the street, he didn't notice any of this, nor did he focus on how he would have to do back-breaking labor the next day at his construction job (which he hated). It was a job he couldn't stand in a town he couldn't stand populated by people he couldn't stand, but none of that mattered because he had his medicine. He drank all of his worries away—at least for one night.

"Show me the way to go home! I'm tired and I want to go to bed! Well I had a little drink about an hour ago, and it went right to my head!" He sang and his slurred voice barely traveled in the fog laden air. He had been troubled by the fog earlier in the day, but at this point he was too inebriated to be concerned.

He didn't have a care in the world. Well he did in fact have plenty, but they were hidden well beneath his drunkenness. He would be happy by artificial means if necessary, as long as he had a few hours in which he didn't have to care about life. Nothing could stop him from stumbling along the street and belting out his cheerful song.

Then something did.

It was a noise, a noise halting Phil in his wobbly tracks, a noise making all of the drunken jolliness disappear. It was a noise Phil had never heard before, but the noise was one that told him doom was coming.

Tttsknknntnchttknchhhhh.

This was immediately followed by a voice echoing throughout the fog. It was a voice he knew and one which made his spirits instantly drop.

"You stinkin' drunk. You good for nothing son of a bitch! You'll live like this your whole life then drown in a pile of your own vomit," his ex-girlfriend and mother of his children spat at him. *"You're the worst thing this sorry sack town has ever produced!"*

Phil was confused. He didn't know what was going on and lacked the faculties to really figure it out. He had only a moment to look around and survey his surroundings before he felt it. It was like someone had gone behind him and grabbed onto his shoulders, attempting to press on his pressure points. But it was not hands that dug into his shoulders, it was piercing *claws.*

Phil's flesh was penetrated and he felt razors dig through his skin and lodge into the joint of each shoulder. He let out a surprised, agonized scream and fell to his knees as the hunter came upon him. Phil barely had time to recognize what had happened, let alone attempt to flee, before the claws sank themselves fully into his shoulder sockets and yanked with incredible force.

Phil's arms were ripped out of their sockets, a horrible deafening pop drowning out the tearing of his flesh and tendons. The noise was followed by splashing sounds as Phil became a kneeling fountain, blood shooting out of both ragged holes onto the sidewalk.

He fell to his side then rolled to his back, staring upward as he began to shake and convulse. It was unfortunate he did not die from the initial strike, as Phil Brooks was forced to see the sight of the tormentor moving in over him. As it revealed itself, moving in for the kill, it began casually chomping on Phil's severed arm as if it were a drumstick. It was then he was able to see its form, and the face of the nightmarish fiend.

In that moment Phil's mind lost touch with reality as all of his darkest dreams, fears, and phobias came to light right before his eyes.

Elise made it home safely, slipping inside and into her bedroom without waking her sleeping mother. She tried sending Ben a text message to let him know she was safe, but, as she expected, it failed to send, an unknown error message popping up on her phone. She tried calling, knowing the action would be in vain, and heard only static as she dialed Ben's number.

She held the phone to her ear longer than she should have. The static was odd, similar to the type caused by bad reception but with other background noises.

The longer Elise listened, the more she could hear the noises growing, obscured by the static but still detectable. Was it whispering, chanting, was there crying?

She heard voices, speaking and chattering in hushed tones. She heard dead voices, and they were growing in quantity and volume the longer she kept the phone stuck to the side of her head.

Elise couldn't understand what they were whispering, but it was becoming louder and more chaotic. It was like she was listening to one thousand ghosts all talking at the same time, each trying to get into her head and drive her mad.

Then she heard something amongst the murmured voices, something much more haunting than any of the other dead voices.

"Tscchnnntchhhh. Eliseeeeeeee. Tschnnkknntchhhhhh. I'm going to rip your pretty little head off. Elissssse, come to meeeee."

She screamed and threw her phone. It hit the wall hard and her battery popped out and onto the floor. Elise looked with disbelief at her now destroyed phone, bewildered to the point of inaction.

Something had called for her. Something wanted to get her. She retreated to her bed like a child, sitting down and holding her knees to her chest. What the hell just happened?

Elise's eyes moved away from her destroyed cell phone and made their way to her bedroom window. Outside the fog had grown even thicker, even in the dark it let off its ghastly gray glow. It was bizarre, it was *unnatural,* and Elise knew that whatever had just spoken to her was out there somewhere in the fog.

Relax. Just relax. It's late and things are getting to you. You might be hearing things. Just lie back and think of something that calms you down, a memory you enjoy. This was a technique Elise used whenever she was feeling stressed out, and she desperately needed to take her mind away from the insanity that had just occurred. She had a particular thought in mind that often soothed her and made her feel secure. It was a memory with Ben, a memory that made her feel the warm feelings of security, trust, and, most importantly, friendship.

Elise thought back to a time when Ben had comforted her, when Ben had been her knight in shining armor. It was a memory that often times made Elise feel embarrassed by her own thoughts; the sentiments were so cheesy after all, but nonetheless it was a memory that Elise would fall back on in hard times in order to feel safe and happy.

Ben and Elise had been taking a walk down Tippman Trail, a hiking path that began in the grass just off Washington Street and ran through the woods around the town and led to Tippman Falls. It was a peaceful, scenic trail with wonderful views of the small, rocky waterfalls just beyond Rowley. The route was a welcomed escape from the drudgery of town; the forests surrounding it were lush and full of life and surprises.

Whenever Elise and Ben were bored they would walk on the trail and talk about life, which for fifteen year old Elise was a welcomed event—Ben was the only *boy* she knew who could hold any sort of serious conversation. Plus, in the summer time the cool pools at the bottom of the small waterfalls were a perfect spot for a quick dip and relaxation.

Elise remembered the entire walk well; it was a day and memory she knew she would never forget.

"What do you think about Greg Fisher?" Elise asked Ben as they hiked through the trail, small branches and leaves crunching under their shoes as they went.

"Greg Fisher? That basketball playing jerk? I think he's an ass," Ben replied, not bothering to hide his resentment.

Elise looked away from Ben for a moment, and her pace faltered. "Hey, he's not that bad you know. He has a lot of problems at home." Elise had been developing a teenage crush on the studly Greg Fisher, and although she seldom took his advice, Ben was the go to friend for these types of things.

"That doesn't give him an excuse to be a prick. He thinks he can do whatever he wants," Ben said in a huff, hating when Elise mentioned other guys. He had just begun noticing her beauty, and every time she brought up one of her more popular, attractive male friends, his mood went right down the tubes.

"Hey, now that's not nice," Elise protested. "Who's being the jerk now, Ben Dowling?"

"Don't call me by my full name, you sound like my mother." Ben kicked at a stone, sending it rolling down the hillside adjacent to the trail.

Elise paused for a moment and looked at Ben. He wasn't one of the "popular" kids like herself or Greg, but she really liked him. He wasn't tall, lean, or tone like Greg either—Ben was of average height and on the pudgy side. His hair was always a wild jungle and he was often too reserved to make his presence known—but Elise knew. One of the reasons she had brought up Greg was to get a reaction out of Ben. Every guy in their right mind had it for Elise and she figured Ben would be no different. Part of her wanted to date Ben, a considerable part of her, but another part told her it was forbidden territory; Ben was too good of a friend to risk losing.

"Why do you ask anyway?" Ben pulled Elise from her thoughts. "Are you thinking of dating him or something?"

There was no sneer or condescension in his voice. Despite Ben's views on Elise's decisions, he never belittled her or held anything against her.

Elise felt her face flush a bit, but she was able to maintain her composure. "Well, maybe, who knows? Unlike you, I have spoken to him and have gotten to know him. He's really a nice guy deep down."

"Shouldn't he be a nice guy all around?" Ben stopped and turned toward Elise.

"Not everyone is like you, Ben." Elise stood firm and met his stare.

"What does this have to do with me?" Ben asked, and Elise could see a drop of sweat developing above his brow.

Elise stumbled on her words, unable to immediately answer. "You-you just seem to compare everyone to yourself. You're great, Ben, but not everyone can act the same way as you."

Ben sighed. "Greg is a good guy deep down I'm sure, but what I think is you can do better. You don't have to fix him, you don't have to find the good in him. You need someone who brings out their own good for your sake. The guy who is compelled to be the best he can be to keep you happy—that's the guy you want."

Elise was moved by Ben's words, however missed Ben's inclination toward the fact he was that particular man.

"Ben—" she began before stopping, choking on her next syllable when she saw what stood in the woods only a dozen feet from Ben. He saw her eyes widen and her body freeze, and Ben turned to see the frightening sight standing in the woods before them.

It was a massive beast, covered with thick, black fur. It stood upon four tree trunk size legs, each equipped with powerful claws. It stared at them with dark, shiny eyes, baring its thick, terrifying fangs.

The worst part was the momma bear wasn't alone; she had brought her cubs along.

Elise wasn't a girl who was startled easily by nature; she had been raised in a rural town and woodland animals were an everyday part of life. She wasn't particularly frightened by bears, but having a three hundred and fifty pound bear a dozen feet from her was a scary sight. Being raised in the sticks, Elise knew the only time a black bear would be aggressive toward people is when it had cubs with it.

Momma Bear wasn't happy.

She took a strong step forward, fallen branches snapping under the immense weight of her paw. She raised her head and let out a growl—no, it was more of a roar. It was a sound that told Elise to run, and run fast, and as the bear took a few more steps forward, with its cubs falling back and behind, Elise turned to make an escape.

She was stopped by Ben as he grabbed her hand, pulling her closer to him. He didn't break eye contact with the bear as he spoke, as cool and collected as Elise had ever seen him.

"Don't run. She will chase you and she will catch you. Calm down. Relax. Follow my lead and step backward very slowly. Do not look away from her and do not challenge her. Do you understand?"

Elise, shaking, was only able to nod and somehow out of his peripheral Ben caught the affirmation.

For the first time the pair held hands, and Ben took the

lead and began stepping backward, skillfully able to stay on the trail while he led them through their backtracking.

The mother bear let out another huff and growl, taking two faster steps forward and howling at the pair. The three cubs looked on with curiosity and amusement, learning the ways of the woods from their mother.

Elise wanted to turn and bolt, but she trusted Ben more than she trusted any other. She wanted to look away from the stone eyed stare of the animal, but she wouldn't disregard Ben's commands. Even as she obeyed, and they began distancing themselves from the bear, the creature didn't relent in its aggression.

The bear kept walking toward them, snarling and growling. She didn't like Ben and Elise and especially didn't like them near her children. She let out another mighty roar, one that caused Elise to jump backward in fear—and this was enough to set the mother bear off.

There was no hesitation from the animal. She charged in a frenzy, her powerful legs launching her massive body at incredible speed, teeth bared and prepared to strike. That was it for Elise; it was time to run. It didn't matter what Ben had said, this was life and death. She spun away from the beast and began to run, her skinny legs pushing off and moving with all the power they had. She barely made it a step before two arms wrapped firmly around her. With a sudden jolt of a tackle, Elise's fragile frame was forced to the ground and held down, but not by the raging bear—by Ben.

Ben tackled Elise and curled up next to her. She began to flail and resist, attempting to rise and run when she heard his voice.

"Elise. Don't move. It will attack us if we move. Play dead, if we're dead we are no threat. Trust me. Please, Elise, trust me." His voice was slightly above a whisper but still held clout. Elise wanted to flee, her heart pounding out of her chest, but there was just something about his voice that told her he was right. If there was anyone in the world she could have faith in, it was Ben.

Elise lay facing Ben, embracing him as their arms wrapped around each other's bodies. She looked into his pale blue eyes and saw the beginnings of what would end up being long repressed romantic feelings. She saw the care and love in Ben's eyes, and for a girl of fifteen she was struck by this. Never before had she seen such passion and conviction, especially in such a simple way. His eyes showed the love and care, and for a quick moment Elise felt everything was going to be okay—everything *had* to be okay in Ben's arms.

The bear's pace slowed when they fell. Elise snapped back to reality as she heard the bear coming to a stop to examine them. Elise closed her eyes and let her trust and care for Ben warm her.

The bear grunted, circling around the motionless friends. Both of their breaths were shallow, both did their best to play dead so they didn't have to *become* dead. The bear went around them once before letting out another grunt and doing something that nearly made Elise shriek.

The bear put her nose down to sniff them and her cold, wet snout touched the side of Elise's face and brushed against her cheek. The momma bear's menacing jaws were pressed right next to her face, with the potential to take the flesh off of her bone in one chomp.

But Elise trusted Ben. She didn't move despite her natural instinct screaming to get away.

The bear nudged her face slightly before pulling away. She hovered over them for another moment before satisfied they were no longer a threat. She turned and left, making her way back to her cubs before beckoning them to leave. Elise could feel air returning to her lungs as she heard the steps become more distant. Eventually there was no sound at all and after two minutes of continuing to play dead, the act was broken.

"It's gone," Ben said, and Elise opened her eyes. She wanted to smile and cry and laugh and scream all at the same time. She wanted to give Ben the biggest hug of his life and never let go. Elise was a teenage ball of emotion *before* this event, and now she could barely contain the dizzying mix of feelings welling up inside her.

Finally tears broke free from her eyes, and gently slid down her cheeks.

"Don't cry. It's okay," Ben said tenderly, using a finger to wipe away the tears.

"I know it's okay. I'm just . . ."

"Relieved? Releasing some pent up feelings?" Ben finished her sentence.

Elise laughed and it was liberating. "Yes. Thank you."

"No need to thank me."

"Yes. Plenty of reason to thank you. You saved my life."

"I care about you, Elise." Elise felt her heart rate increase. Ben was looking at her as if he was going to lean in and kiss her.

Did she want him to? She wasn't sure. He just saved her life and he made her feel safe. Everything felt right when he put his arms around her, but could she *kiss* Ben?

Ben wasn't like the boys she had crushes on. Ben was *too good* for Elise to want to date. Ben wasn't the type of person she wanted to risk losing because of some romantic fling.

Elise broke their stare and sat up abruptly, blushing as she brushed the dirt off her blouse. There was then an awkward silence.

Ben finally spoke. "You sure you're okay?"

Elise forced a small laugh. "Yes, Ben, I'm fine. That was just a lot to go through. Hey, why don't we go back to my house? Mom made some apple pie and I know she wants someone to tell her how good it is."

Ben took a moment to respond. "Yeah, that sounds nice." He rose and offered his hand to help Elise up. She took it and stood to face him.

"Th-thank you, Ben." Elise noticed the bittersweet look in Ben's eyes as she delivered her words.

"Of course. You'd do the same thing for me. We work well together."

Together. There was something powerful about the concept but Elise didn't want to wrap her mind around it any longer.

"Let's get going," she said, and together they made their way out of the woods and back home.

Elise had never told anyone about the incident and as far as she knew neither had Ben. The two also had never brought it up between each other, but Elise had never forgotten. Part of her thought she had taken Ben for granted that day, and in the time since. Greg Fisher had turned out to be a real jerk, and so had Jeremy Brunson and Jake Fulton, Ryan McDonald, and all the rest. Elise had ended up dating a slew of guys who never really cared about her or could take the time to appreciate her, and yet Ben was always there. Was he ready, willing, and waiting? If he was, he had never uttered a word of protest or frustration to Elise about her decision to never give him a shot, but his eyes always seemed to do that for him.

When something is right there for the taking sometimes people overlook it. We want what we can't have, isn't that what they say? Maybe I've been that way. Maybe I've been looking for something I've had all along. Elise bit her lip as she thought that over. She had gone to the memory to feel warm and secure, but the effect had only been temporary. As she glanced out the window and saw the creeping fog she couldn't help but hear that horrible voice again.

Elisssssssse. Something was out there and it wanted her. Elise wasn't irrational and she wasn't a particularly fearful woman, something had *spoken* to her.

Could Ben save her now? Could he be her knight in shining armor and assure her everything was okay? There wasn't a bear out there this time—there was something much worse. Elise didn't know this but she felt it with such certainty she was convinced.

Get it together, girl. You don't need Ben to save you from some imaginary phantom. Maybe it's all in your head.

Elise looked out her window into the creeping fog and felt her blood run cold. It moved unnaturally, it moved *toward* her. It *wanted* her.

For the first time since her childhood, Elise laid with her

covers up to her nose, afraid of every shadow that danced in her room.

She barely slept that night.

Nine

That night the citizens of Rowley began realizing that something was wrong. Although many of them were skeptics and tended to cast issues off as non-problems, they couldn't deny the creeping feelings of doubt, suspicion, fear, and hatred welling up inside them.

As television, phones, and internet connections failed, the populous could only look out their windows at the sight of the ever-growing fog. It was dubious, it had come and they had lost their connection with the outside world—the thick fog was a sign of the isolation to come.

But there was something else strange about the

fog. While some residents felt chilled to the bone upon seeing it, causing them to stay as far away from the windows as possible, others—a good majority in fact—felt compelled by it in a bizarre, mesmerizing way.

Zachary Sherman stared out into the fog and heard voices, but not with his ears—with his mind. At first they were cold dead voices, pleading voices begging him to go out into the fog. But soon the static-like whispers became one voice, and it was a voice Zachary could identify.

It was a voice from the past, the voice of Ernie Stevens, the police officer in town who had stolen Julie Hunter away from him seventeen years earlier. Ernie had come right in and swept Julie off her feet, and took her away from Zachary in the years following high school. This was after Zachary and Julie had been dating for four years; she was the woman he planned to marry.

He hadn't found anyone since and Zachary's hateful grudge ran deep. To add insult to injury, Zachary now had to deal with Ernie Steven's outright audacity as he stood somewhere out in the fog and taunted him over the past.

"I have her now, Zachary. You were high school sweethearts but she wanted a man with a big, thick cock. That's right, I give it to her every single night and she loves it—that sweetheart you used to give little pecks on the lips, well she becomes a filthy slut for my dick! How does being hopeless and alone feel?"

Ernie's voice appeared to be far away in the fog. It was being cast from a distance yet at the same time it seemed to be inside his head. Ernie Stevens was messing with Zachary's mind; he was inside his thoughts taunting him. Zachary clenched his fist and punched the wall next to the window.

His rage was powerful and for a moment he considered running out into the fog to teach that Ernie Stevens a well-deserved lesson.

But despite his overwhelming anger there was still a lingering feeling of apprehension as Zachary stared out into the fog. There was something wrong with it, his instincts screamed at him. The fog was something foreboding.

Something evil.

Although his apprehension held him back from mindlessly charging into the fog, it didn't do anything to quell the bitterness, anger, and contempt growing as thoughts of the past flooded his mind and stung his heart. The flood-gates had opened and his malice spilled over, becoming a raging rapid of hatred.

As his scorn grew, so did the fog.

Molly Carpenter had a similar experience when she gazed out into the fog. Although for her the voice was that of Rachael Ludlow, the catty bitch who got her fired from her job at the insurance agency two years earlier. Her mind raced as the painful memories returned.

Molly had trusted Rachael, as a friend and as a confidant. She had been the only one whom Rachael had told about the affair she was having with fellow co-worker Rich Miller.

It was so deliciously scandalous. Molly's own husband hadn't been able to get it up for the last six months, so Molly figured she had no other choice. Rich was attractive, funny, and a pro in the sack. They had gone on a whirlwind fling for the ages. The most wonderful part had been that there wasn't a shred of commitment. It had been the most carefree, happy period of Molly's entire life.

Then she lost it all.

Molly had seen no harm in divulging her salacious secrets to her best friend Rachael, after all Molly knew everything in Rachael's closest and they were as close as sisters.

Or so Molly had thought.

Turns out Rachael just couldn't keep the raunchy details to herself. The blabbermouth had rode off like Paul Revere and told the whole town about Molly's juicy little secret. Dating, let alone adulterous affairs, were forbidden in the office and subsequently both Molly and Rich were fired when the news got around to their boss. There went her financial stability and paid vacations.

But that was far from the end of it. Molly's husband had divorced her and taken most of their wealth along with him. Judge Paulson wasn't too favorable toward hussies who ran around on their men, especially since he had been the victim of such acts thirty years earlier.

So where did that leave Molly? She had lost her job, she had lost her home, and in the end she even lost Rich when he went off carousing with another piece of ass. Molly had ended up alone, living in a crummy apartment while working two shitty part times jobs for table scraps.

And it was all because of that remorseless *bitch* Rachael Ludlow.

Molly held her rage in for two years, but when she stared out into the fog she could hear Rachael's voice chattering away wildly as she told the story of when Molly had fucked Rich in the break-room to an unknown listener.

"The dim bitch didn't think anyone would find out! Hah!

She deserves all she got!" Rachael laughed and laughed and laughed.

Molly began formulating her plan to murder her.

And the fog grew thicker.

The same could be said about Terry Franklin, who boiled over with rage thinking about the debt Shaun Berger owned him. Jonathan Stuko was convinced his petty neighbor, Bob Dobson, had been the one who vandalized his car a few months prior. That car had been his pride and joy, and Bob had done it just because of a squabble over the new fence Jonathan was putting up. His hatred ran fast and free.

Lillian Roebel had hated Jenny Tanner since high school, where she had mercilessly made fun of her. The old memories sparked a newer, greater loathing that demanded Lillian enact revenge. Then there was Peter Manza who hated Trevor Ambrose, and Allen French who hated Vicki Peters, Heath Holster and Morgan Dimmer . . .

And so on and so on and so on.

And the fog continued to grow thicker.

TEN

The next morning, Nick Laflin was driving down Route 6 from his vacation house off the shores of beautiful Lake Wiladongun, to Rosedale, in order to pick up some fishing supplies and maybe even a breakfast sandwich while he was at it. Nick had taken a week off from work using his saved vacation days, and that meant he and his family would be spending the entire time relaxing on the serene waters of the lake.

It was only their second day up from New York, but already the vacation was going incredibly well. The weather was pristine, and the clear blue skies and warm temperatures told Nick it was a perfect day to take the family out on the boat and enjoy some fishing. A day fishing, drinking a few beers, and sharing some laughs with the wife and kids really would take the edge off and set the mood for the rest of the week.

Nick certainly could have headed into Rowley to pick up his supplies, there were a few places here and there that could accommodate him, but the prices were so high while the quality so low. The town was a tourist trap through and through, so most of the time Nick found himself driving the extra twenty minutes to Rosedale. On top of having better prices and stores, the town actually had a plaza mall which included a Dunkin Donuts, the only one within an hour's drive. Nick could save some money and get a quality breakfast; there was nothing to lose by passing through the little town of Rowley.

Nick thought Rowley was nice enough to look at, but beyond the initial beautiful scenery sat the true identity of the town: a stinking, backwater shit-hole. The people were rednecks and drunks, peddling their second rate antiques and food at you any chance they got, and the kids of the town walked around with blank expressions as if they were zombies.

It's like they don't even have a purpose in life. They walk around waiting for something exciting to happen, and it never comes.

Nick couldn't imagine living in the area all year round. The only thing there for entertainment was the lake, and the locals seldom took advantage of that.

They decided to live here and they don't even buy a boat? What a bunch of redneck morons.

All the people Nick had met on or around the lake had been outsiders. All of the land around the lake itself was owned by weekenders and vacationers; it was like having a little haven of New York and New Jersey in a peaceful, private setting.

The locals only show their faces when you drive into town and they want to sell you something you don't need. They put on those money grubbing smiles when you have your wallet out but as soon as you don't buy anything, you see the bitterness in their eyes. They're happy when you come and happy when you leave. They enjoy being parasites making a buck off of civilized people. It's backward. The whole area is backward.

Nick drove down the slope of 6 as it dipped down and entered the small valley containing Rowley. He noticed something strange as he went down the forested, hilly portion of 6 that would eventually become Main Street: he was driving from idyllic summer weather into a thick, hazy fog seeming to appear out of nowhere.

It was like hitting a wall. He could see nothing past it, but when he drove into it, he could see nothing behind him. It gave Nick the impression he had just entered a different dimension. It was a strange event, and Nick felt a small tingling sensation surging through his body. It was a scene out of a science fiction movie, like he had teleported galaxies away instantly by driving through the fog-wall.

Ha, makes sense. This town is in a dimension of its own.

He cruised down Main Street, barely able to see the businesses that dotted it. Each old building was just an outline behind the fog. The town looked even more creepy and bizarre than it usually did. The haze made the empty streets not appear peaceful, but barren in a foreboding sort of way.

Nick didn't think much of this however; it was just a strange bit of weather hovering over a strange bit of the world. He imagined that beyond the fog, the kids of the town were still walking aimlessly about, ceaselessly searching for something to grab their attention. He imagined the store owners sitting behind their counters and foaming at the mouth while they waited for a customer to come buy their worthless junk.

Just some bad weather in a bad part of the world.

He continued his path down 6/Main Street, traversing the entire stretch of the town in under a minute without passing a single car. This was not unusual. There were times when Rowley appeared completely empty and abandoned. This was just one of those times.

Temporarily void of people, permanently void of character. Welcome to Rowley, Pennsylvania, where all your dreams die.

He passed by the police station as he reached the only stop light in town. The stoplight was only necessary since the traffic going through Rowley traveling on 6 could be heavy during the height of tourist season, especially on the weekends. The light sat at an intersection where 6 continued forward heading toward Rosedale, passing through the hamlet of White Hills along the way. The road intersecting it was Beecher Street, which was the last stretch of residences before Main Street simply became 6 West and the town of Rowley ended.

The light was red, though Nick could barely see this through the mist. He sat for a moment as no traffic went by in any direction, and waited until the light turned green to go on his way.

Then something peculiar happened.

As Nick drove through the stop light and continued down 6 the fog grew even thicker. Nick had to slow to a creeping pace just to stay on the road; 6 was notoriously winding and poorly maintained. One slip up and a driver could end up rolled over in a ditch or wrapped around a tree.

That was one of the many things he couldn't stand about driving in the area. Sure, there were often no other motorists to deal with, but there were plenty of other hazards. There were pot holes, treacherously winding roads, deer and other animals jumping across the road, and those damn trees everywhere.

When a storm blows a few into the road no one ever seems to be in a rush to move 'em.

Nick was frustrated. He clenched the wheel tightly and began to think if any of those obstacles were in his way he would be unable to see or avoid them. A nasty voice in his head kept snapping about how awful the rural area was, and he began wondering why exactly he continued coming to an area he secretly hated.

It's peaceful.

Yes, but the people and the way of life here drive you mad.

It's a get-a-way.

Yeah, from the people you like to the people you hate.

The lake is nice.

It's about the only thing that is.

He returned his focus to driving, which took precise care. He had no clue how far down 6 he had gone at his crawling pace, and he hoped he would see the plaza that signified he had arrived in Rosedale and found civilization.

For ten minutes this continued, Nick driving at a snail's pace in zero visibility, leaning over the wheel as if he was a grandfather. He couldn't even see the trees surrounding the road. He could have been convinced he wasn't even on a road at this point. It was a miracle Nick didn't drive off of the road or slam into one of those steadfast trees.

Nick took his time and drove carefully, hoping he would eventually see something. He wasn't normally a worry-wart of a man but when something did go wrong he usually over-reacted. That was the opposite of what he needed while on vacation, so the sight of his destination would be a welcomed relief from the unknown of the all-encompassing fog.

When finally an object emerged out of the haze it was somewhat of an oddity. It was something that didn't exist on Route 6 West between Rowley and Rosedale.

A traffic light.

It was red, and Nick stopped. He was puzzled and filled with disbelief.

Where am I? Did they put a new stoplight in White Hills? This isn't the one near the Rosedale Plaza Mall. No, they don't need one in White Hills, there's nothing there. Maybe I drove off onto a side road and got lost?

That possibility was erased when he saw the green street sign attached to the metal pole holding the stoplight.

Beecher Street. He was at the intersection of 6 and Beecher, the exact same location he had been ten minutes earlier.

Perplexed, Nick surveyed his surroundings. To his shock, he could see the outline of the Rowley Police Department in the not so far distance, discernible by the large sign they kept on the small patch of grass between the station and the sidewalk.

What in the hell?

The light turned green, but Nick kept his foot on the break, unable to comprehend what had just happened. He hadn't got turned around nor done a U-turn. It was impossible for him to have ended up in the same location; in addition, he knew there wasn't any road that would have looped him back to Rowley that quickly.

This was inexplicable, this was mind-blowing, and for Nick Laflin it was too much.

His knuckles whitened on the steering wheel and he began taking deep breaths. Nick wasn't the type of man who dealt with the unexplained well. Logical thought failed him as stress and tension took over.

What, am I in the goddamn Twilight Zone? He wouldn't have been surprised if Rod Serling himself stepped out in front of the vehicle and went off on one of his famous monologues, describing how the tourist who visited the area he could not stand was now destined to be trapped in it forever.

"Case in point, we have Nick Laflin, everyday man trying to enjoy an escape with his family. Only this time he's taken a detour, one filled with bizarre occurrences and irony as rich as it can only be . . . in the Twilight Zone."

HONK! A car stopped behind him beeped as he sat at the now green light.

Nick jumped, jolted from his thoughts. "Fucking hell." He held back the urge to give the driver the finger and hit the accelerator and drove through the intersection. He continued down 6 West as he had previously, while the car behind him made the right onto Beecher. He should have been relieved to see someone else alive in the fog, but his mind was preoccupied with making sense of and rectifying the impossible scenario that had just played out.

He drove faster now, disregarding his safety in order to get away from the strange bit of madness which had just occurred. He sped around each turn and bend with desperation, wanting to find Rosedale and a return to normalcy.

Fuck this, whatever just happened, fuck this. I want to go get a bagel with some cream cheese, a few fishing supplies and then head on back to the house. Gotta get to Rosedale and leave this mess behind me. Nick Laflin couldn't stand the town of Rowley to begin with, now he was dealing with the possibility that he couldn't escape it.

He sped but drove with precision, making sure not to leave the pavement of the road. He was positive that he didn't veer off of six and onto some side street. This time the trip took only five minutes, but as his car flew through the fog something appeared that made Nick Laflin's heart stop.

A stoplight. The stoplight at the intersection of 6 and Beecher. He was at the place where he started—again.

He stepped out of his car, leaving the door open. Standing in the middle of the street he raised his arms to the sky and cried out, "What the fuck is this? What the fuck is going on?" He fell to his knees, defeated by the inexplicable series of events that had just occurred. A mentally weak man, Nick Laflin was losing his composure, wit, and a small shred of his sanity. He wanted to get out, to get away, and to go anywhere that was not this town—not this intersection.

But he was trapped.

Nick Laflin was trapped in what he thought was some type of sick nightmare.

And it was only the beginning.

Eleven

Dead silence.

That's all Tom Williams heard, no matter what number he dialed into his cell phone.

Absolute dead silence.

No phones worked. The television showed only static, which by now had gone from a noisy ruckus to a still silence, and to top it all off he had tried to use his computer only to find he couldn't access the internet.

This had been the exact same case yesterday and not just for him, all of Rowley was cut off from the world.

For the first time in his years of service for the

town of Rowley he was deeply troubled. Whatever was going on was far beyond his control; it was the type of situation a small town sheriff should never have to deal with. His job was supposed to let him kick back and relax until he had to deal with the occasional drunk or fender bender. For fifteen years it had been that way.

Until that day. Something was going on, and he couldn't find out what.

Tom wanted to know the conclusions drawn about Mitch Joiner's body. Was it an animal attack or had the wounds been inflicted by a man? Mitch Joiner's body was at Rosedale Memorial Hospital, and when Tom had awakened, he attempted to call them in order to inquire as to the state of the autopsy.

He couldn't get through. He couldn't find out a thing.

The worst part of all of this was the knowledge of how ill-equipped the Rowley Police Department was to handle such a case—they didn't have a crime investigation unit or forensic technology. All they had were a handful of bumbling peacekeepers, who would do their best to make sure the tourists never had anything to distract them from their leisure times. There were never more than two cops on duty at a time in Rowley—there was never a need.

Most likely, if true foul play was at hand, the case would be turned over to the State Troopers. They would have the equipment necessary to deal with and investigate the crime. Tom Williams had no issue passing on the responsibility, especially when he lacked the resources to adequately handle the matter.

I've put in too much time here to have to deal with something screwed up like this. None of this is supposed to happen in our town, our quiet, beautiful, peaceful, happy town.

But it was happening, and now it appeared things were in Tom's hands until he was able to contact the State Troopers.

No phones, no internet, no TV. I suppose I can drive out to the Barracks if I want to get a hold of someone. But first I'd have to get the word on the autopsy. That'll take up a lot of time, and if there really is a nutcase out there the town is going to need me.

Tom knew deep down he didn't want to face who or what had torn Mitch up so badly, but if duty called, well then duty called. Despite his anxiety Tom still had a sense of responsibility; after all he *was* the sheriff of Rowley.

As he glanced out of his window into the thick fog, a sizable majority of his conscience wished he wasn't the sheriff. That portion of his conscience wished he was on vacation, because the more he peeked out the window at the fog the more he felt a sinking sensation that something was terribly wrong. The fog itself was strange, but the murder, the phones, and everything else put together seemed all too odd to be coincidence. Tom shook his head. Any thoughts of these things being associated was crazy. *I'm not in a Hollywood movie, I'm in real life,* he told himself.

Since it was real life, Tom had to take initiative and go out and begin solving some of these problems by driving to the hospital, phone company, cable provider, and the State Police Barracks if necessary. He would get answers and take command of his town. Sheriff Tom Williams would show the residents of Rowley that he was in control and he could handle any situation.

He gulped, hoping he could not only convince the townsfolk, but himself of this image, and began getting dressed.

He had a feeling it was going to be a long day.

Around the same time Sheriff Williams had woken up and begun to dress, Ben Dowling pulled himself out of bed after being awakened by the speed of his beating heart and the feeling of thick, slimy sweat decorating his skin. He knew he had another nightmare, but was thankful to realize he couldn't remember it. All he could remember was the intense feeling of terror that had shaken him during the dream. Like aftershocks from a massive earthquake, waves of discomfort radiated through him as his mind did its best to piece together the scene of what had so startled him in his slumber.

He only could come up with concepts: Fear and Darkness. Desolation and Hatred. Loneliness and Pain.

Ben quickly surmised it may have been the exact same dream he had the night before. He knew he was fleeing those awful concepts in the dream, and the source of them was very likely the dark shadowy figure chasing him through his dreams the night before.

It didn't matter. What did matter was he could see the fog through his window and it was thicker than ever, as if someone had painted the glass of his window a muddled gray. Something was wrong, that was for sure, and as he stared at the plane of gray blanketing his home and his town, he was hit with a new sharp stab of fear.

Elise. The name shot into his head and his worry hit an all-time high.

She never had called him the night before, or maybe she had but couldn't get through. Ben experienced the same difficulties when he tried calling her before going to bed. Whatever was going on, it was interfering with phones, with technology overall. The strange event was leaving the town without any form of communication.

It's trapping us. It's trapping us and maybe it has already gotten Elise. Maybe it chased her down like it's been chasing me in my dreams but she wasn't able to escape. Termination. It has her. It's killed her. It's gone and cut up her beautiful face and dragged her into the darkness . . .

"No," Ben said to convince himself. "That's ridiculous, Elise is fine." He did his best to reassure himself, but the sudden jolts of fear along with the unwelcome thoughts left Ben rattled.

He needed to confirm that Elise *was* okay. Something was going on, something dangerous to everyone in Rowley. Ben decided he was going to get to the bottom of it so the unknown could torture him no longer. He was going to start by making sure Elise was all right, and that would be the most pressing and important matter of the day.

I'd die for her. Only now in a moment of distress had Ben's mind subconsciously accessed the sentiments that had laid dormant for years.

Purpose in mind, Ben changed his clothes in preparation for what he also imagined would be a very long day.

He hadn't the slightest inkling of what was to come.

The long day had begun for Tom Williams in all the wrong ways. His short drive down River Street was usually relaxing. That particular day however, he could not see the river; he couldn't see anything and the scenic drive lost all of its charm as it was suffocated in a coat of gray.

The gray-out conditions had nearly caused him to veer off the road at the winding turn just before Main Street. If not for his quick reaction he would have plowed through Bob Dobson's picket fence and torn up his pristine lawn. His out of control car would have only been stopped when it smashed into the gigantic, ancient oak tree that decorated Bob's property and had been the subject of countless quickly snapped photos. Just like that, a cornerstone of the town would be ruined and the citizens of Rowley would have to peel Tom Williams' face off of the scaly bark of the tree.

Tom muttered as he took the left onto Main Street, mainly on a leap of faith since there was no real way of telling if traffic was coming. He cruised toward the police station, wondering just how he would rally the troops to solve the growing problem Rowley was facing. Only McNair and Stevens would be in, although Tom held out hope that some of the other officers had actually taken initiative to come assist in the effort. Jenkins and Dowery lived outside of town, and Tom wondered if they were experiencing the same types of problems with the phones and technology. With no way to call in or out of town, it was actually possible both of them were completely unaffected and unaware of what was going on in Rowley.

As Tom was rehearsing the big, bold speech he would use to spur McNair and Stevens into action, all feelings of power and composure faded when he cast his eyes on the police station.

It's like a goddamn mob, he thought, as he spun his car into the lot, parking at the very end to avoid the crowd gathered outside of the station doors.

In truth, it wasn't a mob. It was only ten people waiting outside the station for help and/or guidance. Joe Handlan (whose presence as a police officer had been one of the many reasons his brother Jack had never gotten in trouble with the law) had been working the late shift at the station, all by his lonesome. He was slated to close it up. After ten, the station closed down and all police response was in the hands of the State Troopers, Pine Grove and Rosedale each had posts about a half hour drive from the town

Handlan had not been surprised by the lack of calls he received, but he hadn't the foresight to even check the phones without being beckoned by one ringing. It had not occurred to him that the phones might have gone from buggy to completely out of service. Joe had never gotten in touch with the slew of citizens who were becoming concerned about the disappearances of their loved ones. Additionally, with phone service out, these concerned citizens had been unable to contact the State Troopers for assistance. Due to this, and the ever growing panic quickly spreading through Rowley, a small group of citizens had gathered at the police station, desperate for answers.

Tom was overwhelmed as the crowd swarmed his car, some beating their hands on the side and clamoring for his attention. He was used to being a big fish in a very small pond. When he shouted orders and made speeches to small amounts of people, they held merit. Now he was surrounded by panic stricken people, who would demand answers he didn't have. What would they do then? What would they do when he couldn't just sweep the problems under the rug?

Tom pushed the door of his car open, forcefully budging Jen Roberts out of the way. Hands immediately found their way to his body, grasping at him desperately as each citizen tried to explain their situation.

There was Paul Roberts's wife, Jen. Tom also noticed Kate Rhine, the closing manager at Braylon's Market, Tim Dolan, a member of the seldom used Rowley Volunteer Fire Department, Jeff Hossler, one of the mechanics at the Rowley Garage, Tiffany Bent, stay at home wife of George Bent, the town dentist, and Todd Miles, a twenty-something that worked at the local gas station and used the money to support his drug habit. Tom did not recognize the other four people, although the town was small he didn't personally know everyone.

There were two teenagers, who seemed to stand as one and gravitate away from the group. Both ratty looking, Tom correctly assumed they were a couple. Additionally there was a fat, balding man about Tom's own age, whose wispy white hair could barely contain the shining baldness of his head, and a woman of about forty, with dark red hair and a figure so thin it looked like a mild gust of wind could pick her up and carry her away.

Tom did not have time for introductions, pleasantries, or even basic procedure; he was under attack by a swarm.

"Sheriff! Sheriff!" Jen Roberts screamed as she beat her hands against his chest frantically. "My Paul, my Paul, my Paulllll! He hasn't come home from his morning deliveries and he's NEVER late. Where is my Paul?"

"There's a huge blood stain in the parking lot of the park!" The male teenager stepped forward, then seeming surprised by the boldness of his declaration, he slid back behind the rest of the crowd.

Todd Miles grabbed Tom's arm and yanked him forward, forcing Tom to look at him face to face. "There's no fucking way out of the town. I can't get out of the town. What the fuck is going on, Tom? What the fuck do we fucking do? Is this a goddamn dream?" Tom had no idea what his words meant, or what the hell had happened to him, but by the crazed look on Todd's face, Tom could tell it was big. Suddenly, the man who had been planning his save-all speech a few moments ago wanted to disappear and get as far away from the desperate crowd as possible. Sheriff Tom Williams wanted nothing to do with Rowley, its people, or any of its problems.

"My father!"

"My friend!"

"My daughter!"

"My Paul!"

They all clamored and pulled at Tom, and for the first time he understood what it was like to be claustrophobic. He was being engulfed, he was being suffocated. His face turned bright red and he wiggled away the best he could from the prying hands, before he had enough and had to let it all out.

"EVERYONE STAY BACK AND CALM THE HELL DOWN BEFORE THINGS GET OUT OF HAND!" He didn't even realize he had drawn his pistol until he saw the frightened looks of the townspeople. Just like that the big concerns had vanished and been replaced by the concern of the moment, the fear that Tom Williams was about to start firing off some rounds.

Tom gasped, surprised by his own actions, and fumbled his gun back into its holster. "J-just . . . relax! Okay, just everyone calm down and we will get to you. One by one line up in front of the station."

The woman Tom did not know protested. "But they locked the door! They won't see any of—"

"STAND IN LINE," he bellowed again, each person freezing with the fear that the shout was a prelude to a gunshot. In their brief moment of paralysis, Tom scrambled past them to the front door of the station. Barely able to hold the keys straight, it took him a few moments to make his way in. Tom slammed the door behind him, wishing he would wake up from the awful dream. He wished he would wake up to his bumbling, boring everyday life, the life where he had more time than responsibilities.

There was no escaping the nightmare.

TWELVE

Dan McNair was not known as a particularly friendly man, or even as one who would give someone the courtesy of engaging in pleasant small talk. Unlike most residents of Rowley, Dan didn't even care enough to *pretend* anyone in the town mattered to him. Dan was callous and blunt, if he didn't like the way someone dressed or behaved he would let them know. He wasn't prone to gossip like the rest of the town, but he wasn't immune to the petty hatred deeply seated in the town's culture.

Dan McNair was not a tolerant man, and if Rowley was a larger area with a more diverse population that may have been a problem. But in a small, out of the way town like Rowley there wasn't enough crime for Dan McNair to exercise his bitterness and abuse his power. There simply was no opportunity like that in a town averaging less than one emergency phone call per day.

With Tom Williams as sheriff, Dan McNair had been reduced to playing sidekick to a bumbling idiot, someone who was as incompetent as they came. In Dan McNair's eyes, Tom Williams represented all of the satirical portrayals of inept cops. *He's the type of cop who really does go out of his way to get donuts,* Dan would often jest to himself. Making caricatures of Tom Williams was one way Dan got through the day.

Dan himself was no superstar cop. He wasn't even particularly adept at the job when he *did* have something to do. Dan didn't consider this however. Dan was the type of person who couldn't deal with his own vices; he much preferred scorning others for their own. By devaluing others in his mind he was able to justify his own shortcomings, and rationalize to himself the idea that he was, at least in most ways, superior to the general population.

Dan McNair had been unable to handle his shortcomings since he was a child. His deep-seated insecurity and power complex had a source. His uncle, Chad Weiss, had molested him multiple times over a period of two years. His family had eventually come upon the truth years later, but the scandal would threaten family unity and their image in Rowley. In a town where not too much went on and small successes were the apex of achievement, image meant everything and a setback as large as that would have put their family name in the dumpster for generations. So the McNairs had kept quiet, and most in the family had raised their eyebrows when Dan, the boy who had been hidden from the eyes of the law, decided to become a police officer himself. His mother mused that it was because he wanted to do justice, since justice had never been done in his case—and although this theory would certainly be plausible, it had nothing to do with Dan's choice.

Dan wanted power over his life. He wanted the control and influence that had been stripped away from him when he was a child. His desire for power was influenced by his many encounters with his perverted uncle, however Dan had no drive to put an end to the pain and suffering of others—he only aimed to put a Band-Aid on the ever-growing emotional scar cut deep into his psyche.

But even as a police officer, the control and influence he wanted never came. Dan was in no position to use his authority to coerce others—in Rowley there was never an opportunity. At thirty years old, Dan was stuck in a sidekick role, relegated to driving drunks home from Mac's Bar a few times a week. He was subordinate to a man who was his inferior, doing next to nothing in his job, and all of this in a town he had always despised.

Staying in the town served as a constant reminder of what had happened to him as a child. Even as an adult, Dan McNair continued to have nightmares about his uncle.

His pencil snapped, and Ernie Stevens gave him a curious look. Dan couldn't stand Ernie. He was an ass kissing, compact version of the bulbous idiot who was their boss. *What are you looking at, shit-face?* Dan thought bitingly.

Stevens opened his mouth to say something but caught

the look on McNair's face and decided against it. Dan wasn't sure how he would react if Ernie had said anything; he was closer to the edge than he had ever been before. First it had been Mitch, a situation that spooked Dan despite the golden opportunity it provided him to make a name for himself. Along with the death was the fog, which a bizarre chain of events seemed to follow.

But it wasn't the TVs or the phones that bothered Dan the most—it was the *voices.*

The voices drifted out of the fog, and after he left the scene of Mitch's murder he could not stop hearing them. Every time he stepped outside into the haze he would be forced to listen to them. At first they were hushed, sounding almost like children whispering secrets to each other in the back of a classroom. Then there were more voices, and every time they spoke they grew louder and louder, each hushed word more intensified than the last.

Dan remembered standing on the sidewalk outside of his home, looking into the fog with disbelief. They were talking to him, they were *beckoning* him. They wanted him to *join* them out in the fog. His mind heard them calling out for him. And then he heard a voice shooting out through all of them. It was a voice he recognized.

It was the voice of his dead Uncle Chad.

At first the voice simply spoke his name along with the others, but in a mocking tone that implied to Dan his uncle was scoffing at who he was—at what he had done with his life. Then his assumptions were confirmed when he heard Uncle Chad's raspy voice permeate from the mist.

"You little faggot, I know you wanted it. You were just beg-

ging." His uncle laughed heartily. *"I made you what you are today, queer boy, it's all 'cause of me! You want some more dick? Do ya boy? Want some more of your uncle's big, hard schlong? Come on in and get it, come get a taste, you fuckin' whiny queer!"* The laughter was overwhelming, filling Dan with a malevolence he never knew existed.

But was he hearing it? His ears were detecting nothing, although his mind was alive with voices. His uncle was around him, not physically, but in spirit, and in his head, and . . .

In the fog.

Dan had wanted to rush in there to join the voices and fight his uncle. He wanted to let his hatred be felt and consumed by the fog—but something in him wouldn't let him. There was a portion of Dan that was frightened, no *terrified,* of what was in that fog. It was something Dan hated, but it was the type of hate a small, helpless child felt toward a merciless bully. He detested whatever was out there but he also knew whatever was out there could take advantage of him just like—

Just like Uncle Chad took advantage of me when I was a young boy.

Dan McNair snapped back to the scene at hand. He once again saw his legs positioned on the desk in the back office of the police station. He saw the lanky figure and un-groomed salt and pepper mustache of Ernie Stevens standing in the corner of the room, shifting and repositioning himself every few moments.

McNair was fortunate to be brought back to reality because, unbeknownst to him, he was quickly losing the last shreds of his sanity. His unresolved issues and pains had been growing for twenty-three years. He had been emotionally unstable for most of his life and the insanity he had dealt with within the last twenty-four hours were the final cracks in the foundation.

"What do you reckon we should do, Dan? We can't keep all of those people waiting forever."

Ernie Stevens was diminutive. When it came to decision making, he always found a way to relinquish responsibility to either Dan or Tom, with Tom often turning and passing the responsibility back down to Dan or simply dismissing the issue all together.

"We wait for Tom. He's the sheriff. Something big is happening here, Ernie, something real fucking big, so we need the good ol' sheriff on board before we do anything." Dan's voice was so calm it came off as apathetic.

"Something big? What the hell are you talking about? Some strange stuff has been going on but what in God's name is all of this? People are starting to lose it, and what if some of those things that guy was yellin' about are true?" Ernie was looking to Dan with eyes as wide as the moon, hoping his superior would console him or at least reinforce him in the belief that reality in Rowley had not been warped.

"What things are you talking about?" Dan's tone held no emotion.

"About not being able to leave." The response was quick and solemn.

"Do you believe that?"

"No!" he replied too quickly. "No, not at all, that's some crazy talk. That's some bullshit is what that is." He looked at

Dan with trepidation. "Right, Dan?"

"I don't know, Ernie." It was the most clean, honest thing Dan McNair had said in years. "I do know something is going on in this town. Now, I hate this damn town but it's still MY town, so we're going to do something about it, whatever it happens to be. I have a feeling this is all related to Mitch Joiner's death."

"Wait, that butchering? But how? Why?"

"I don't know."

"Then what the hell do we know?"

"That the phones don't work, a few people have gone missing, and it's pretty hard to get out of town in this thick fog. Other than that, not too much, but I'll tell you what, I got a bad feeling about this."

Ernie Stevens didn't need his superior to tell him to feel bad about this situation; he had felt sick all morning. He had tried to tell himself he was being paranoid, but with the way that particular day was beginning, Ernie Stevens couldn't help but get even more distraught, and fast.

The chaos had just started, and both men could tell the situation would get much worse before it would even begin showing signs of getting better. These fears were only exacerbated when they saw the disheveled, fearful figure of Tom Williams rush through the office door and quickly slam it shut behind him. He leaned back against it like there was a need to brace the door and set up a barricade.

He looks like a scared, lost child. This was Dan's initial thought, and he knew the day ahead would be a decisive one for Tom, himself, and the rest of the people of Rowley.

Maybe, just maybe, his opportunity really was at hand.

~

Ben walked out of his house and onto Church Street. He would have to head down Church and through the intersection at Main until he could take the right onto Willow and get to Elise's house. He had chosen to walk rather than drive, despite his growing concern about the fog and what might lurk behind it. He felt compelled to face the situation rather than avoid it. He had learned at a young age that problems were best solved when they were dealt with immediately and not left to fester and grow.

Ben walked at a leisurely pace, surrounded by the fog that had too quickly acclimated itself with the town. It had only been around for a day, but to Ben and the other townspeople it seemed like much longer. Despite how awful the fog was, part of Ben was already used to it, and that fact troubled him perhaps more than its existence.

He walked by the brown, brick Presbyterian Church that gave the street its name. In the fog it did not look like a welcoming sanctuary of God, but a foreboding, dark structure straight out of a horror movie. The charm of Church Street and the town was fading as the fog obscured it, making everything dark shadows set behind a wall of gray. Even the Livingston's house near the intersection at Main, which usually was lovely with its white color, green shutters, and flower-covered lawn, looked listless and unfriendly. Somehow the house looked like it was dying. What was once pretty was now exuding feelings of gloom, and as much as Ben wanted to attribute these things to his wild imagination, this was no longer an option.

As he walked down the slight decline leading to Main

Street, Ben noticed there were an unusual amount of people out of their homes and on the street. Normally he'd only see a few pedestrians here and there throughout the town, but as he got to the intersection he noticed a bunch of scattered people, all wandering from their homes and talking to each other.

At first Ben was puzzled, but then he scolded himself for being so. He had told himself that something was wrong countless times over the last twenty-four hours—he wasn't the only person aware of this. At breakfast, his parents seemed blissfully ignorant, choosing to attribute all of these strange happenings to a bizarre weather spell rather than considering other options. Ben had a feeling his parents had suspicions of their own, but Ben didn't want to aggravate the situation; he didn't need to begin the day with fear *and* drama.

Ben walked toward the gathering, and out of the fog a figure appeared, making Ben recoil slightly before he realized it was just another person—a person he recognized.

Derrick Laurel had gone to high school with Ben at Wiladongun Area High. They had not been close friends, but were acquainted enough to be on speaking terms. Ben had only seen Derrick a handful of times since graduation, and each of those times had been pleasant enough.

No longer was Derrick calm, relaxed, or laid back. His cool and easy demeanor was a far cry from his current expression. He looked fearful and confused. Ben opened his mouth to address him, feeling obliged to since he nearly walked into him on the sidewalk, when Derrick began chattering away.

"Ben, Ben, do you know what the heck is going on?" Derrick looked at Ben like he had never looked at him before. The casual diffidence was gone, replaced with a hopeful yearning—a yearning for answers and guidance.

"I-I don't know. What's wrong, Derrick?"

Derrick shook his head, seeming to try to snap himself out of a long thought. "A lot, man. The TVs don't work, the phones don't work, this fog won't go away, and a few people have started saying they can't get out of town. I know it sounds nuts, right? But a whole bunch of people are saying it." Derrick had never been the brightest of bulbs, that was the main factor behind him staying in Rowley after he graduated, but even someone as scatterbrained as Derrick wasn't impervious to what was going on around him,

"Can't get out of town?" Ben asked in a hushed tone. As if beckoned by his question, a car flew through Main Street at a reckless speed, veering in and out of its lane—the driver, who was on his fourth lap through town, had enough of retracing his path over and over despite which way he tried to leave town.

"People are starting to lose it, and it's only morning." Derrick knew there were greater things to come. "I think this is real bad, whatever this is."

"I think you're right. Something isn't right about this fog. I think you should stay inside, buddy."

"Something isn't right with the fog," Derrick muttered, mostly to himself.

"Just be careful, okay, man? I got some things I have to get to, but I hope to see you around."

"Yeah, yeah, have a good one, dude." Their handshake was weak, uncertain, and they both parted ways feeling less assured than before.

Ben passed by a few other stragglers, some walking around aimlessly as if they were in the aftermath of some type of disaster. There was confusion, fear, and a general feeling of being lost. What little Ben could see of their faces revealed that much.

He overheard two people talking at the intersection, both male, one was playing the voice of reason to the other who seemed frantic and inconsolable.

"Just relax. I'm sure there is something to explain all of this."

"I'm fucking telling you! No way out of the town! Not for me, or Lilly, or whoever else who has tried. There's no fucking way out of the town!"

"Steve, that isn't possible, none of that—"

"I don't fucking know what is possible! All I know is what I saw, man!"

Ben sidestepped the conversation, not caring to hear more; he believed what the frantic man was saying to his friend. He believed things were going crazy in his town all too quickly.

He tentatively made his way through the intersection, hoping another driver wouldn't fly down the road, driving blindly and erratically, and strike him as they drove. He made it safely and continued down Church Street, unable to take in the beauty of the oak and willow trees lining the sidewalk, or the charming houses positioned down the street near the bridge over the Lackawillen.

The walk was only about a mile in total, but it seemed eons longer. After passing the smattering of people at the intersection at Main, Ben seemed to walk into isolation. The fog was so thick he couldn't see a thing. It was as if he was stranded walking on a sidewalk in the clouds.

It was eerie but Ben stomached it, knowing he was close to Elise's house which meant he was close to Elise, and despite the situation that was a warming thought. Their shared fear over whatever was happening to their town seemed to have brought them closer the night before, and more than ever Ben felt compelled to be there with her—to be there *for* her. The situation was most certainly dire, but Ben would make sure that no misfortune would befall Elise.

Whoosh. He heard the sound in the distance. It was different, it was unnatural. Ben froze despite every instinct in his body screaming at him to run, run far, far away.

Whatever made the noise, ceased to make it again, or had gone too far away to be heard, but whatever it was certainly wasn't human. Ben knew this, and it frightened him that he knew it with such certainty.

He paused for a moment longer before walking on, now power walking at an increased pace, and soon all inhibition gave way as he began to run, fearful he would hear the noise once again.

It was out there, and Ben had the creeping feeling it was *watching* him.

Ben ran as fast as he could, nearly stumbling and face-planting onto the road below, but he managed to regain his balance and keep up his healthy pace. It was only moments until he arrived at Elise's home, but it felt like forever.

He ran up to the door and without looking back rang the bell.

Thirteen

Andrew Murphy was a pyromaniac. There was no way to smooth it over, to sweeten it up, or to avoid the fact in any way.

Andrew Murphy was a full-blown pyromaniac.

Of course, Andrew had never looked at his "problem" in the way everyone else had. He never felt there was something wrong with his appreciation for the almighty flame. On the contrary, he viewed himself as the only true appreciator of such a fine art.

Short, frail, red-headed, blue-eyed, and freckle-covered, Andrew wasn't an imposing form. He didn't strike those he met as threatening or even capable of being threatening.

But they did not understand what lay beneath.

Andrew had started playing with fire when he was five years old. He took his father's matchbook and within a handful of minutes most of his toys were up in a blaze in the middle of his bedroom. The fire subsequently spread to his carpet, and then the curtains—if it hadn't been for the quick actions of his father, armed with a fire extinguisher, the whole house would have ended up in flames

Glorious, glorious flames.

There had been a number of incidents in the eight years since, most of which went unnoticed or were covered up by Andrew's parents.

The Murphys couldn't have a child with problems. After all, Janice Murphy's sister had children who were prodigies, one an all-state gymnast, and the other had taken up three instruments by the age of eight. Janice Murphy couldn't be known as having a *freak* for a son.

So the solution for the Murphys was not to acknowledge any problem. Andrew was curious, as many little boys were, and he liked fire, but with all the explosions in the movies now-a-days, what little boy didn't?

The Murphys would slap Andrew on the hand when necessary, but for the sake of their own image they never made a scene about any one of Andrew's spats and, fortunately for them, he had never done anything big enough to attract attention to the family.

That, however, was quickly going to change. For despite what his family knew about his condition, there was still a great deal they did not know about Andrew Michael Murphy.

He was also a sociopath.

Andrew had never been an expressive boy, but the Murphys figured that was because he was shy, or perhaps a bit socially awkward. They never suspected Andrew didn't care whether they approved of him or loved him. They were unaware he didn't fully understand these concepts. Andrew had no grasp of love, fear, or hate. Andrew only knew what Andrew knew, and what Andrew often knew was impulse.

There were things that felt good, and things that felt bad. *Do things that feel good. Avoid things that feel bad.*

And for Andrew, there was only one thing in the entire world that really made him smile inside. There was only one thing that could light up his blue eyes and fill him up with a warm, legitimate delight.

Fire. Glorious fire.

Andrew found fire had become even more fun since he hit puberty. It had always allured him, entranced him like a temptress, but as he had grown older it began to have a *physical* effect on him.

Fire made him erect. Fire stimulated his libido like nothing else.

He would lock himself away in his room for hours on end, lighter in one hand, penis in other, and the world was his oyster—there was absolutely no limit to the joy he could experience.

The warmth of the flame, its power, and its delicious essence was right before him and he could touch himself. He could feel the tingling sensations building up within him; he could feel his excitement rise to levels he never thought possible.

All because of fire, all because of his maiden.

If Andrew Murphy was capable of loving something, he would be considered in love with fire, but what he truly shared with the element was more so desire; a gripping *need* for it.

Without the exhilaration fire gave him, Andrew wouldn't have found a point in living. Life was about doing things that felt good, and avoiding things that felt bad. Without fire life would be bleak and miserable. It would lack substance, and Andrew was convinced he would kill himself if fire was ever taken away from him.

But it was there. It would always be there.

Andrew flicked his lighter on and off in his hand, drooling as he stared at the flame in a mesmerized fashion. He was home alone, his parents had left early for work and would not be back until much later, though for some odd reason Andrew felt they would never be back at all. To most children this would be a daunting feeling, but to Andrew it was no considerable matter. If they did not come back, they did not come back; it was as simple as that.

I'd still have fire, he thought longingly.

Then he heard something that jolted him from his thoughts, something able to pull his intent gaze away from the flame.

"Annnndrewwww, Annnndrewww." The voice sounded like a whisper, but if it was possible, a *deafening* whisper, and it wasn't just one voice, it was a few, or more, or thousands.

At first Andrew was confused. He was fairly certain he had

not physically heard the voice but more so *thought* it.

"Burnnnnn, Andrew. Burn it all. Burn it to the ground." The whisper was sweet now, having the same alluring qualities as his beloved flame. Andrew looked out the window—the voice was coming from the fog.

"Don't be scared, Andrew. Come out and burn it all. No one will stop you. Burnnnn it all."

Andrew was curious. His curiosity hinged on suspicion, but Andrew was not in the least bit frightened—he was incapable of fear.

What he was not incapable of was desire.

Andrew felt stiffness in his pants as his erection pushed against the firm confinement of his blue jeans. He wanted to listen to the voice.

*"The fog will turn a beautiful orange, lit up by the power and majesty of the fire. The glorious fire!"*His parents were gone, they were not coming back. Somehow he knew this. With so much fog, no one would be able to see, no police officer would be able to track him down, and he had a strong feeling something was going on that was distracting the whole town. If Andrew had emotions, he would have acknowledged it was something awful, something terrible—but that was not the case, and such things were no concern to Andrew.

Do what feels good. Avoid what feels bad.

Andrew knew what would feel good. Andrew knew the voices were right.

It only took a few moments for Andrew to gather the containers of gasoline his father kept hidden in the storage closet within the garage. There were three full containers, along with a half full can of kerosene. Andrew wasn't quite sure what he could do with this amount of fluid, but he was in an adventurous enough mood to go and find out.

There was a gleam in his eyes, stronger than any gleam there had ever been before.

Andrew Murphy was a pyromaniac.

He was also a sociopath.

Fourteen

Christine Sutter was a considerably attractive woman for her age, with barely a wrinkle showing on her still-soft skin, hair as silky and full as ever, and her face holding the seductive allure that had won her so many starry eyed admirers when she was younger.

Elise had inherited her mother's good looks, and if Elise was a little bit older and Christine a little bit younger, it would have been very easy for them to pass as sisters. Ben admittedly always had a physical attraction to Christine. He had permitted himself to think that way about Elise's mother rather than sully their friendship with sexual thoughts about Elise herself. In short, for a good while Christine Sutter had been Ben Dowling's childhood fantasy.

Her vibrant eyes and her trademark smile were now gone as she greeted Ben at the door, replaced instead with a deep expression of wear and worry which added years to her face in just one day.

"Hello, Mrs. Sutter," Ben said, still stuck in the habit of formality.

Some life returned to her face upon hearing Ben speak. She had always thought favorably of him and although she had never expressed it, Christine secretly hoped Elise would come to her senses and date the boy.

"Oh stop this Mrs. Sutter stuff, you know to call me Christine. You're going to make me feel old."

Ben laughed and it was a welcomed sensation. "Old habits die hard, Christine."

"Don't talk like that, Ben! That reasoning will land you in Mac's Bar for the rest of your life."

Ben laughed again, this time more heartily. Christine had not only passed on her fine looks to her daughter, but her wit and sense of humor as well. "In that place old habits don't die at all!"

She smiled and suddenly her face looked younger. It looked like the face Ben used to dream about whenever he had stayed over at Elise's house. It was the face he wished would walk into the guest room, lean over the bed, and plant a big kiss right on his lips. He found himself smiling uncomfortably at Christine, thinking about the fantasies of days past. In some ways the awkward thoughts had endeared him to Christine even further—she was his big childhood crush after all.

"So, are you looking for Elise, or are you just here to give me a few good laughs?"

Ben blushed. "Well, can't it be both?"

Christine kept smiling. "She's right upstairs. Poor thing hasn't come out of her room all morning though, says she has a head cold. I bet seeing you will cheer her right up."

"I think we all need a little cheering up," Ben said with a tone more solemn than he intended.

Christine's face tightened and she looked a decade older once more. "Yeah, with this weather and whatever else is going on I think we all need to smile." There was an awkward silence and then Christine stepped back, motioning for Ben to come inside.

"She's right upstairs, go on up."

Ben walked upstairs and took the first right to Elise's room. Just as he raised his hand to knock on her door it opened, and Ben found himself face-to-face with Elise.

The moment was tense. They stood unblinking, sizing up one another and wondering what the others' thoughts were. Ben was hit with the sudden urge to kiss her. He wanted to hold Elise and keep her close and safe. Instead he stood motionless, eyes locked with Elise's, unsure if the moment was as powerful for her as it was for him.

His thoughts were doubtful. *Am I just adding more meaning to this than there really is? Wouldn't it be a joke if I tried to kiss her and she wasn't even thinking anything near the same thing?*

Elise decided to end the silence. "About time you got here."

Ben's face broke out in a goofy, embarrassed grin. "You were expecting me?"

"Phones are out, no way to communicate. I knew you would be worried about me getting home safely. Looks like chivalry really isn't dead."

"Maybe it's just on life support," Ben replied, playfully nudging her shoulder, causing Elise to readjust her balance. She lightly slapped his hand in response.

"Way to ruin a moment, jerk." All tension left her voice. They both smiled at each other.

"That's all I'm good at, you know that by now," Ben said while trying to contain his grin.

"I'm getting too used to it, pretty soon I'll stop noticing," Elise replied, the corners of her own mouth curling up in a smile.

"I pray for when the day will come."

"You're an ass."

"You love it." They each wore a giddy smile once more. Ben took a minute to revel in the dynamics of the moment before he brought things to a more serious level.

"Are you okay? Your mom said you were sick." The worry showed in his voice.

Elise's face dropped as her voice became a whisper. "Come in, we'll talk about it." It was as if Ben had spoken a word of taboo.

Ben nodded, already having an inkling as to what this was about. He stepped inside the room and Elise closed the door behind him.

Dan McNair sat at his desk with his hand to his chin, thinking long and hard about the insane stories just presented to him. Tom Williams looked like a plumper version of Frosty the Snowman—his skin white as snow and his eyes as wide as chunks of coal. Ernie Stevens looked like he had come down with Alzheimer's and was trying to figure out where the hell he was and what the hell he was doing.

Dan appeared to be the only one in any sort of stable mood after what they had encountered. He was the only man not completely rattled by the slew of reports they took from the group of citizens outside of the station.

After Tom Williams fled from the crowd and inside, Dan decided they should have a little pow-wow of sorts. In their brief meeting, Dan came up with the idea to try and gather as much information as they could from the individuals in the crowd in order to get a grasp of what they were dealing with. He put Ernie Stevens outside of the station with a shotgun in hand and instructed him to point it at the crowd. If anyone got out of line he was told to blow 'em in two. Ernie didn't object to this seemingly brutal order. Like the lap-dog he was, he was happy to obey and receive a pat on the head for his efforts. Ernie stood outside of the station on crowd control, instructing them that Tom and Dan would take reports of the incidents one by one in an orderly fashion.

It had gone smoothly enough. While Ernie did his duty, Tom and Dan interviewed each of the concerned townsfolk and took detailed reports. Tom had stood idly by during the whole process, seeming all too happy to pass the buck to Dan. As Tom stood by passively, Dan realized his inability to deal with tragedy truly indicated Tom wasn't the man meant to be in charge of this whole situation—he was.

It's your town, Dan. The thought was loose and dreamlike but somehow still strong. He was happy to get to his responsibilities and begin solving the crisis at hand.

The reports they filed did not help them get a clear view of the situation. Rather, they left them in a state of bewilderment comparable to that of the desperate townsfolk. If what they were hearing from these people was in any way true, complete madness had befallen Rowley, Pennsylvania.

Jen Roberts's problem had been simple enough to comprehend. Her husband Paul had gone out to deliver the daily copies of the *Rowley Times* like he did every morning. That morning, however, he didn't return home and according to Jen this was uncharacteristic, especially since he never missed a warm meal at home.

The stories got stranger from there. Kate Rhine also filed a missing person's report. Between her hysterical tears, Dan discerned that she had seen her nine-year-old daughter on the front lawn just as the morning began, playfully kicking a soccer ball around the yard. Then a wave of particularly thick fog came in and Kate lost sight of her. Although this was strange, she took it as nothing more than nature being nature until she noticed she could no longer hear her daughter or the sound of the ball sliding across the dew-soaked grass.

Barely twenty yards from the house, little Amy Rhine had gone missing, and the story struck a chord with Tom Williams. Dan McNair saw tears welling up above the man's blubbery cheeks. This wasn't the case for Dan himself. He was cool, calm, and collected in the face of this unknown danger. He had to keep it together to continue to have a hold on the town.

His town.

Tim Dolan reported there were blood stains along the sidewalk near Mac's Bar, and they continued down Main to the pizzeria. Talking out of his ass, he explained that in his experience dealing with car accidents the amount of blood he saw on the sidewalk was more than enough to cause a fatality. The two teenagers had a similar story, although this one was set in the gravel lot of the town park.

Jeff Hossler said he had heard some banging noise at the house next door. A woman named Lisa Grogan lived there with her boyfriend Neil Bergen. Hossler thought nothing of the noise until the next day when he saw the door to his neighbor's home had been ripped off the hinges, and his two neighbors were nowhere to be found.

Tiffany Bent and Todd Miles were near hysterics as they tried, to no avail to convince the officers there was no way out of Rowley. Both had tried to leave the town limits and both had found themselves back on Main Street multiple times. The stories were each bizarre, and on first take not believable, yet it struck Dan how well the stories matched. Despite the insanity of their claims, the stories each gave an all-too-perfect description of the *same* events. Although Dan was understandably skeptical of their tales, he decided it would be foolish to discount these two once level-headed people.

The most interesting stories to Deputy McNair were from George Riley and Wanda Sepinsky, the two individuals Tom Williams had not recognized outside the police station. Their stories involved a sighting of what Dan *knew* had to be the suspect. Each of them had heard and seen something. Both of their accounts on their own were on the verge of absolute lunacy—but like many of the other accounts Dan and Tom had encountered that morning, they *corroborated* each other.

George had seen someone, no *something* as he described it, lurking in the fog.

"It didn't move like any person, it moved in unnatural ways."

"What do you mean, unnatural ways?"

"It floated, and . . . flew."

"You're saying this guy can fly through the air?" Dan raised his eyebrow, making his skepticism evident.

"No, I don't mean flew like an airplane. I guess, hover, that's a better word. Hovered just barely over the ground and floated instead of walked. It was like nothing I've ever seen."

"This is like nothing I've ever heard."

He said he only caught quick, fleeting images of it since it was moving around so rapidly. But it did stop and turn his way for a moment and look in his direction.

"It was huge. Bigger than huge. It was impossible." His eyes were wide and still seemed to be laden with shock, but they were the eyes of a truthful man. Dan McNair could tell that much. Whatever George actually saw was in question but what he *believed* he saw was being honestly reported to Dan.

"It was dark, like maybe it was in a cloak or a robe. Ya know the type a weirdo cult member would wear. Couldn't see any bit of its body though, just . . . black."

"What did he do?" Dan asked.

"It looked toward me. And then it started whispering, crazy whispers all around, like this cloaked fella or thing was chanting with a thousand voices. They was hateful whispers too, the types of things you wouldn't want anyone hearing."

"What specifically was he saying?"

"It wasn't saying anything. It was just hatred, awful hatred. No words . . . just hate."

Tom shifted uncomfortably.

"Then what?" Dan asked, even-mannered despite the lunacy of what he was hearing.

"It looked at me. It wanted to kill me. Then . . . I was so scared I thought of the Lord and how much I loved him and the life he gave me. Well, then I look up from the ground and it's gone."

"Just like that?"

"Whoosh and gone away," George said nodding.

"Of course, whoosh and gone away," Dan said in a flat tone.

Wanda's story was similar. She gave the same description of the dark menace with the same account of its motions and strange whispers.

"It growled too," she said, looking like the memory was going to cause her to have a heart attack.

"Growled?" Dan snapped.

"Or more like a hiss, a scraping noise, or both, or more . . . I don't know what it was. It was just some terrible sound."

"Did he growl at you?"

"No, it was growling at something else. It wasn't after me. It saw something else out there in the street and went for it. Like it was an animal."

"Could you see who he went for?" Dan inquired.

"*It* went off into the fog. It was too thick to see where. I locked myself in my bedroom for an hour after seeing that thing. It was unholy. I swear on my mother that wasn't any person, I don't care how crazy I sound."

"I guess if you're crazy, Wanda, then today the whole town is," Dan said with a sigh.

The stories *were* crazy, over the top. All Dan could piece together was that there was someone out there who was big and dressed in a black hooded robe. This someone gave people a seriously bad vibe and he was likely the one abducting some and hacking others to bits. He was aided by the strange weather and able to make his way place to place essentially undetected. He was a psychopath who was a real threat to everyone in the town.

But could that really be it? The stories—they worked too well together. The people were honest about the madness they had seen—it wasn't them just being fearfully irrational.

Was it possible that whatever was out there, actually was an *it?*

Although initially he found it unlikely, Dan couldn't find any evidence to discredit the possibility.

"What the hell do we do, Dan?" Tom burst out, ending the short moment of silence that ensued after the departure of Wanda Sepinsky. "What the hell do we do? Those stories are goddamn insane! Is everyone losing it? What in the world is going on in our town?" The situation had only begun and already Tom was falling apart.

“Can’t be true, not one bit of it.” Ernie was happy to dismiss the situation as utter nonsense, though the fearful look on his face said he wasn’t fully buying his own conclusion.

“Well, boys,” Dan said, leaning back in his chair, “it’s clear that something is going on here, something bad. We don’t know what it is and it sounds like no one else does either—but whatever it is, it’s bad and has to be taken seriously.”

“Don’t tell me you believe that there’s some crazy monster out there tearing people apart! That’s insane!” Tom was desperate to believe anything else.

“What I’m telling you,” Dan’s voice held a belittling connotation, “is that whatever is going on is serious. We have several reports of missing people and evidence of multiple murders. We have stories of someone lurking out there in our town and it appears that person is going after people. We have lost communication and whatever is going on with this weather seems to be disorientating people. So regardless of what the cause is we have to get together and keep order before this whole town falls apart.”

Ernie Stevens nodded and looked toward Dan hopefully, happy to have a superior in such a decisive moment.

“B-but what do we do?” Tom asked as if he were a hopeless child. “We don’t have outside contact, no outside resources, no—”

“Don’t you have a goddamn spine?” Dan McNair shouted at Tom for the first time and was surprised to see the large man recoil like a frightened mouse. “We’re the police, for God’s sake! We deal with our town and we keep order. If someone is out there, we go get the bastard. And we sure as hell make sure the town doesn’t lose its composure in the meantime. This is our responsibility! We don't have to run off to the staties for help at the first sign of trouble."

Tom looked at him and mouthed silent words, his grip over himself and the situation quickly fading.

Dan stared him stone-cold in the eyes and made the decision the voice in his head was demanding he make.

"Give me your badge, Tom."

"W-what? What are you talking about?" Tom choked on his words.

"I'm the sheriff now, Tom. Give me your badge," Dan said sternly.

"Who gave you the right? What the hell is this?" Tom was gaining some defiance now. The title of sheriff was all the man had going for him.

"You can give the badge to me and I can get to solving this crisis or you can keep it and deal with all the problems on your own, you know, since you're such a capable leader and all." McNair didn't bother hiding the sarcasm in his voice.

"Dan, we don't need to do something like this," Tom appealed.

"Dammit, Tom, I'm the one doing all the work. I'm the one coming up with all the ideas and I'm the one who is going to get our asses out of this situation. It's time you stepped down and let a real leader save this town."

Tom looked at him, shocked by his words. His expression also revealed, however, that he didn't want to handle the responsibility. The cowardly part of Tom's conscience was all too willing to hand leadership away. Why should the weight of the entire town be on *his* shoulders? He was just as frightened and confused as the people outside.

This isn't what I signed up for! This isn't what I signed up for at all! he thought frantically and his mind could only come up with one option for escape.

Tom placed his sheriff's badge squarely in Dan McNair's hand.

And so the reign of a tyrant began.

Fifteen

"What did you hear? Don't be scared to tell me." Ben put his hand on her shoulder as she began to cry lightly, tears staining the beautiful canvas of her face.

"Voices, terrible whispering voices coming from the fog. They wanted me."

Ben shifted uncomfortably. "What do you mean, wanted?"

"They wanted me to go out there into the fog. They wanted to *have* me." Elise looked away briefly before scooting closer to Ben.

Ben spoke gently. "There's something evil about

the fog. It's doing strange things. People say that they can't get out of town and I believe them. Just like I believe you." He put his hand on her shoulder to reassure her he was there for her and she loosened up slightly.

"There's more people missing, too. Word travels quickly in this town, even with the phones being out. Lisa Grogan and her boyfriend are nowhere to be found and the door was ripped right off her house, and I mean *ripped.* It was thrown across the street, pieces of wood strewn all over. The house was an absolute wreck. My mom is terrified."

"Where's your dad?"

"Out of town, across the state looking for some bargains on antiques at some expo. I'm glad he isn't here—the more people out of town right now the better. Something is going to happen."

"Something is happening," Ben said, their eyes locking together once more.

"Ben," she began tentatively, her eyes revealing how unsure she was. Ben saw she was opening up and wanted to share something deep and secretive.

"Yes?" He hoped this was going in the direction he was thinking.

"There's something I have to tell you, but don't . . . don't judge me over it."

"Never. What do you have to tell me?" He felt an eager anticipation now. Maybe this tragic moment had made each realize what they truly meant to each other. Maybe Elise was about to admit to the same feelings growing within Ben.

"I think I know where it is. Where it's hiding out or living or doing whatever the hell it does." Ben was dead wrong in his assumption and his heart nearly stopped as he dealt with the transition from thoughts of love to those of the tormentor of his dreams.

"What do you mean?"

"I have these feelings and I think you've had them too. They're about this whole situation and how something is wrong."

Ben nodded and said nothing.

"Well, I have a feeling I know where it is. I took one look at the place the other day and the worst sensation I've ever experienced came over me. I've seen the place before too, it was nothing new, but what I sensed was completely new to my *heart*. I could *sense* a new presence about the building, one that was never there before. The hairs on my body stood up and I felt a strange tingling sensation, like I was being mildly electrocuted. Something evil and terrible is in that place. I know it wasn't just my nerves getting to me." She paused and raised her head to look at Ben with an unsure expression, biting her lower lip in a manner Ben found positively adorable. "You don't think I'm crazy, do you?"

Ben wanted to tell her she wasn't crazy. He wanted more than anything to open his mouth and reassure her she was not only sensible, but wise and beautiful in every way. He wanted to hold her close and console her and assure her that everything was going to be all right.

Instead he bottled his emotions and gave Elise a more reasonable response. "I think instinct is what we have to rely on in a situation like this. Sometimes our feelings are privy to things our minds just can't pick up. What place are you talking about?"

"The old stone building, the one that used to be the old garage years ago. The one right down the road."

Ben's heart sank and all the warmth fled his body.

The garage, that creepy, rundown old garage, he thought. *Somehow I knew it, too.*

The old Rowley Garage was the stone building he had found himself leaning against in his dream when the shadowy figure had come upon him and was preparing to finish him off. He hadn't fully realized it until the moment Elise mentioned the building, but as soon as she did there was no doubt. He knew that was where it was living, at least while it was in Rowley.

"Ar-are you okay Ben? You're shaking." Elise now put her arm on his shoulder to steady him.

Ben nodded solemnly. "It's there. I know it's there, too. You aren't crazy."

"You too?"

"Yeah, me too. Except it was a dream for me," he confided.

"What do we do?" she asked in a grave whisper.

He paused, and then gave her the soundest answer he could think of. "We investigate."

Considering their fear, investigating the supposed lair of the unknown shadow beast seemed asinine, but Ben and Elise were both of the belief that if you loved something you had to fight for it, and neither was willing to sit passively as their town was destroyed by an unknown assailant.

They also realized their gut feelings may not go over too well with the people of the town, even though they too were realizing something was wrong. There was a difference between thinking something was off and jumping to the conclusion that a shadow man was taking refuge in an abandoned garage.

This was something Ben and Elise had to do by themselves. This was something they were meant to do *together.*

"You want to go to that garage then, that's what you're saying?" Elise tilted her head and Ben couldn't read her demeanor.

"I think that's the place to start."

"This isn't a video game, Ben, this is real life."

"What does that mean?"

"It means that if you lose a life here you don't get another one. It means if you make a mistake it's game over for good. This isn't a Scooby Doo mystery we're dealing with. We aren't going to be pulling off any silly rubber masks. This is serious."

Ben felt his face grow hot. He detested Elise talking to him like he was a child. "I know, Elise. I'm taking this very seriously and—"

"Ben . . ."

He continued, "and I think . . ."

Elise wouldn't be halted. "Ben, I know you're taking it seriously and I trust you with all my heart. I just want to make sure that we're careful. I don't want anything to happen to you. I . . . care about you."

Ben's face was still hot, but this time because he was flustered. "Thanks. I care about you, too. We're both taking this seriously, and we're both going to look out for each other. It's going to be all right."

Elise smiled. "You know how to win a girl over."

Ben didn't know what she meant and didn't have the immediate courage to ask. "Let's get going then."

They didn't think to take any weapons as a precaution. It was an investigation, not a war. As they went downstairs and prepared to leave they were met by Christine, who questioned her daughter as she was about to step out the door.

"Where are you going, honey?" Christine asked as casually as she could. Her eyes betrayed her, showing her worry.

"Going out with Ben," Elise said smoothly.

"Yes, but where?"

"Just for a walk around town."

"I don't think that's a good idea." Christine crossed her arms.

"I have to get out of the house for a little bit. It'll help me feel better." Elise's tone revealed she had no intention of bowing to her mother.

Christine bit her lip in the same tentative manner Elise had before. "Why don't you go to Ben's instead?"

"We may end up there," Elise lied. "Right now I just need to get some air."

"It's not safe," her mother shot back.

"Don't worry, Christine," Ben interjected, stepping forward. "I'll be with her and I'll keep her safe."

Christine smiled politely. "I'm sure you will, Ben, it's just—"

"Trust me. It's going to be all right."

Mrs. Sutter shifted back and forth uncomfortably. "Okay, I trust you. Just don't be out too late, okay guys? There are a lot of strange things going on."

Elise hugged her mother and gave her a peck on the cheek. "I know, Mom, we'll be fine. I'll be back before dinner."

Christine forced another shaky smile. "All right, I'll see you then. Ben, you're welcome to join us—we'll have plenty."

"I just might do that, Mrs. Sutt—err, Christine."

There was a prolonged silence before Elise opened the door. They all shifted their eyes back and forth, watching each other with collective nervousness. Finally Elise opened the door and after a small wave from Christine, she and Ben exited the house.

The pair walked down Willow and onto Church, taking it until they reached the small cul-de-sac called Penn Court. At the end sat the ruined remains of the town's very first service station. For the majority of the time they were silent, walking with purpose toward their goal. Each was unsure of what to say about the situation and their brewing feelings for each other, so the only thing to do was press on. It was Ben who eventually broke the silence as they took their first steps onto Penn from Church.

"It's like we aren't even in Rowley anymore. All this fog makes it look like a ghost-town."

"It doesn't feel like Rowley, not the hometown I know." Elise looked around suspiciously as if the shrouded scene around her was an illusion bound to change at any moment.

Ben shared her sentiments. It seemed like Rowley was fading away. Less and less could be seen as time went by and the fog gobbled up the town. Its presence had turned Rowley into a gloomy shell of its former self. Soon there wouldn't be much left except for the suffocating haze.

"We're going to get to the bottom of this. We'll get our town back," Ben proclaimed with the certainty of a child on a make-believe adventure.

Elise was relieved to see some optimism amid the dreary landscape. "Your attitude is infectious. I'm thoroughly creeped out but I also have the feeling we can do something about this. In a weird way, I think we were meant to." Conviction shone in her voice, a conviction they shared due to their faith and trust in one another. They were comfortable. As long as they had each other their determination was rock solid.

Or so they thought.

It started to wane when they finally reached the end of the cul-de-sac and laid eyes upon their destination. The garage popped out of the fog like a lurking phantom, the sight of it leaving them both breathless.

Topped with a hastily put together wooden upper half and roof, the faded red brick walls of the building looked ready to topple. It resembled a partially finished renovation project gone completely wrong. The windows were either boarded up or smashed, the roof was caving in on the left side, and graffiti covered the heavy wooden barn-style doors which once served as the bay, the markings expressing generations worth of angst from the youth of Rowley. The building was ominous on a sunny day, but in the fog it appeared wretched and horrifying.

The building was suited for the scene. The fog and it had a relationship, Ben could feel this. The thought was confirmed when he saw the fog was pouring *out* of the garage. It seeped out of each crack in the building like it was its very source. The building was causing the fog and projecting all of the town's problems, worries, and fears.

The weathered building had a new presence about it. It had always been aesthetically off-putting but now it was emotionally devastating. The aura coming from the garage was the worst vibe Ben or Elise had ever felt, and they knew their suspicions about the place had been spot on.

Something had changed. Whatever presence had come to the Rowley Garage was a dreadful one.

"Having second thoughts?" Ben beat Elise to her own question.

"Third and fourth thoughts actually," she responded.

"Do you want to do this?" Ben asked.

"No."

"Want to go back to your house?" Ben's tone was gentle.

"No. I don't want to do this but my gut tells me I have to," Elise said with more confidence.

Ben nodded, understanding completely. "Only way to beat your fears is to face them, right?"

Their eyes met and Ben wanted to face his fears right then and there. He wanted to plant a kiss on Elise's lips. He could release all of his pent up emotion and be honest with her and himself. Her eyes studied him. Ben's heart did a flip as he realized his inability to read her only made him adore her more.

She was leaning in toward him, her eyes sparkling with an allure he had never seen. She was going to initiate the kiss. He felt his body tingle and his face grow hot as her face came closer. Ben wasn't sure how he was going to react but he would let impulse dictate the moment.

She tilted her head. She was so close he could feel her warm breath. He smelled her perfume and thought he was in heaven. The grand moment was finally at hand.

Then Elise pulled back and answered his last question.

"Let's hope so. How about facing them by finding a way inside."

Ben felt like he had been punched in the gut. He was light-headed and thrown for a loop. He was able to nod and in a shortness of breath he said, "Y-Yeah. Yeah, let's do that. Maybe there's a back door or, or something."

Neither acknowledged the near moment of romance and instead diligently began their search.

It wasn't difficult finding a way into the building. They needed only to walk around the weed strewn yard surrounding the garage to find a door leading inside. It had been chained shut in years past in order to keep the hoodlums of Rowley out of the condemned building. When Ben and Elise walked up to it, however, they noticed all restraints had been removed from the door and it was slightly ajar.

"That's odd," Elise commented, although didn't believe that in the slightest.

"Kind of what we expected," Ben replied, correcting her.

They shared one more meaningful glance. With a deep breath, Ben pushed the door open and they took their first steps into Hell.

Sixteen

Dan McNair barely had the badge in his hand for ten seconds before the three police officers heard the screech of tires in the parking lot and the surprised shouts of those still congregating outside. Dan McNair wasted little time getting up and rushing out to assess the situation, while Stevens and Williams meandered behind him at a much slower pace, both less than eager to deal with the unknown happening.

McNair burst out of the station and saw Tiffany Bent and Jeff Hossler sprawled out on the ground. Not far from their position was a parked and still running white Honda CRV which had narrowly missed the two (among others) when it veered into the parking lot at a reckless speed.

The crowd around the car was alive with anger. Still, no one acted when the driver, Nick Laflin, pushed his way out of the car and stormed over to Dan McNair.

McNair put his hand on his holstered gun when he saw the look in the man's eyes. It was borderline deranged, and under Dan's rule there was no room for crazies who tried to test his authority.

"Stay where you are, pal. You almost ran down some innocent people right there and I don't take too kindly to that." Dan was surprised by the force behind his own voice.

Nick stopped for a moment and looked at Dan McNair with uninhibited rage. "What do you take kindly to? Being stuck in this backwater shit-stain of a town? What's going on, Copper? What the fuck gives? I've been driving around for over an hour and I can't get the fuck out!" His scream conveyed both his frustration and developing madness. The crowd quieted, paying close attention to the drama unfolding before them.

"I don't know what the heck you've been through or what the heck is going on, buddy. What I am sure of is that I'm going to maintain order. You nearly running people over doesn't quiet mesh with that. Whatever you're going through we're all going through, so don't make this harder than it has to be." There were murmurs of approval over Dan's words.

"Who the fuck do you think you are? You're just some two bit pig in this nowhere town! You don't know what's going on! What use are you? I'm not one of you people! I come from a civilized world, so let me the hell out!" Nick's eyes were far away and cloudy. They were turning as gray as the fog surrounding him. The once laid back father of two now appeared to be a raving madman. When he took a strong step toward Dan, the newly crowned sheriff didn't hesitate to draw his pistol and point it directly at Nick's chest.

"Not another step." Dan's voice was ice cold. He wasn't scared of what this man could do physically, what he was afraid of was what would happen if someone were to undermine his power.

"What are you going to do, shoot me, you hick cop? You ever even pull that trigger? I'm from the Bronx. This ain't the first time I've had one of those waved at me. Who do you think you are anyway?"

"I'll shoot." Dan's voice lacked emotion yet was resolute. Behind him he could feel the fear and helplessness of his deputies. He sensed Stevens and Williams were pining for McNair to lead and handle the situation.

It's my time to shine and save us all. Then everyone will see how truly great I am. They will be so upset that I wasn't given this job sooner. And I'll revel in it just like I deserve to. I'll let everyone know just how great it feels to be the man with the badge. His thoughts teetered over the edge of fantasy and he was only brought back to reality when he heard the scolding words coming from Nick Laflin's forked tongue.

"You won't do shit, Howdy Doody. I'm not scared of you or any of your two-bit officers." Nick Laflin took one fateful step forward and called what he thought was McNair's bluff.

BANG! The deafening noise echoed through the silence and everyone, save for McNair, flinched as the shot rang out. No one expected him to fire, no one expected to ever hear a gunshot go off within the town limits let alone witness Dan McNair shoot an unarmed man in front of a crowd of concerned citizens.

Dan's aim was true and the bullet hit Nick square in the heart. It passed through without resistance and Nick barely had time to register the pain or the copious amount of blood spurting from his chest before he collapsed backward. Nick Laflin was dead before he hit the ground.

His body fell and landed with a hard plop. It gave one final spasm before it lay completely still, a pool of blood forming around his slain form.

There was a collective gasp, which was about to turn into panicked screams. Dan killed the process before it started by firing two warning shots into the air. Everyone froze, paralyzed by fear.

Dan recognized his opportunity and seized it. They were willing recipients to what he had to say. Finally he would have his chance to win them all over and convince them he was what they needed. This was his town and this was his moment.

His voice was smooth and articulate.

"As you all realize, we are in an emergency situation. Whatever is going on is something that must be dealt with in an orderly manner or we risk our town falling into unruly chaos. Already most of you have witnessed terrible, unspeakable, inexplicable things. Rather than give way to panic we must unite under strong leadership to defeat whatever is tearing our town apart. As new sheriff I am enacting Martial law. No, right now it ain't legal but we're not exactly in a situation to be considering legality. This is survival, folks. Something isn't right and I'm not about to sit by and deal with bureaucracy while our town is being destroyed, you got me? This is for the safety of you, your friends, and your loved ones. We don't have any time to debate while there's something out there hurting those we care about."

Understanding dawned across the faces of the crowd. They began to see his way and grasp his method. They needed safety in such an unsure time and their fear compelled them to agree with him. Some wanted to be followers to whoever had the most guns—that had to be the most surefire way to ensure survival throughout this ordeal. In Rowley's time of crisis, freedom, liberty, and due process were the first things to crumble.

"As of now, I am forming a new town police unit, filled with anyone who wants to volunteer and follow my lead. Together we will maintain peace as we try to solve this terrible mystery, and we will not rest until safety and order are completely restored. As you can see," Dan motioned to Laflin's dead body, "in this emergency situation insubordination will not be tolerated. Any act against the police force is an act against the town and shall be dealt with accordingly."

The faces of the crowd grew grimmer as they understood exactly what that last statement meant.

"Now, any men who want to join the force do so right here and now and then I'll send a few of you out there to get more recruits. Bring all the guns you got—I have a feeling we're going to need 'em." Many in the crowd couldn't help but be drawn toward Dan McNair and his principles due to the magnetism of the words he spoke. So quickly they were willing to forget he had just shot an unarmed man dead in front of them, so quickly were they willing to abandon freedom for safety, and so quickly were they willing to heed his advice and support his hastily crafted plan. They looked to their new leader with hope and they looked to him seeking direction, despite the fact he horrified them. He was simply the man with the guns and the plan.

"So, who's with me?"

Nearly every man in the crowd volunteered.

SEVENTEEN

Andrew Murphy stood outside of 311 Evergreen Street and smiled like he had never smiled before.

The house was Victorian, white with a green triangular peaked roof and matching shutters. It was one of the largest and oldest houses in the town and one of the few Andrew actually enjoyed staring at while he went on his occasional bike rides.

Now it was up in flames, and it was more beautiful than ever before.

He had only put a container's worth of gasoline on the door of the home and along the front stretch of it. Upon lighting the fire with a match he was hit with disappointment as the fire barely caught and spread ever so slowly. For a time he thought he would have to add more gas to get the fire going but then, as if spurred by his own desire, the fire began catching and spreading at a rapid pace. It caught onto the siding and burned under the wood below where it consumed the house from the outside in.

Andrew didn't know if anyone was home and didn't have an opinion on the matter. He didn't care whether someone died or not—he just wanted to see the fire. He wanted to see his mistress dance unabated in the cool summer air.

And now she was dancing as a brilliant powerful blaze, the heat came at Andrew in waves making him feel warm all over. He smelled and tasted the burning air—the essence was intoxicating. He was high as he watched his lover dance and flail high into the sky.

It was art. It was a masterpiece. It was euphoria and bliss in their most pure forms. For Andrew Murphy, it was completion.

Eventually the flames reached the roof and the fire waved its way out into the gray sky, the entire sight a shining beacon on a bland, colorless day. The existence of the fire gave soul to a town lacking any remnant of character or culture.

Andrew felt tears come to his eyes. For the first time he was beginning to understand an appreciation for beauty. What he saw was awe inspiring and breathtaking. The power and dominance of his love was undisputable. He had helped her rise to prominence and lay claim over such a wonderful home.

It was destroyed by the fire.

The glorious, glorious fire.

As the smoke poured into the sky and became lost

amongst the fog, the fire consumed the entirety of the home like it was a party appetizer. The lovely home had deferred to the almighty flame and the sight was a testament to Andrew's passion for fire. It was his monument to a goddess.

At the point when the flame overcame the wood, Andrew reached down into his jeans and grabbed his penis. He slowly tugged it as it he watched the fire.

Just as the fire had spread slowly, he started gently massaging his member and warming it up, increasing the speed of his hand with the spread of the flames. The fire within him burned and his lust was at its peak. He jerked and tugged his member until he felt something new, a sensation he had never before felt.

Andrew Murphy experienced his first climax as he stood touching himself, looking at the destruction wrought by the fire he had started.

After it was over, after his body relaxed and his spasms ceased, Andrew's typically stoic face broke out in a wide grin. For the first time in his life, he approached a feeling close to genuine happiness. There was meaning and substance to this action. This was Andrew Murphy's conception of love.

For that one moment, Andrew Murphy was in heaven.

Do what makes you feel good, avoid what feels bad.

After his climax and prolonged satisfaction passed, Andrew was wrought with desire. He wanted to experience that addicting feeling once more. He wanted to be rewarded for his love over and over again.

He looked to the remaining containers of gasoline and started laughing.

Andrew Murphy was a pyromaniac.

He was also a sociopath.

Eighteen

Ben and Elise walked into a hell far worse than any of their nightmares could possibly conjure.

As soon as they entered, they smelled it—the absolute unadulterated smell of death and decay. It was thick and powerful. More overwhelming than any sensory perception either had ever dealt with. Elise held back the natural reflex to vomit as she took her initial steps into the dank dungeon.

The air was rich with the putrid stench of decomposition. It was so overpowering they struggled to gain their bearings and assess the situation before them. Both were ready to turn and run but instead each clenched the other's hands tightly. The only thing holding both in place was their endearing commitment to one another.

At first glance nothing was particularly out of place in the large room. To make their way across the expansive room, Ben and Elise zigzagged in between two broken down cars that had seen their heydays in the seventies, stepping over a hodge-podge of discarded tools and car parts on the ground. These things were to be expected in a garage, and despite the rotten smell filling their nostrils, their eyes at first could see nothing off putting. The walls were mostly barren except for few work benches attached here and there and—

Then Ben noticed the one workbench on the far wall, across the room from where they stood. As he stared at it, Elise noticed the object and saw why Ben's attention had been directed to it. Unlike the other workbenches, this one didn't have trash strewn on top of it—there was something more.

Both crept slowly toward the far wall. They walked with caution, as if whatever was on the bench was about to jump off and come after them. As they drew closer, the scene revealed something much more horrifying: tangible evidence to the grizzly horror show playing out in their town.

Ben was the first to notice the chunk of mutilated meat decorating the top of the workbench. It looked akin to a slab of meat one would find in a butcher shop. Still wet and juicy, the prime cut had not been removed very long ago and had come from something sizable—the chunk was over a foot in length.

Terrified, but captivated by the sheer horror of the scene,

Ben and Elise walked closer and closer. A dried pool of blood had seeped into the wood, leaving a trail staining the bench all the way to the floor.

They walked within a few feet of the bench and got a more detailed look at the slab. It was actually a cut with a clearly defined shape. As Ben reluctantly peered at the meat he saw one edge was distorted. Its form and shape were symmetrical all around until it came to that bottom edge. There were small chunks of meat missing from the slab that looked like they had been intentionally torn or cut away.

Ben only needed to turn his head slightly to see what had caused this distortion. Neatly lying next to the grizzly hunk of meat, covered in drying blood, was a simple fork and knife.

A fork and knife.

Someone—something, the shadowy thing—had been standing over the bench casually eating the severed mass of meat with a fork and knife. Ben's thoughts ran rampant. *Did it have a relaxed, civilized dinner? Did it enjoy the dark setting and ambiance while slowly cutting into and eating someone's back muscle?* The image was chilling.

The fact that this thing had the wherewithal to use a fork and knife while eating human flesh made Ben sick to his stomach. Elise let out a mortified gasp and buried her head into Ben's shoulder, sobbing instantly. Both wanted to say something to assure the other but the sight before their eyes left them in a mild state of shock and their minds crawled at a snail's pace over the available options in such a harrowing situation.

What do we do now? We were ready to take this on and it looks like we're in over our heads. We were like little kids going out on a make-believe adventure and now reality has knocked us flat on our asses. With that thought his eyes continued scanning the workbench, where more atrocious items waited to be discovered.

There wasn't only a slab of meat on the table. There was a jar—a jar filled with a sickly, greenish fluid that somehow seemed to glow and flicker in the dark room.

In the jar, fingers extended, was the severed hand of Mitch Joiner. The fluid had left it bloated and sickly, his blue varicose veins looking ready to burst out of his paper-thin skin. His boney fingers were contorted, bent and clawing out in Ben's direction as if they were reaching out to get him.

It put someone's hand in a jar. It put someone's hand in a fucking jar! What the hell is it and what does it want?

Elise removed her head from Ben's shoulder. Her face was tear stained but she looked upon the scene in the same solemn manner as Ben.

"Do you want to leave?" Ben asked

"Yes, but I don't think we should." Her voice was a squeak.

He held her hand and gripped it tight. "There's a hand there. It . . . it put a hand in a jar."

"There are fingers there too," Elise noted, weakly pointing to the far side of the workbench toward another horror Ben failed to notice.

There were fingers of all lengths, widths, and thicknesses cut up and stacked into a grotesque pile. They had been systemically chopped off and gathered from the bodies of a dizzying amount of people. At first glance, Ben guessed there were nearly thirty fingers cut up and thrown together on the far side of the bench. They were the thing's personal collection of severed fingers as trophies, or maybe they were the creature's idea of a quick snack. Ben shuddered as he envisioned the thing picking up a finger and popping it in its mouth as if it were a peanut or potato chip.

This time the only thing keeping him from running was Elise's hand in his own.

"What do we do?" she asked, looking to Ben for guidance.

He didn't know where he was getting his courage from, and he wasn't sure if the reserves could last much longer. His boldness surprised even himself. "I think there's more we have to see," he said, looking over to a door positioned to the far right of the workbench. It was a door to some type of office or storage room, and it stood half open.

Even separate from what the building emanated, there was a feeling permeating through the doorway—there was something awful back there and Ben felt he *had* to see it. There was no inkling of want or desire, or even curiosity. It was purely a sense of duty.

It was time to face the fear.

Holding Elise's hand, Ben walked toward the door and led her farther into the lion's den. They both walked with trepidation, but each step was steady and with purpose. Their steps echoed across the musty garage until they reached the old metal door. With little effort but great courage, Ben pushed it open and revealed the horror that lay within.

NINETEEN

Near the same time Ben and Elise entered the room, Nathan Wright was walking down Washington Street on patrol as a loyal servant of the newly formed Rowley Emergency Police Squad. Dan McNair had been so convincing in his speech that forty volunteers presented themselves within an hour, each wanting to do their part to keep the town safe.

McNair had his plan of action worked out by the time all of the volunteers gathered at the police station. He would break the men up into ten groups of four, and each group would patrol their designated areas to make sure order was maintained and the murderer apprehended. This mandate helped ignite McNair's popularity with his volunteers. The men who had come out to join him were underachievers, go-nowhere slackers whose greatest moments were a good punch line at Mac's Bar. Young or old, the men had no motivation, little pride, and little to do with their lives—but in this tragic situation that had all changed.

Dan McNair needed them, their town needed them.

They now had power.

Sheriff McNair had authorized them to use their own judgment when assessing the situations that would present themselves while on duty. He appointed each squadron a group leader, responsible for making the final decisions and reporting back to McNair. They were to keep order and peace, and specifically make sure every other citizen remained indoors—by force if necessary.

This made sense to the volunteer squad. Although they wanted duty and importance, they weren't particularly used to working hard or diligently. All that really mattered to them was their title and the pride that came with it. But power and privilege are dangerous things, especially when they are given out carelessly. This was the case when it came to Nathan Wright.

Nathan was thirty-three and he made a living cooking up food in Rollie's Cafe. He worked for minimum wage and got by on the food-stamps he received from good ol' Uncle Sam. He had four kids with three different women but, like him, they were not people who were particularly fond of commitment or responsibility. Therefore, raising children properly was never a concern Nathan had to deal with.

But now Nathan had a responsibility he was proud to uphold. McNair had appointed him the leader of his squadron of four volunteer officers. Nathan was overjoyed. He got to be the commander, he could call the shots, and his boys would have to listen. Here was big bad Officer Wright coming to save the day and make all the correct calls—it was a dream come true.

Things only got sweeter when McNair gave him Washington Street to patrol. Washington Street was the home of Eddie Rader, the two-timing schmuck who Nathan had gotten into a spat with while he was enjoying a few drinks at Mac's Bar.

Nathan had been drinking and having a good time. Between a sip of Yuengling he made a comment about how he was glad the Jets were "sucking it up" in the preseason football game playing on the lone television in the bar.

Nathan wasn't into football, but he identified himself as a Patriots fan. He decided it was best to side with the winner. He could always gloat and feel better than other sports fans with that logic. Turned out Eddie Rader was a die-hard Jets fan and he had enough booze in his system to be offended by the comment.

"Hey, fuck you, Nate! Fuckin' bandwagoner! You don't even know the difference between a quarterback and your own asshole," Eddie spat.

Nathan had a few drinks in his system as well and although Eddie was much larger, he mustered up the courage to respond, "Yeah, yeah, say that all you like, but the Jets won't ever win the big one again. So you can kiss my ass, or my quarterback, whichever one tickles your fancy more."

In two quick steps, Eddie Rader was upon Nathan and just as Nathan stood to face him he was struck down with authority.

POP! Eddie hit him square on the point of his chin and Nathan saw stars as he plummeted toward the floor. Luckily for Nathan, Phil Brooks and Jeff Hossler jumped upon Eddie before he could move in for the kill. He had been planning to straddle Nathan's downed body and lay down some heavy handed punches courtesy of Eddie Rader and the entire New York Jets fan base. Phil and Jeff had been able to hold Eddie back and convince him to leave the bar before the police were called.

Eddie didn't think Nathan was worth spending a night in the slammer so he had backed off and the situation had diffused nicely. The only real damage was a nice cut on Nathan's chin and a badly bruised ego. Despite his retreat, Eddie Rader had outright won the first round.

But who's the one with power now? Nathan thought. It didn't matter how big Eddie was or how strong he happened to be—now Nathan was the one who had the upper hand.

He smiled sadistically as he led his band down Washington Street, intent on going straight to Eddie Rader's house and embarrassing him in any way possible. Eddie would have to listen to Nathan and obey all of his orders. Otherwise he had to face the consequences.

Oh the consequences, Nathan thought with a cruel smile.

Revenge was sweet to Nathan and he found the creepy setting of the fog-covered town perfect for his vengeful plot. He would boss Eddie around, bully him, or just give him a hard time for nothing. The point was to prove that Eddie hadn't won and now Nathan was the big dick in charge.

They marched down Washington Street, Nathan Wright leading Ryan Giordano, Matthew Hawkins, and a kid who he had never met before named Derrick Laurel. During the first stage of their patrol, they only had to tell two people to get inside. Since they were brandishing three rifles and a double barrel shotgun those incidents had gone without a hitch.

They listen. They listen to me and my orders. Nathan had never felt so important. It was an addicting feeling for a man who was used to having orders barked at him. This was his sweet liberation.

Nathan was a bit worried, however. He wasn't sure what *exactly* he was going to do to humiliate Eddie once he got to his house. He was a police officer now, so it wasn't like he could just go out of his way to bother Eddie without some type of cause. He would need *reason* to stray from his duty and harass Eddie, otherwise the new position he coveted could be stripped away from him.

The only way Nathan could justify bothering Eddie was if Eddie was somehow breaking the new laws Sheriff McNair had enacted. That could be the case if Eddie Rader wasn't in his house but *outside* of it. Nathan could only hope this would be the case.

As the small patrol group reached the stretch of Washington where Eddie Rader's house sat, Nathan saw that fortune was continuing to smile upon him.

Eddie Rader stood outside on his lawn, looking off into the distance where even through the thick fog an orange hue could be seen dancing, flashing, and growing. Nathan had no concern for this glowing light. He didn't even take the time to consider that the glow was being cast because of a raging fire ceaselessly consuming homes. Nathan knew nothing of Andrew Murphy or his devious actions. No, all Nathan Wright knew was revenge.

Sweet, delicious revenge.

He upped his pace and the others followed behind him. The posse approached Eddie Rader, who hadn't even looked away from the distant orange light when Nathan opened his mouth and said, "Hey, asshole!"

Eddie Rader turned, his initial anger fading as surprise overtook him. "What the hell do you want? What's going on here?" he snapped.

Nathan kept up the bravado, fueled by a Winchester in his hand and a posse of armed goons behind him. "New law in town, pal. The sheriff has enacted some emergency provisions to deal with whatever the hell is going on. He appointed me as the leader of this patrol. Now get your stupid, Jets-loving ass back inside before there's trouble."

The humiliation and defeat that were supposed to dawn on Eddie Rader's face never did. Instead his expression became one of amused disbelief.

Then he laughed. He *laughed* at Nathan and his authority.

"Who the fuck do you think you are, Nate? The dumbass sheriff gives you a gun and a fake title and you think you're king of the world? Fuck you and the horse you rode in on. This is America. I'm not going anywhere."

Kill him. The thought came so suddenly and strongly that it shocked Nathan. Had he thought it? It was strange, like it came from another source, like it just floated from (the fog) somewhere and implanted itself in his head.

Although he was shaken for a split second, soon he couldn't deny he *liked* it. Part of him *really* liked it. It was the part that lay buried deep within his conscience, the part of his being that harbored hatred and murderous intent.

"Maybe you didn't hear me, jack-off, new laws, new rules. Get inside the house or you'll be in trouble."

"What, are you going to fucking make me?" Eddie Rader was a rough and tumble type of guy. Being at the brunt end of intimidation just wasn't his thing.

Kill him. Kill him. Kill him. The thoughts chanted in his mind.

For an awful moment, Nathan lost all control of his rationale and it gave way to the most sick, depraved type of thinking the mind can muster. It was the type of blind hatred that disregarded Eddie Rader as a human being and caused Nathan to look at him as only something he couldn't stand. This malevolence was the source of all the problems the town was experiencing at the moment, and it was the fuel giving Nathan the strength to do what he had only thought of doing when he was alone at night, his secret musings well hidden from the judgment of others.

Nathan Wright raised his Winchester rifle, pointed it forward, and without even a warning pulled the trigger and shot a round into Eddie Rader's head.

Eddie's head snapped back as the round lopped off a small upper portion of his skull. Part of his head exploded, flesh, bone, and brain matter scattering his lawn as he fell backward and landed on the ground.

The bang of the rifle startled everyone but Nathan. He felt no fear or remorse over his action, only more fiery contempt.

Even after he had used his hatred to pull the trigger it hadn't been satisfied or quelled. It felt *stronger* than before.

He turned around to face his flabbergasted men, all looking at him with a mix of horror, shock, and fear.

"W-what . . . w-w-wh-hat the hell, Nathan?" Matt Hawkins stammered, his eyes wide and his heart pounding out of his chest.

"That was law," Nathan replied coolly.

"Law, what do you mean law? You shot him dead for nothing!" Ryan Giordano exclaimed.

"Martial law. I gave him a chance, didn't I? We don't have time to deal with bullshit. You heard Dan. I'm in charge and I can make the calls when people are out of line. He was breaking the law and I made the call, as your leader I have been given full right to do that. "

"I-I can't handle this," Derrick Laurel said through panted breaths. "You, you killed him! This is crazy. This whole town is going crazy. Screw this, I'm out!" Derrick threw his gun to the ground and ran off into the fog. Neither Ryan nor Matt made a move to stop him. Acting on instinct, Nathan Wright raised his rifle once more and pointed it at the quickly fading figure of Derrick Laurel.

"Holy shit, Nate, you're not gonna—" Ryan began, weakly reaching out in his direction before the crack of the rifle cut him off.

The raging bullet hit Derrick Laurel in the upper back, just below the neck, severing his spinal column as it tore through him and exited through his chest. He barely had time to register what had happened as he fell forward onto the ground, scraping his face as he landed on the unforgiving pavement.

He shook and let out a weak moan before he passed, only having to suffer for a minute before darkness overcame him.

Nathan stood remorseless, looking upon the sight of Derrick's dead body with a sense of accomplishment—there would be no deserters in *his* unit.

Both Ryan and Matthew were without words. Both had come up with the idea of shooting Nathan right then and there, but those thoughts quickly disappeared when he turned to them with dark eyes that pierced right into their souls.

"No deserters. McNair put me in charge here. Either you listen or you end up like him."

As lifelong followers, neither man had the gall to challenge Nathan on his statement. They nodded and submitted to his authority.

The insanity was spreading, burning hot and bright like the flames already spreading throughout the town, the raging inferno still a mostly well-kept secret behind a wall of fog.

There was fire.

There was death.

Twenty

There were bodies. Dead, mangled bodies hanging from the rafters via large, metal meat-hooks piercing through each victim's chest. They were lifeless, yet managed to swing lightly in some nonexistent breeze causing the chains of the meat-hooks to make a soft, eerie jangling noise.

The first body was missing an arm—there was only a pulpy mess in the socket where it should have been. It was also missing a face. The wet muscle clinging to the bone was a mess—patches were stripped away, leaving only shredded, meaty strands hanging loosely from the skull. The eyeballs had been removed (eaten) straight from their sockets, and the jaw of the victim hung wide open. His tongue lay off to the side of his mouth, and his corpse was forever frozen in the expression of a silent, tortured scream.

Like the two others, this body had been gutted. A long slash ran from slightly below the meat-hook down to the pelvis. The ragged, red slit revealed the body had been cut through and opened up cleanly, and from what Ben saw all of the major organs had been removed.

The second body had been a teenage girl, from what was discernible. The only sign of that was the clothing: a blouse and a mini skirt.

She had no head but the decapitation had not been a smooth process. Instead, jagged, boney ends of her spine poked up through her neck-hole, spouting out from gnarled flesh. The head had been crushed, ripped away, or even eaten right off her neck. Unlike in the movies, this beheading was not painless and quick—this had been an agonizing, drawn out process. She was probably still alive while her head was being mutilated and consumed.

The third corpse was that of Phil Brooks. This was certain by his all-too-recognizable bushy beard, which was now decorated with a crusty mix of blood and vomit. This combined with the stink of cheap alcohol caused a pungent smell. The stench of death added to the mix made an abominable odor.

Other than his face, which was only missing small bites from it, nothing else could have been used to identify the corpse as Phil Brooks. He was gutted like the others, but additionally his limbs had all been removed directly from their sockets. There were no stumps or any flesh to indicate limbs had ever been there.

On his torn shirt, near where the arms should have been, were dark blood stains and concave openings where bits of gore were crusting and hardening. His jeans had gone from blue to red and were shredded to only a few tattered bits of material, barely long enough to cover his genitals. Like the first corpse, his tongue was hanging out, but it had been bitten in half.

By teeth that weren't his own.

They had found the thing's killing-ground—they had stumbled upon its personal slaughterhouse and butchery.

Overwhelmed, Elise fell to her knees and stared down at the floor, letting out a pitiful whimper. She couldn't leave Ben, but she also couldn't stand to see another tormenting sight. This was more than she bargained for, and she was about to burst into tears when she felt Ben's arms embrace her.

She shook uncontrollably in his grasp. He opened his mouth to ask if she was okay but nothing came out. Ben was as rattled as Elise by the sight of the mutilated, partially eaten bodies so carefully hung up for preservation on the rusty hooks.

It was saving them for later. It took out their organs and their eyes and whatever parts it couldn't wait to sink its teeth into, then left the rest for later. It wants meals, it wants to collect us and eat us at its own leisure. Ben's thoughts were haunting and he tried his best to block them out.

"B-Ben." Elise's voice was little more than a squeak.

"I'm here."

"We should . . . we should go. We've seen enough." Her shaking worsened.

"Okay," Ben responded, letting go of her but grabbing her hand. They both turned away from the sight of the hollowed out victims of the shadow creature. They were relieved when they left the scene of the butchering and closed the door of the grizzly room behind them.

Both took belabored breaths, and Elise put her hands on her knees to brace herself.

"I didn't think something like that existed, or could ever exist." Elise's voice was stunned and filled with a horrified disbelief.

"It ate them. It was tearing them apart and eating them."

"It called for me," Elise blurted. "It called out for me in the fog. It wanted me to go out there so it could get me. If I had gone I would be one of those dead bodies strung up from the ceiling!" She began crying and Ben put a hand on her shoulder.

"It won't get you, Elise. I won't let it. This thing is going to be stopped. We know where it is and we can get the cops or the army or whoever to come here and kill it."

Elise shuddered. "I don't think any of those things can stop it. We don't even know what this thing is but it has a way of making us *feel* what it is. And those feelings are bad, Ben. I know you feel them too."

"It's hatred," Ben said matter-of-factly. "Hatred and fear in their most unadulterated forms."

"How can it be stopped? How can we get out of this nightmare?" Elise was now looking to Ben like he was her savior and protector. It was a glance Ben had secretly always wanted to see from Elise, though certainly never under those circumstances.

"I—"

CRASH! The door they had used to enter the building smashed open, flying from its hinges. Something dark and shadowy bolted in with incredible speed, at first appearing to be just a blur before it stopped and revealed itself. Elise put her arms around Ben, clinging to him as they saw the reality of the nightmare enter the room. All they had speculated about had chosen to reveal itself.

The monster was gigantic. It easily stood seven feet tall, perhaps even taller. The figure was clothed in some type of flowing black hooded robe. The hood hung over its head and it wasn't possible to see a face, instead there was just a deep darkness, void of any light. Through the darkness, Ben felt eyes, powerful, evil eyes, staring right through him into his core.

If the figure had legs they were obscured by the flowing, torn robe. It appeared to be hovering, with the bottom of its robe flowing out and moving—pushed by a breeze it seemed to generate. Its body swung back and forth lightly, head bobbing ever so slightly along with the rest of its motions.

The only discernible physical traits were the tips of fingers, barely seen from behind the sleeves of the Grim Reaper-style robe. They were white, not quite bone white but a clammy sort of grayish white. *A dead white.* The fingernails were a blackened yellow, chipped and jagged.

It started coming toward them, swaying back and forth methodically. It was as if the figure was a snake, slithering its way through the air en route to them. It was moving with a confidence that frightened Ben. It moved like a predator nonchalantly toying with its prey. It had no worry or concern—it knew it was about to slaughter them.

It slid through the air, accentuating its motion so much that it looked like it was actually swimming. Gravity had no effect on the creature. Its motions were completely its own and in a bizarre way the beast was graceful.

Then Ben felt it. It was a dreadful feeling, a sinking feeling making him feel like he had never experienced happiness or joy. It wasn't quite sadness, anger, or hate, but a sick combination of the worst of them all.

It had busted the door down like it was nothing at all. It had strength, power, speed, and a demonic aura to boot. Ben's brief assessment of the beast told him it could rip him and Elise limb from limb if it chose to.

If this thing wants to it can make me and Elise its afternoon snack.

Elise!

She had turned a ghostly white. Her mouth was agape with horror as she stared at the beast that was destroying her once peaceful hometown. Like Ben, Elise had not only seen the horrible sight, but felt the evil radiating from its core. This was the only certain thing Elise could understand about the being—she didn't believe her eyes were showing her the true nature of the beast.

Tssskknnkktchhhh. Its dead hands curled up as the fingers reached toward them, grasping and molesting the air like a child reaching out in anticipation for a new plaything.

It was hungry for them. It wanted to eat their souls and make them a part of its infinite blackness. Ben and Elise were trapped, and at the mercy of the beast.

It had none.

Tsskknknkknnnkknch. Fog poured into the building as if beckoned by the beast's cry. The fog was putrid, smelling like death, and further pressed the feelings of hopelessness into Ben and Elise's psyches.

"Fuck you!" Ben shouted, lashing out against the being. "Fuck you, you piece of shit! You're killing my town, my friends, and everything I love! Go back to hell where you came from!" Ben didn't have a method to this madness but he wasn't going to lie back and let the thing kill him and Elise without a fight. He reached down to the ground next to him and found a dust covered metal pipe, about two feet in length. He held it forward like a club, ready to bash away at the creature.

If it wants Elise that bastard's gotta go through me first, he thought with resolve.

Tssknknknncccchkkk. Was this an utterance of pleasure? Ben felt the thing grow pleased from his anger, as if the energy he had let off gave the creature an exhilarating rush. The fog grew thicker and filled the room more quickly.

"G-get out of here! Leave us alone!" Elise's cry was not authoritative but fearful, and the creature arched its head back and let out another long cry. Like Ben's anger, Elise's fear seemed to drive it, to *arouse* it, and after it took a moment to breathe it in, it snapped its head forward and intently focused on them.

There were dead eyes under that hood, eyes that sank infinitely into darkness. They weren't eyes in the familiar, physical sense, but Ben knew they were looking through him and into his soul. It was picking out the parts it found the most delectable. This wasn't the first time it had done this. It had ravaged and consumed souls for years and years. Only God knew how long the thing had been roaming around and murdering people.

It's been around for a long, long time, and no one has stopped it. Ben gulped, and he squeezed Elise's hand tighter.

It stopped floating and instead began walking toward them on feet that didn't appear to exist. It was twisting its head side to side, turning it slowly but to impossible degrees, loud pops and cracks accompanying the motions. If it had bones, Ben would have guessed it was breaking them. But his intuition screamed that it didn't have bones, or even a real body.

This thing couldn't operate by the laws of physics. It did things that were impossible. Was its body even real? Ben's mind was dizzy with questions even as fear kept his heart in a vice-grip.

Then it started jerking.

Its motions were spastic and borderline frantic, as if the creature's nervous system had suddenly been jolted by a wild surge of electricity. Its arms moved in sudden jerks, bending in sickening, unnatural ways as they reached out toward him. It almost looked to Ben like its left arm had three joints.

Snap. Snap. Snap. Ben heard snapping as it continued its motions toward them. The creature appeared to be breaking its limbs one by one as it forced its body into grotesque contortions. It bent its body nearly to a ninety degree angle sideways and Ben heard whatever was inside the monster violently snap, pop, and churn.

Crrrrunch, snap, snap! Ben and Elise looked at its fingers, now slightly more visible, and watched in horror as the decomposing fingers bent backward then sideways, snapping and breaking in all different directions. It looked like someone had taken a hammer and smashed those evil hands and broken every bone in them, but the fingers continued to move and contort, dislocating and relocating constantly while reaching for them.

Then for a horrible moment they weren't fingers at all, but piercing claws. They were alien-like hands, hard and shelled with long fingers tipped with dark, spear-like claws. Long, thick, and as black as night—they looked like they could shred whatever stood in their path.

Tssschnkkktchchhhnnktcchh.

"Let's run," Elise whispered.

"It will catch us. It's faster than it's letting us know."

"How do you know that?" Her hushed voice was frantic.

"I feel things from it. I know without . . . having to experience."

"What do we do?" Elise's fear was at a peak now. A crushing wave descended upon Ben as he realized he had let Elise down. He was not her hero or savior. He was just as helpless as she was. He had a pipe but that wouldn't be enough to stop the thing.

His body froze in place. *What do you do, Ben? What do you do? Think, think, think.*

Ben didn't have time to think. The beast lost interest in playing with its food and moved in for the kill. It utilized its amazing speed, spanning the six feet between them in an instant. Ben barely had time to register what had happened and was fortunate that passion spurred a knee-jerk reaction.

Elise stood beside him and no matter what he wouldn't let

that thing hurt her—even if he had to die in the process. He grabbed Elise's forearm and yanked her backward with him. Ben *felt* the air in front of his face part as it was cut through by those ungodly, razor sharp claws. They sliced through space so fast they were just a dark blur, and ended up a mere inch away from tearing off both Ben and Elise's faces.

They were stunned but Ben retained the wherewithal to pull them backward again and away from the second swipe. They turned and ran from the nightmare.

Whoosh. It was in front of them once more. With little effort, the beast had appeared directly in their path.

Ttsskkkkkkknntntnchhh. It was amused by the futility of their efforts. No matter how fast they ran, Ben and Elise could not escape the demon.

Termination, Ben thought. *It's here to consume us and end us once and for all, and there's nothing we can do. But I can't let it hurt Elise!* Despite the all encompassing fear, Ben did not lose sight of what mattered most to him.

Anticipating its next strike, Ben pushed Elise backward and leaped backward as well, shielding her body with his own. This slowed Ben enough to where he was unable to completely dodge the next attack.

It shot forward with incredible speed and slashed again. Ben felt a hot, searing flash of pain as the tip of the dagger hit him in the lower right section of his stomach before slicing up diagonally across his entire sternum. Ben dropped the pipe, let out a gasp, and fell back, blood already shooting out from beneath his ripped shirt. He hit the concrete floor of the garage and smacked his head on it, topping off the sudden physical trauma with a concussion.

Elise shrieked and the now-hazy Ben barely heard it. The beast let out a triumphant cry and crept toward Ben to deliver the final blow.

Ben looked up at the assailant. He still did not have his bearings after falling onto the concrete, and could do nothing to defend himself against the terror. He placed a hand over a portion of his bleeding wound and awaited the inevitable.

Then something was upon him. He was shielded by something he did not see coming—something quite the opposite of the horrible, dark creature.

Elise threw her body upon Ben, embracing him and covering him. She would protect him from what she could, even if it meant sacrificing her own life.

The Harbinger continued toward where they lay, and just before it was over them, Elise turned her head toward Ben. Their eyes locked and Ben had no reason to hold anything back; nothing could be left hidden any longer.

His mind gave way to his heart, his reason gave way to impulse, and he let it happen. If this was Ben's last chance at proclamation he would make clear to Elise what his heart had been telling him since the whole ordeal had begun.

"Elise, I love you." The words were simple but the emotion powerful. All pain faded from her face as she felt the same love for Ben free itself from the static of fear and desperation. When he pushed his lips forward she met them with her own. The kiss was completely liberating, filled with a ripe passion greater than anything either had ever experienced.

Their embrace brought warmth back to their bodies. If they were going to die, they would be happy and content dying in their lover's arms.

TSSSKKNNTNCCHHHH! The sound was no longer a hissing whisper but a loud cry, and Ben and Elise felt the pain coming from it.

They separated their lips and turned to see the creature. It no longer approached them. It was hunched over, in a defensive position, and the outward aggression it had displayed only moments prior was long gone.

Ben and Elise each stared at the monster with disbelief. Why had it stopped its charge? What had hurt it? Why did it suddenly seem to be behaving *cautiously?*

There was a standoff where both parties did nothing but stare at each other. The creature appeared to be sizing up Ben and Elise again, but this time with hesitancy. Ben didn't know why or what it meant, and for a moment he thought this would be their chance to escape. But the moment came and went, and the beast stood tall again and extended its claws. It prepared to strike once more.

"I love you, Elise." The words escaped from Ben's lips again without a thought. It was the only thing that mattered, regardless of the monster's actions.

"I love you too, Ben." As the last syllable left Elise's lips they heard the beast let out a cry of pain once more.

Tsskknknnkncchh! Tssknktnchhh! It stumbled backward, flailing at them like it was trying to shoo them away. It thrashed violently and its claws reverted to the dead zombie hands. It grasped its hood and writhed side to side in pain while letting out another cry.

Tsskknknnkncchh! Tssknktnchhh!

"I love her," Ben said it in the direction of the creature

and this time saw the physical reaction as it jumped backward and whipped its arms around. It struck an old wooden work bench with its hand and shattered it, sending splinters and discarded tools scattering across the entire garage. Old wrenches and screwdrivers landed on the floor with loud clinks. Ben raised his arms to brace himself and Elise from any falling debris.

"I love her! There's nothing you can do about it!" He felt the rush of passion as he proclaimed it once more and the creature recoiled more fiercely. "I am always going to love her!"

It spun away, darting around in circles like a trapped animal. It let out low hisses and grunts and other sick guttural noises as it flailed in protest to Ben's statement. It had gone from a foreboding, vicious monster to a pissed off child throwing a temper tantrum. After a handful of seconds of this behavior it made its final decision.

With just as much speed as it had used to rush in, the beast became a blur and darted across the expanse of the room. The threat was gone—the dark shadow had actually been the one to run away.

Ben tried to think about what this meant when Elise reacted to his wounds.

"Oh my God, you're hurt! We have to get you help!" Her voice was shrill. She reached out and pushed aside his tattered shirt to get a better look at the slash wound. Ben looked down and was shocked to see what was left of his blue shirt was dyed red. He reached down and grabbed either side of his shirt, tearing the garment away so they could see the true extent of his wound.

He felt the actuality of the pain for the first time as he stared down at his injury. The slash ran from just below his right nipple to just above his left hip, barely missing his belly button along the way. On first glance the wound appeared alarming. Its size was overwhelming and the blood seeping down his abdomen accentuated the perceived damage.

After a brief moment of self-examination however, where Ben put his hands to his chest and felt the area of the wound, he realized it wasn't that bad. If the cut had gone deeper, the gash would most certainly be fatal, but from what Ben could see the claw had barely grazed him—it was nothing more than a flesh wound. It was a *large* flesh wound certainly, one that would keep on bleeding if he didn't patch himself up, but at least it didn't appear to be a mortal injury.

Whereas Ben was quickly calmed by examining the extent of his wound, Elise's fear was heightened.

"Shit, Ben! We have to get you to the hospital. You're going to bleed to death!" Her eyes were wide with fear, and her tears fell without resistance.

"Elise," Ben began in the calmest tone he could muster, "I'm going to be all right. It barely nicked me. It isn't that deep."

"Barely nicked you? Look at all that blood!" Elise exclaimed. "We have to stop the bleeding!"

"Take my shirt, what's left of it, and wrap it around me and tie it tight. Get it over the wound." Ben was calm in the face of hysteria.

"That's not going to be enough."

"It's going to have to be until we find something else to stop the bleeding. Now come on, help me out," he said, putting a hand to his knee and standing up. He spread his arms so Elise could get to work.

Elise wasn't squeamish. She grabbed the blood dampened shirt and tore it to further stretch it out and make it more of a rag. She glanced at Ben for a moment and all fear was gone as she took on the responsibility of properly bandaging his wound.

She threw a portion of it over Ben's shoulder and brought the rest down and around, making sure the shirt was tightly pressed over the entirety of his cut. Moving behind Ben, Elise made the make-shift bandage tighter by tying it firmly together over his upper back. It was crude, but it appeared the shirt was containing most of the bleeding.

Ben turned and smiled at Elise. "Ever consider a career in medicine?" He tried to lighten the mood and won a small victory when Elise rolled her eyes in response.

"And you thought I was going to die," Ben said keeping up the fight.

"You aren't safe yet. You need someone to take a look at that. You've lost a lot of blood and then there's the risk of infection."

"I saw you about it, there's no better."

"Stop it."

"I'm serious," he said with a grin.

"So am I." Elise let her frustration show. "You almost died there. You're lucky that thing didn't cut you clean in half!" The tears showed in her eyes once more.

"Why did it leave?" Ben asked.

"Maybe it had something to do," Elise guessed.

Ben shook his head. "The only thing that thing does is kill

and it had an opportunity right there."

"It didn't like what you said," Elise answered, her eyes meeting Ben's but showing some hesitancy.

"D-did you?" Ben asked tentatively and there was a pause.

"Let's get the heck out of this garage. It's a nightmare in here," Elise responded, avoiding the question.

Ben nodded. "We walked right into hell." He shivered as the magnitude of what they had just witnessed dawned on him.

Both were relieved to step out of the dank, dim dungeon and get outside—even if the outside was dreary as well. Elise stood near Ben, hands slightly extended as if ready to catch him if he stumbled.

"I'm fine," Ben assured her.

"You're arrogant is what you are," Elise retorted.

"We have to stop it before it kills more people, before it does what it did to those poor souls in there."

"Stop it? How do we stop it? You saw how that thing moved! We're lucky to be alive and you think we can just stop it?" Elise exclaimed.

"What it did to me is nothing compared to what it's doing to our town."

"Wake up, Ben." Elise raised her voice to him for the first time in years. "Wake up! Were you asleep that whole time in the garage? That thing is bad. Not cartoon villain bad or monster in the closet bad, but real hardcore rip-your-head-off-and-eat-it-bad!"

Ben raised his own voice in response, partially insulted by Elise's lack of faith in his argument. "It ran away, Elise. We stopped it. It didn't kill us."

"Didn't kill us? It nearly ripped your guts out. And who knows why it left. Maybe it's just messing with us. Maybe it's out here in the fog just waiting to strike."

"No!" Ben shouted and Elise's eyes widened with surprise. "It didn't like that I loved you—that was it. It ran away because I love you."

Elise fumbled her thoughts and emotions before responding, "S-so what does that mean? Does that mean because you love me you can kick its ass? That doesn't make sense."

"Nothing makes sense right now."

"Then how can you pretend to know what you're doing?"

"I just do." His indignation shined.

"Just because you love me doesn't mean that we're safe." Elise softened her tone now.

"You saw how it reacted though. You saw how it recoiled. Something about what we did hurt it in some way. Maybe we can figure out a way to stop it."

"You're just trying to sneak in another kiss aren't you?" The sly remark blindsided Ben.

"N-no, wait, what are you—"

Elise smiled and let out a chuckle. "Okay, lover boy, I'll give you that much. What you said and what we did . . . our kiss . . . seemed to throw it off. But what does that mean? What if next time it doesn't work like that? There are no guarantees in any of this and I'm not going to let you run out there armed with just your heart."

"That thing is hate," Ben reasoned, "so the fact that it doesn't like love makes some sense. The only thing that stops hate is love, right? Maybe that thing wants our hatred. Maybe it wants our whole town's hatred. What it doesn't want to deal with is love, so maybe we can find a way to use that to our advantage."

"That's a stretch of a theory," Elise replied.

"It's not much to go off of, but right now I don't want to sit back and let that nightmare tear our town apart. We have to do what we can and we have to do it quick."

Elise was troubled by how stubborn Ben was, yet at the same time she was becoming enamored with his new sense of bravery and commitment. He had saved her in the garage and now he wanted to save the entire town. Ben Dowling was becoming a man right before her eyes.

Elise sighed. "We don't do it alone then. It's too dangerous and I don't want to risk you getting hurt. And we need to get you to a doctor first."

"I'm fine. I don't need a doctor. We don't have time to waste."

"No," Elise said firmly. "You're hurt and that dirty shirt is just going to make things worse."

"How can we go to the hospital? It's too far away. We can't run now. We have to stop this thing as soon as possible."

Elise paused in thought. "The least we can do is properly bandage you up. Then maybe we can get together with some other residents and fight this thing."

"We need to come together. It doesn't like love, so maybe if we get people to love we can get it to leave."

"Get people to love?" Elise took the tone of a youngster instigating a punch line.

"You know what I mean," Ben said with a sigh. "Okay, we'll go to your house and clean me up. Then we'll get everything going."

"We can't go inside," Elise commented. "If my mom sees what happened she won't let us out of the house and I don't want to drag her into this. Out back we have some sheets drying. We can use one of them to bandage you up, maybe use the hose to clean you off a bit too."

Ben looked at her strangely. "I thought you wanted to *properly* bandage me."

"You're too stubborn for that. Besides, if we go to the police station I'm sure they have first aid kits. That would be a good place to start if we're going to rally the town."

Ben nodded in agreement, and then smiled. "Sounds good. Let's do this together." He offered his hand and Elise took it. As their hands met, Elise relented, letting Ben see some of her worry, fear, and uncertainty.

"I want to do this together, but I'm scared. I'm scared of what I saw in there, I'm scared of that thing, and I'm scared of losing you."

Ben gripped her hand tighter. "I'm scared, too. I'm not going to lie to you. I'm scared of all of those things and I never want to lose you. But this is something we have to do. This is something we were *meant* to do."

"Together?" Elise asked.

"Together," Ben affirmed. "We don't have to be crazy or go charging in like commandos. Let's just take it a step at a time. I think going to the police station is a good step one."

"Look at you," Elise said as Ben's words eased her tensions. "You save the day with a kiss then you take the girl in your hand and lead her to the final battle. It's like a movie. Very well scripted there, Casanova." Elise's personality shone despite the harrowing situation.

"Hey, I wasn't the only participant in that kiss."

Elise blushed and put on a sideways smile. "Now you're really throwing on the romance, huh, lover boy? Stroke your ego later—we have things to get to. Lead the way."

"So now I'm the leader?" Ben was happy to relish in the small, carefree moment.

"Oh Captain, my Captain . . ." Elise began.

"Don't," Ben replied and felt his face blush. If things worked out in saving the town, maybe he would have a shot with Elise. This thought was so strong it nearly made him forget about the horror he had just lived through.

Stop it, Romeo. There are bigger things on your plate right now. You nearly got cut in two and you're planning a honeymoon in your head. His thoughts were right. They had to get going and organize. It wasn't like he had won the battle and outwitted the beast. He was lucky both he and Elise hadn't ended up strung up on the rafters like those unfortunate victims.

He shuddered with the thought and came back to reality. "Let's go then." Hand in hand Ben and Elise walked away from the garage toward Church Street.

Neither knew the magnitude of the chaos awaiting them.

Twenty-One

It's out there. It's out there and it's hungry.

That's all Charlie Braylon could think about as he took refuge in his office, the door barricaded by his desk, chair, and an assortment of other items he had found lying about the room. He was trapped like an animal in a cage. He was a prisoner in his own business.

But Charlie knew Braylon's Market was his no more. Perhaps the building could still be considered to be owned by him but Braylon's Market had ceased to exist. Outside his office there was no longer the friendly atmosphere of a small town supermarket, only a gore splattered slaughterhouse.

Braylon's Market had turned into a blood-bath.

There were many things Charlie Braylon was: an adulterer, a heavy drinker, a bad husband, a worse father, a cheat, a scoundrel, and oftentimes an outright coward.

But one thing Charlie Braylon had not been was stupid.

When Charlie noticed the state and security of the town was crumbling, he knew he had to act quickly. He wasn't sure exactly what was going on, but he could tell it was bad enough to incite widespread panic. Unrest and chaos were already rearing their ugly heads and at the rate things were progressing, it wouldn't be long before the entire town went mad. Charlie Braylon didn't want any part of that strife. Charlie wanted to be safe, sound, and comfortable just like he had been the majority of his life.

Charlie felt no trace of any of those feelings, however, as he sat huddled in his office, holding back a flood of tears. The things he had just witnessed left him with scarring memories that would haunt him for the rest of his life. That was if he even managed to survive.

He thought back to how he got himself trapped in such an awful situation, back to how his efforts to preserve himself had sickly and ironically blown up in his face.

Despite the strange circumstances, Braylon's Market had opened up that morning as usual with most of the staff reporting for duty. Charlie wasn't there when the store opened—this was customary and accepted. The few appearances he made were only when the newspaper had a story to report pertaining to his business. Then he would stand proudly and talk about how his efforts were perpetuating a business that was a crucial component to the lifeblood of the local economy—he was a hometown hero after all.

That morning, Charlie decided to make an appearance at the market for a new reason. When he became aware of how out of control the town was becoming he knew exactly where to find his safe haven.

Charlie Braylon was somewhat paranoid. He was adverse to the idea of ever *having* to struggle to achieve. His greatest fear was losing the comfortable life he was so adept at living.

His worries were sometimes outlandish. He wondered what would happen if anarchy ensued and roving bands of looters took control. If there was some type of disaster, he could lose all of his comfort and security. Just like that, his life blood would be taken from him and he'd have to struggle to survive. If those awful things really did begin to happen, he had to know what his first priorities would be. If anarchy was imminent, what were the highest priorities for self-preservation?

Food and shelter.

Those priorities were why Charlie had decided to go to Braylon's Market that day. If something was going wrong he wanted to make sure to have enough food and supplies to hunker down and wait for the crisis to be alleviated. He planned to secure his business so rioters or gangs wouldn't bust in and take all of his goods and threaten his sanctuary. He knew his methodology was jumping the gun slightly, but he figured it wouldn't hurt to be safe, secure, and surrounded by sustenance. Charlie hadn't bothered to invite his wife or two children—they were closer to nuisance than necessity.

If the town's problems persisted for the long run he knew he wouldn't be able to stand being stuck for days on end with them. They were too needy, demanding, and blatantly annoying.

The moment he arrived at the store he ordered it closed and ushered all customers out. The few there complied willingly and without incident. After this he ordered his employees to barricade the two automatic doors on either side of the market and instructed Darren, the pudgy cashier, to climb up on a ladder and nail boards over the large windows that made up the majority of the front wall of the building.

Many of his employees scoffed and one even called him a raving lunatic. Trish Rader, wife of the recently deceased Eddie Rader, and morning manager of the market, even stormed out despite the threat of being fired. Three employees went with her. Charlie fired them all as they left, but it didn't matter.

What mattered was that order was disintegrating. What mattered was the town's devolution.

What mattered was Charlie's safety.

Six of his employees stayed and helped him turn the supermarket into a hastily-constructed fortress. The doors were sealed off by layers of stacked shelves and carts. The windows were boarded up by sheets of plywood found lying in the back cargo bay of the building.

The employees wanted an explanation as to what was going on and why they had been commanded to do such things, but Charlie didn't see the need to give them one. He was the owner and the boss, therefore all they had to do was listen.

The reason he ended up giving them was that he "paid their goddamn salaries," so as long as they finished up the work he gave them they would get paid and could leave.

"Do we get paid for the full day if we leave?" Ronnie Thompson asked.

"Yes, you get paid. You all get paid for helping," Charlie responded impatiently.

"Then what's the point in staying here?" inquired Linda Logan.

"There is no point, go, all of you go!" Charlie snarled.

"Mr. Braylon, what's going on? Why are you hunkering down here?" Scott Pascal couldn't help but ask. "I mean, I did this because you're the boss but it all seems kinda nuts." He looked down and away. Poor little Scott wasn't used to questioning authority.

"I'm doing this because I want to—that's all you need to know. Now if any of you want a paycheck you better get your things and—"

Scrrrrrrrthhh. Scrrthhhh. The sound of something clawing against the outside of the windows halted Charlie mid-sentence.

Everyone stared at the window. It was the type of noise one couldn't simply ignore. It wasn't quite low enough to be dismissed and it wasn't quite loud enough to cause an instant stir. It was just enough of an oddity to seize their full attention.

Then, for some odd reason, the supermarket suddenly became ice cold. Each of the workers shivered as the store became as chilly as a refrigerator.

"What was that?" Ronnie was the first to break the silence. He looked around hoping to find an answer, but was met only with shrugs.

"It better not be some people trying to break in already," Charlie replied with scorn.

"Break in?" asked Scott. "Why would anyone want to—"

CRACK! The sound of shattering glass cut Scott off and caused everyone to leap back from the windows. More shattering and splintering was heard as something smashed through the large glass window and found its way through the flimsy plywood sealing off the supermarket from the rest of the world.

Charlie was about to shout and give hell to whoever was breaking into his sanctuary. He would let them know he'd have their head for defacing his property and ruining his plans. He opened his mouth but then choked on his own utterance as he heard the unknown agent who had just smashed his window. His fiery rage was soon turned into icy fear by the guttural noise coming from the other side of the wood.

Tssskkknntcchhhnntchh.

Linda Logan shrieked and ran farther back into the store, taking refuge behind one of the cashier's stations near the far wall. Everyone else looked at each other puzzled, waiting for an explanation or order. The sound was so unusual, so *unnatural,* that a wave of confusion quickly swept over and paralyzed the remaining employees.

Charlie was shaking uncontrollably, his arm forcefully slapping against his hip. It wasn't just the fear either, but the *cold.* He was *shivering* from the bone-chilling essence permeating throughout the store.And then it wasn't only the cold that assaulted the trapped workers—there was also a terrible smell. It was a rotten smell, a decomposing smell, a dry, *dead* smell stabbing Charlie's nostrils and sending pangs of fear surging to his heart.

The air around him was filled with death.

There was another moment of silence. Darren, being closest to the window, looked back to Mr. Braylon to ask what he should do.

Then it happened.

The wood splintered open with a resounding crack. The plywood was so thin it tore like paper as the hand shot through the barricade and reached into the supermarket.

It was a dead hand, pale white with bits of flesh missing near the tips of the fingers and the palm. Under the torn skin lay dead muscle and tissue, white, clammy, and putrid. Its finger nails were long and ragged, with a slight blackish-yellow tone. The sickly hue of the nails was juxtaposed staunchly by the all-too-white skin of the creature.

They had to be staring at the hand of something dead. It was a rotting, decomposing hunk of flesh—but still somehow it was *alive*. It was alive and it *craved* them.

It snatched out into the air viciously, clawing blindly for its prey and stretching its fingers out to incredible lengths in the process. *Pop. Snap. Pop.* Its fingers popped in and out of its joints without effort, attempting to stretch out long enough to reach the horrified employees.

Pop. Snappppp. Crack! Tssssskkkkkknnntch. It wanted them. It wanted them badly.

The sound of the creature's growl brought bile into Charlie's throat and it spilled over his lips, forcing him to lean forward and let his stomach contents fall to the floor. Linda Logan wanted to find another, safer hiding spot but her legs had become a sick mix of cement and Jell-O—too heavy to move and too weak to support any of her actions. Ronnie Thompson and the rest backed up to where Charlie was standing, a good twenty feet from the dead hand, but Darren stood frozen in place, a mere ten feet from the predator.

Darren thought he was dreaming. What he was seeing was impossible. Dead hands didn't exist, zombies didn't exist, and nightmares like this only occurred in bed.

It couldn't be real—he tried to force himself to believe this. Then the popping and cracking got louder. The creature broke all of its fingers and each of the shattered sections moved independently of one another. Broken segments of finger churned and thrashed like each was desperate to reach the victims on its own. Just when everyone thought they were staring at the culmination of all their worst fears, things somehow managed to get even worse.

Suddenly, the hand changed form completely. It was no longer a rotting, dead, white hand with grotesque broken fingers—it was the clawed hand of a beast. It was a black, hard, and somewhat scaly hand with foot-long fingers capped by shining, razor-sharp claws. Each of the claws looked more than able to mutilate anything having the misfortune of falling into their grasp.

There was no transformation process—the hand simply *became* this in a moment incomprehensible to the human mind. Too overwhelmed by the disorientating sight, no one reacted until the beast let free its cry once more.

Tssckknnnkkttthhh.

This was all Linda Logan needed. She ran from behind

her register and headed for the back of the store. Her legs were still not ready to carry her, however, and she sprawled out and collided with a display of tomato sauce. The containers fell with her, smashing on the ground. Shards of broken glass cut her as she landed harshly upon them but all evidence of her wounds was hidden amongst a lumpy mess of tomato sauce.

No one even heard her fall. They only focused on those terrible claws.

It happened too quickly. There was a loud shattering noise, a mix of glass and wood breaking as the being leaped through the reinforced window. It yanked two large sheets of plywood from their position on the window, one of them falling and striking Darren on the head. He toppled to the floor, holding his head and writhing as hot pain throbbed through his skull.

With the breaking of the glass came a rush of air—a rush of *fog*. It blew past them and overran the supermarket, limiting visibility to a couple of feet in a second flat. The terrible dead stench that had been merely a whiff was now encompassing them and filling up the entire store.

This series of events was enough for everyone else. They ran backward, fleeing farther into the building, a few of them tripping and falling over displays and shelves. The visibility had become zero and the victims lost their bearings.

Everyone ran except for Darren and Charlie. Darren tried to stand up and did a poor job of it. Charlie was intent on seeing what this nightmare was before he ran. Despite his fear, his curiosity held him in place for a moment.

It moved too quickly. It surged through the window and

the wood in a dark blur. It was striking to see something so large shoot through the opening with such grace and speed.

All feelings of awe stopped, however, when Charlie got a look at the monstrosity before it sprung on Darren with its ungodly speed.

It was the Grim Reaper—that was what his mind told him. *The Bringer of Death,* he thought. It was tall and impossibly thin. Despite its massive size it was gaunt to the point of emaciation. Its black robe disguised its feet (if it had any) but revealed those hard, alien-like claws. Charlie's curiosity was a thing of the past as he realized he *never* would want to know what the thing looked like under that cloak. The sight would drive him insane, or kill him, or drag him straight to hell.

Charlie knew he had to run. Before he had the opportunity, the monster sprung into action and initiated the massacre. The Harbinger lunged at Darren and the gruesome scene to come would be forever ingrained into Charlie's memory.

It traveled the ten feet between them in less than a second. It moved like a darting shadow as it flew at Darren, regaining its form as it stopped directly in front of him.

Darren, on his knees, had time only to glance up at the predator before his life was cut short.

TWAP! The noise was sick and wet, and Charlie felt the specks of blood rain on his face before he was able to piece together what happened.

With one quick swipe, the creature decapitated Darren, sending his head toppling through the air end-over-end like a desperate last second Hail-Mary pass. It continued to sail, spraying blood all over the floor and ceiling before landing with a sickening thud on one of the cashier's check out stations. It rolled over once more, and then settled into place.

Charlie saw Darren's head had landed neatly on the station, right where the groceries were supposed to be scanned. If the station was turned on, there would have been a bleep confirming the purchase of one recently severed head.

Darren's dead face stared at Charlie. His tongue had been nearly bitten off by his teeth and hung listlessly by a thread of meat from the side of his mouth. His blue eyes were still moving, rolling backward into his skull. What blood was left in his head now gushed out of his torn neck, turning the conveyor belt of the station into a bloody river.

Darren's body was on its knees for a moment longer, neck spraying blood into the air like a geyser or a twisted fountain. Droplets of blood rain scattered out to surprising distances, transforming Charlie's once friendly market into a scene out of the goriest of horror films.

Darren's body then fell over and began to spasm, causing a blood puddle to develop quickly near check out station one. These twitches only lasted a second or two before the boy's body lay still.

Clean up! Get a mop down here! The sudden thought made Charlie ill. He saw the beast look over at where he stood and he *felt* it looking at him. Under that hood there was no face, eyes, or any discernible features—only a hateful darkness. It stared hungrily from the total darkness, wanting him to join it. The cold gaze penetrated his soul and he felt violated. The culmination of all of the world's ills stared him directly in the face.

He ran.

Charlie ran as fast as he could away from the horror, weeping as he realized his life was likely coming to an end. The monster could move with lightning speed—catching him would be no issue.

He ducked into one of the aisles, his own tears nearly blinding him. His heart sank as he stumbled over a wayward can on the floor and nearly lost his balance. He braced himself on a shelf, knocking an assortment of products to the floor in the process, before regaining his stride. The hairs on the back of his neck stood up as he felt the beast gaining on him. The shadow was nearly upon him and the game almost over.

Tssskkknnntcchchhh. Everything started to go dark. The creature was directly behind him. Its aura dimmed everything around it and extinguished any last traces of hope. Charlie prepared for death when a twisted bit of fortune unexpectedly prolonged his existence.

As aisle four ended, Charlie collided hard with a figure appearing from the fog. It had become so dense Charlie didn't see the figure until he was literally upon him.

There was a flailing of limbs and an array of desperate cries. At first, Charlie didn't recognize that what he hit was not the creature. He jumped to his feet quicker than the other figure, his employee Chris Cullen, and continued running, not even bothering to assist the man who had put in countless overtime hours to help keep the market in business. Chris was on his feet a split second after Charlie, but it was too late.

The beast reached him.

Charlie foolishly looked back and caught a fleeting glimpse of what happened to Chris, his loyal employee until death. The monster stopped in front of Chris, mouth agape as he stared up at it, witnessing the embodiment of death. He stammered and choked on a scream. Before he was able to release the cry, the creature forced its massive claws straight into his body.

There was no resistance, the massive daggers seamlessly slipped into his chest and mid-section. He was impaled and then lifted up into the air, the entire weight of his body falling upon the claws. They ripped through muscle and grinded against bone, accentuating Chris's already agonizing torment. He struggled, kicking, punching, and screaming even as blood poured from his lips. The Harbinger did not slaughter him as quickly as it could have. It was amused by his pathetic struggles. His prolonged suffering was the utmost entertainment.

Charlie heard the grotesque ripping sound. It was complemented by a series of crunches and breaks. The creature sunk its claws deeply into Chris's midsection, grabbing a hold of each side of his ribcage. Then, yanking in both directions with little effort, it tore him open.

Chris let out a gurgling scream as his ribcage was separated and his sternum broke in two. His ribs shattered, piercing through his flesh like jagged spears. A ragged cut appeared in the center of his chest as he was ripped in two, his skin tearing away like wrapping paper. The monstrosity had opened Chris up like Christmas present.

Chris was dead by the time his abdomen was ripped in two. He was opened up from his neck down to his pelvis, his intestines revealing themselves through the bloody slit before falling onto the floor with a wet plop. Then the creature threw the broken body like it was a rag doll, tossing its discarded toy ten feet through the air into the frozen meat container lining the back wall of the store. Chris Cullen's shredded corpse was left with his organs spilling out onto the frozen packaged meat below.

Charlie Braylon was already running away. His gut swung side to side and he panted with the effort. He passed the bread aisle (Buy one loaf get another free!), then the beverage aisle (24-pack only $5.99!) before he made the turn into the small hallway leading to the managerial offices.

He ran to his seldom-used office. The heavy blue door was the only thing standing between him and safety.

"JESUS CHRIST NO! AHHURRGHGHHH—" The scream was cut off too quickly in the distance. The beast had found another victim.

Heart pounding, Charlie reached for the door knob and turned. To his horror he found it locked.

My keys, my keys, did I bring my office keys? He couldn't even remember when he last saw them. The store had become so irrelevant to his life that he hadn't even taken the time to place his office keys somewhere accessible.

Tssskkknnnntkkcckkk! It cried out triumphantly. It was close now, Charlie could sense it—and he knew it had claimed another. His supermarket was becoming a slaughterhouse.

"Goddammit! Fucking goddammit! Open you sonavabitch!" Charlie rattled the handle and began throwing his shoulder against the door. Time was running out.

Tttscckkknntchhh. It was closer this time. It was getting closer and taunting him at the same time.

Charlie took a few steps back and threw himself at the

door. *Thud. Thud. CRACK!* On the third try his overweight frame proved good for something as the lock gave way and the door burst open, causing Charlie to sprawl forward and fall face first onto the carpeted floor.

He spit dust out of his mouth and scrambled to his feet, flicking the light switch on before getting into action.

Charlie had done the best he could creating the barrier now sealing him inside of his office. His heavy metal and wood desk was the main pillar of this barrier, supported by two office chairs and a filing cabinet serving as further braces. It wasn't the greatest defense system, but it gave Charlie an ounce of hope that he could hide in the room and ride the disaster out. He had come in and looked around briefly, hoping there was a window in the office he had not remembered, but that was not the case. The room was windowless to prevent anyone from being able to break in from the outside. This feature only succeeded in making the office room a trap rather than a real means of escape.

Maybe it won't find me. The thought did nothing to console him. Somewhere deep down, Charlie knew this creature could find him no matter where he was. Whatever this monstrosity was, it didn't operate by conventional means. It didn't give a shit about the laws by which humans operated. This thing did whatever the fuck it wanted to *get* whatever the fuck it wanted, whenever the fuck it wanted it. It didn't need to see to find Charlie, and he was exactly what it craved.

Then what in God's name do I do? How the hell do I get away from this thing? He tried to think of another strategy when he heard a noise stopping both his thought process and heart.

Rattle. Rattle. Thud. Thud. Something had tried the doorknob—something was trying to get in.

"No," Charlie sobbed. "No, no, no no! Leave me alone!" He was about to break down fully when something strange occurred: Charlie heard a response.

"Charlie, are you in there? Jesus Christ, let me in! Open the door, Charlie!" It was Linda Logan.

Charlie took only a second to objectively evaluate the request.

"No! Go away, Linda! Find your own spot. You're going to lead the fucking thing to me." He had tried to be authoritative but his voice came out shrill and terrified.

"Charlie? This is serious, Charlie. Let me the heck in. What's wrong with you? Let me in, let me in, let me in!" She was pounding on the door now, throwing herself against it. Charlie's makeshift barrier rocked but held firm.

"GET THE FUCK OUT OF HERE, LINDA! I DON'T FUCKING WANT YOU HERE, YOU CUNT! LEAVE ME THE FUCK ALONE!" His shouts were desperate. The nightmarish being would soon notice the commotion Linda was making and then be upon them.

"Charlie, can you reall—" She went quiet and there was a light thud against the door. The sudden silence was horrifying. Charlie listened hard to hear anything from Linda.

"L-Linda? Are you . . . are you still there?" His voice was barely above a whisper, perhaps even too meek for her to hear on the other side of the door, but he got a response nonetheless.

It was a coughing noise, a sputtering choking, barely audible from beyond the door. It was short-lived and the disturbing sound was followed again by deafening silence.

The silence wouldn't last long, however.

Cracckkkkkk. The sound was wet, and soon Charlie could hear a ripping noise accompanying it. It sounded like someone pulling and breaking something apart.

Was it there?

There was a loud sickening pop, followed again by the horrid ripping noise. Charlie couldn't help but imagine Linda's body beyond the door, lifeless as it was held up by the creature and played with. In his mind he saw it tearing away at her, ripping her arm out of its socket.

POP! Rip! Crack! Charlie was certain Linda wasn't making those noises on her own. It had her. It was mutilating her for its pleasure.

Charlie's pants were wet with urine as he cowered against the back wall of the office. He pressed back against the wall, trying to get as far away from the door as possible. He wished there was some way he could push himself through it.

Then came the chewing.

The chewing was thick and wet and the gnashing resonated with Charlie. The noise reminded Charlie of a sound he heard as a child, a sound that had become the staple of a fond childhood memory.

At age seven his parents had taken him to the Bronx Zoo and he had enjoyed a day seeing the sights and wonderful animals. One of the highlights of the day had been seeing Charlie's favorite animal, the powerful lion.

Lions were Charlie's favorite since he was a young child. They were so regal and majestic, and on top of it all they were born into their role as kings of the jungle—very much in the same way Charlie had been born into his place in life. He could relate to the proud lion and the life it lived, so when he saw them at the zoo he was overjoyed. He had laughed and jumped and pointed—the day could not have been more fantastic.

Oh, but then it could. Young Charlie had the opportunity to see the lions being fed. For a young sport at the age of seven this was quite a sight. Every little boy has a taste for action, and seeing the lions tear at the pieces of meat being thrown their way was truly an awesome sight.

He remembered the sound vividly—the ripping and tearing following the loud chewing noises as the lions wolfed down those big hunks of meat.

Wet, thick chewing. The memory of the sound was no longer a pleasant one. It was the same sound he was hearing outside his office door. Wet, thick, voracious chewing.

It's out there. It's out there and it's hungry.

"L–leave me alone. I–I never . . . never bothered you," he pled in vain.

CRASH! The barricade was broken with an incredible force and Charlie had no time to react. The heavy metal desk serving as his protector flew across the room, bouncing off the floor toward him.

He tried to stand and avoid the threat, but the desk had been launched his way too quickly and it collided with him. Charlie slammed against the wall and he felt his ribs break as he was sandwiched between an unstoppable desk and an unmovable wall. Gravity then took full effect and the desk fell from the air and landed on his legs, pinning them to the floor while simultaneously wedging the rest of his body to the wall. He was too weak to push the heavy desk off. Only his upper chest, arms, and head were free and he couldn't move the rest of his body to garner any pushing force. With each motion he wheezed and panted, attempting to deal with the pain and gather air back into his lungs.

The pain was rich and deep. He didn't have time to consider the damage, but he had broken or fractured every rib and punctured a lung. His barrier had done more damage to his body than it had sustained in his entire lifetime.

The worst part wasn't the debilitating pain—it was the fact that he was stuck in a trap that he had unwittingly set for himself. He was pinned to the wall and left helpless as The Harbinger made its way into the room.

It stood in the middle of his office, its black robe flowing and fluttering from a nonexistent breeze. The fog poured in behind it, and Charlie, who already was having trouble breathing due to his injuries, began choking on the thick, acrid haze as it filled his lungs.

It looked at him as if it were further examining him, though Charlie felt it knew him through and through—nothing could be concealed from the beast. It swayed from side to side at first, hovering slightly and keeping its head stuck out farther than everything else. It moved with a smooth rhythm as it assessed its prey, and for a brief moment Charlie was mesmerized by the dance.

This was short lived. With one quick snap its entire form went rigid and it stood erect before him, jerking and twitching.

It seemed the creature was enacting a sick fetish before it fed. The movements were accentuated and overly spastic. It moved in ways possible only if its body had joints in places it shouldn't.

It cocked its head and turned it a full 270 degrees, the hood and cloth of its robe twisting around with it. It then slowly turned its head back and continued to size him up and complete its pre-feast ritual.

Tsskknnkktcchhh. Tssknnnktkchhhh. Charlie heard the hunger in his mind. His ears perceived nothing new in the sound but his mind could recognize a starving quality. He sensed he was some sort of delicacy.

Charlie tried with all he could to free himself from his position, but it was hopeless. He was trapped. Even if he forced his way out from beneath the desk there was no way he could get around the demonic figure and escape from the office.

"What? What do you want?" Charlie babbled, already knowing the answer. All warmth was now gone from his body—even the piss in his pants left a biting chill on his damp skin.

Tttskkknttchnnkntck. It wanted to feed.

It reached out with one of its hands, once again that of a dead white corpse, and grabbed at Charlie. He violently swung his own arms around in a last ditch effort to keep himself out of the thing's grip. He was able to avoid a few weak swipes from its hand but his efforts only served to frustrate the beast.

The thing could feel no anger however, and Charlie sensed it actually was gaining some type of *pleasure* from seeing him struggle. It was the same type of gratification psychopaths received when they tortured defenseless animals.

Charlie was a rat in a cage.

It soon tired of the game. Moving with lightning reflexes, it seized control of his right wrist. The coldness of the creature's hand made Charlie's blood run cold and an icy paralysis mercilessly plagued him.

It leaned forward and pulled his arm toward its hooded face. Compared to its strength, Charlie's feeble efforts to resist were nothing. A sensation of impending doom fell over him and the single hope he clung to was he wouldn't have to see what the beast truly looked like. No matter what he was about to go through, he knew he did not want to gaze under that hood. The sight was the nightmare of all nightmares—the most terrible evil that the devil made into a single form.

Charlie closed his eyes and turned away, accepting his fate as long as it did not come with a visual. He felt his hand slowly being pulled under the hood of the beast. He knew this because he could literally *feel* the cold darkness surrounding his flesh and taking him in. He felt all blood flow to his hand stop and then the excruciating experience began.

Teeth. An uncountable number of teeth were now gnawing on his hand and tearing into his flesh. It was not a mouth. The teeth were too numerous and spread out to be contained in a physiological mouth.

He felt an individual jagged tooth on every inch of his skin as his flesh was slowly chewed away. They were gliding and grating over each in independent motions—each tooth had a mind and preference of its own.

The monster then let go of his wrist. Charlie's instant reaction was to pull back and remove his hand from the horrible void. He yanked with all he had.

And his hand did not budge an inch.

It was like his hand had been pulled into a wood-chipper. The small teeth had latched onto him and dug in. Now they were beginning to consume him while slowly pulling him farther in as they progressed.

The grinding came next. His fingers were now being chopped off bit by bit as the teeth moved across them like razors in a synchronized precision. They lopped off small bits of flesh and bone indiscriminately, consuming every bit of matter. The process was agonizingly slow and the pain Charlie felt was indescribable. His hand was being hacked into the smallest of pieces and eaten at a rate so slow that he could feel every individual wound inflicted on his body.

His entire hand went next, surrounded by tiny teeth and slowly diced into bits. Soon his arm really did resemble a branch being fed into a wood-chipper, held rigidly in place as it was pulled in and annihilated. He was forced not only to feel every bit of the pain but also to hear the crunching sounds that came with the chewing and breaking of his own bones. It took its time and tortured him for as long as it could to marinate the moment and sweeten the flesh it was eating.

As he suffered, the creature became more ravenous, chomping into his forearm with more speed and ferocity. Each bite brought loud snaps and crunches as the bone was easily bitten through. In a matter of seconds Charlie's arm had been reduced to a length no farther than his elbow.

His convulsions started. Mercifully, numbness overtook him and he stopped experiencing the pain. It was almost over. The soul-wrenching agony was nearly at its conclusion.

Chomp. Crunch. Rip. It made its way past his elbow, then suddenly the process halted.

The Harbinger pulled the stub of Charlie's arm out of his hood, causing Charlie to do something he promised himself he wouldn't: open his eyes. Fortunately for him, the creature's face was once again well hidden amongst the darkness that lay under its hood.

It stood up and away from him, looking around as if contemplating what to do next. It had already claimed Charlie, but there were other bits of prey still running about the store—some of them about to *escape*. This was something the monster didn't like. This actually *bothered* it.

Tsccckkntchhhk. This time the noise was angry. Without a moment's hesitation, the creature spun and became a dark blur as it left the room, leaving Charlie and his stump of an arm pinned to the wall.

Charlie Braylon wasn't in the mindset to consider what was happening or why the being had left. The world was cloudy around him, and not because of the fog that had seeped its way into his store. He had lost too much blood and felt everything fading away. He glanced at the ripped stump of his arm and saw the torn flesh and jagged edge of his bone. Blood vessels were spraying blood onto his desk like some ghastly waterfall, running down the desk into a newly formed blood-lake on the carpet.

In his right mind, Charlie Braylon would have been horrified. He would have screamed and kicked and tried to get free. Instead, he weakly waved his mostly amputated arm, unable to believe this damaged nub was once his fully functional limb.

Charlie Braylon had lost his spirit. Any inklings of self-preservation or self-worth had been drained from his body when the nightmare tore into his soul. His flesh, blood, and bone had not been the only things the monster had taken from him.

Barely a minute after the beast left, Charlie's head fell backward and thudded against the wall behind him. His last thoughts were of the majestic lion, eating away at raw meat in gigantic, savage, ravenous bites.

Twenty-two

Things weren't going according to plan—and for Dan McNair that was an insult that simply could not be tolerated. This was his opportunity to prove his power and worth, and any slip-ups would be representations of his own shortcomings and weakness. Those were things he did not want to face. Those were things he *could not* face.

His reign was only in its second hour when he saw his plans to maintain order failing miserably. If anything, the provisions he put in place had exasperated the chaotic situation rather than diminish it. His own men had engaged in looting and violence, causing fear to run rampant and dissent to prosper. How could the people of the town believe in Sheriff Dan McNair if his men were going around committing atrocities as severe as their unknown assailant? Dan couldn't afford to lose control, not with so much on the line for his town.

Or for himself.

It wasn't only the stress of the decision-making process getting to Dan. It was also the fact that his uncle's voice had returned from the fog.

Dan had tried to ignore the voice at first, but now he caught himself throwing sideways glances out the window from his office. He held back the urge to yell slurs at his deceased uncle as he hid like a coward behind the veil of mist. What kind of man called out someone's manhood then ran and hid? The rage he felt for his uncle was more powerful than ever, and Dan McNair was nearing his breaking point.

"What's the matter, you little faggot? Can't even handle this hillbilly town? You're a fuckin' girl, that's what you are. That's why I gave you my dick nice and deep. Yeah, you remember it, you little queer? You remember that tickle it gave ya? Want to feel it again? Do ya, huh, huh?"

He snapped a pencil in his hand and was about to stand up and deal with his uncle when his office door opened and former sheriff Tom Williams walked inside.

Dan smiled openly as Tom walked in, wearing a sad-sack expression on his face. His light blue eyes looked ready to burst into tears and the ever-present bald patch on his head looked like it had grown in the last few hours.

Dan snickered.

"Danny, I need to talk to you." Tom Williams used his very

best big boy voice.

"That's Sheriff McNair to you, Officer Williams," Dan corrected him with the tone of an educator.

Tom looked hurt, causing Dan to fume. *Oh, what does he expect? For me to reminisce about the good ol' days when I was his useless lapdog? He wants us to be buddy-buddy like he thought we were? The only reason I didn't spit insults at him every day was because he was my boss. Fuck him. Fuck him, his fat ass, and his useless piece of shit brain, too. This is my town and these are my rules. It's about time the chain of command reflects actual competency.*

"Sheriff McNair," Tom conceded, "we have some problems."

Dan laughed viciously. "Some problems? Really, you think so, Tom? What exactly gave you that impression anyway? Did you come up with that conclusion before or after people started going missing? Was it that maniac who almost ran down Tiffany Bent? Did he clue you in to the fact that something was wrong? Hmm, or maybe it was the appearance of this crazy fucking fog?"

"Come on—" Tom pleaded, but Dan was too far gone on his tirade to stop now.

"No, Tom, tell me. Tell me what finally got through your thick fucking skull to tell you we had problems. I'm fascinated to know."

"There's anarchy out there, Sheriff. Cars are smashing into each other in the streets. People want to find a way out but they can't. Most of our new officers aren't coming back and we got people runnin' over here talking about roving bands of gun-wielding madmen. Those are the men *you* gave guns, right on a whim, and now they're making things worse. What do we do? What in God's name do we do?"

Dan couldn't avoid the truth that his own actions had temporarily made the situation worse, but Tom pleading like a lost child was too much for him to handle. Even though Dan had led him into a shittier situation, Tom had turned around and begged Dan to come up with the answers. The man lacked gall or any remnant of a spine.

"At least someone still has faith in you, Danny, you little queer! Maybe fatty's got a crush on you! Maybe he can give you some more dick, you cum-guzzling faggot!" His uncle's voice laughed heartily from outside in the fog and suddenly Dan was sweating profusely.

"What do we do?" Tom insisted on his question being answered.

"Shut the fuck up! Just shut the fuck up, both of you!" Dan shouted, standing with the look of a crazed man.

Tom recoiled, looking at Dan with shock. "Who . . . who else is here?"

There was an awkward moment of silence before Dan sighed and regained his composure. "I'm sorry. I'm just under a lot of pressure. I thought this would pan out a little better than it has, but it turns out you really can't rely on anyone, can you?" Dan was looking for empathy, but Tom was too confused and afraid to offer any.

"Look, there are car wrecks littering the street and people are getting violent. All the power is out and people are going mad. We have to do something quick."

Dan nodded. Tom was right about something. "Everyone here stays here. As more of the scouts come back from patrol, we tell them to stay here, too. Small groups can't be trusted, but the fact of the matter is we need numbers to contain whatever chaos is going on out there. We band together as one mobile militia, all the men we got, and we go out there and maintain order. Security is the priority and there will be power and safety in numbers."

This plan of action did nothing to quell Tom's rapidly growing fears. "Militia, maintain order? Just exactly what are you planning, Dan?"

"It's Sheriff."

"To what end is this militia?"

"Together we'll be strong and we can look after our troops. No one will step out of line when the commander is right there to witness it. People are fragile on their own and buckle under the pressure of responsibility. But they get their asses in gear when they don't have to think and have someone telling them what to do. The men will listen out of fear of direct punishment and any problems we encounter will be dealt with swiftly. We'll send a message that no out of line behavior shall be tolerated."

"Violence breeds violence, Sheriff." Tom's tone was solemn and for the first time in his life his words were sagacious.

"Strike first, strike fast, worry about the consequences after. You want to question me? I'll throw you straight to the dogs, Tom," he paused for dramatic effect before adding, "and you know they're hungry."

Tom gasped. "I'm . . . I'm on your side, Dan. Why are you talking like that?"

"Yeah, cocksucker, why are you talking like that? Look, you hurt his feelings! Give him a kiss, queer boy! Or maybe it's just

my lips you want. Do you miss how they feel on your neck? Oh I remember how the first time you let out a gasp and then I moved my hands . . ."

"It's Sheriff McNair. Get it wrong again and you'll be alone in the streets." Dan's voice was ice cold. This was a stinging proposition for Tom Williams, the former proud sheriff of the Rowley Police Department. In less than a day he had gone from a happy, carefree leader, to a dejected has-been clinging to the arm of his own tyrannical usurper for safety. Tom mostly lacked pride, but being treated this way was provoking what little he did have. He was concerned about his own safety but the more and more he conceded to Dan, the less safety appeared guaranteed.

But what was Tom to do? He didn't want to end up dead on the streets he once patrolled. Dan wasn't making anything better, but did Tom have any choice by this point? With one word, the mob would take him out and leave him bloody and beaten in the streets. Was that the direction his town was destined to go? He wanted to change it, he really did, but he didn't have the oratory presence Dan did—Tom was no gifted wordsmith.

Begrudgingly, Tom accepted Dan's call, but his mind began formulating an ulterior plan of his own.

"So, you want me to gather everyone together then? Make the announcement?" Tom's question came out in a feeble tone.

"No, I'll handle it," Dan replied with a sneer. "I have a way of rallying the troops, after all."

"Don't let our town fall apart, Sheriff." Tom's words were a warning. The farce couldn't persist for much longer.

"You're in good hands." Dan's statement sent an icy chill through Tom's body. He had passed the buck onto Dan—he was the one who put Dan in charge and now Rowley was suffering the consequences.

His thoughts echoed his concern. *I hope this is going to be all right in the end. Am I going to have to step up again? Am I going to have to try to lead? He won't let me, but maybe there are other ways. I don't think I can sit back and watch this for much longer.*

"Well, let's—" Dan began before the door to the office flew open and a frantic Ernie Stevens ran in.

"We got a big problem!" he said desperately

"What now?" Dan's tone was even.

"People are saying almost all of Evergreen Street is up in flames. A few houses caught and now it's spread across a few blocks. Pretty soon Logan Street is going to catch, too. Lawns, trees, houses, and everything in between. People are abandoning their homes because of the flames!" Ernie flailed his arms at the end of his report in a ridiculous attempt to further portray the severity of the situation.

Dan's words were quick and concise. "Tim Dolan is out there and he is still the chief of the Rowley Volunteer Fire Department. Get him and whoever else he needs and send them to get the fire engine. They can go deal with the situation."

Ernie's eyes were as wide as plates. "But are you sure that's enough? I mean a *whole* street is blazing!"

"It's going to have to be enough, Ernie. It's all we have right now. There are many more problems to deal with. Now go."

Ernie gave a quick nod and ran out of the room, leaving

Tom and Dan alone once more.

"You know what you're doing, Sheriff?" Tom asked, despite knowing the answer.

"*Yeah, you know what you're doing, Sheriff Shit-Head? If you knew how to run a town half as well as you knew how to suck a cock this crisis would have been solved by now. Hahaha!"* Uncle Chad's laughter was overpowering and Dan McNair finally took the last steps down the descent to complete madness.

"Yes," Dan replied with glossy eyes. "I know exactly what I'm doing."

Twenty-three

Twenty minutes later, the only fire truck available to the Rowley Fire Department was blazing down Main Street, sirens wailing into the air. Tim Dolan led a crew consisting of one experienced firefighter, himself, and Billy Brissler, Jeff Hossler, and Rollie Peterson.

The situation was grim and he knew it. Tim had been fighting fires for over a decade and none of those guys even knew their way around a fire truck, but they would have to suffice—they were the town's only option.

As Tim Dolan drove the truck through the fog, weaving in and out of the wrecked cars piled up on the streets of Rowley, he couldn't help but feel an overwhelming sense of trepidation descend upon him. It was so powerful it almost convinced him to abandon his responsibility as a firefighter and turn the truck around.

But he couldn't do that. Fighting fires was what Tim Dolan did. It was what gave him fame and recognition in the town. It was the reason he was complimented and heralded whenever he ate breakfast at the diner. It was the reason he found pride in himself—in short, it was the justification for his existence. There was no way he could abandon his duty in the town's darkest hour. It wasn't only his town at stake, but his very identity.

And so he swallowed his apprehensions and kept on driving, heading toward the glow of the orange flame and certain impending doom.

Standing at the intersection of Bell and Evergreen, Andrew Murphy let out a triumphant cry of victory. He raised his arms to the sky and realized he had never accomplished anything so magnificent in his life.

He had given sustenance to the glorious, glorious fire. Because of him, she ran wild and free, consuming Evergreen Street and subjecting all houses on it to the power of the almighty flame.

Andrew believed he now understood what it meant to truly live. This had to be his purpose, it felt so right, and as he stood and watched the flame run wild, he felt *complete.* So often he had felt hollow and out of place. Throughout life he was isolated due to his inability to understand others and their inability to understand him.

But that was a problem no longer.

Andrew understood fire and fire understood Andrew. They co-existed, with Andrew as the one who provided nourishment and fire the one who provided pleasure. Together they formed a beautiful union, one so powerful the entire town would feel its wrath.

And to think, it almost had not happened. If it weren't for the shadow thing in the fog, Andrew's brilliant plan would not have come to fruition. He briefly thought back to the fortunate encounter.

Forty minutes earlier, Andrew was confronted by Mr. Richter, a resident of the block on Evergreen Andrew was lighting up in flames. He had been able to do his duty with stealth due to the cover the haze provided, but Mr. Richter caught Andrew setting the Shultzs' lawn on fire, and ran to stop him.

"What do you think you're doing, you little bastard? You're the one who started these fires! Put that can down," Mr. Richter shouted, charging Andrew's way.

Andrew obeyed, calmly setting the container of gasoline on the sidewalk while he awaited Mr. Richter. He sorely wished Mr. Richter didn't have a way to stop the fire—hopefully it was too widespread to contain entirely. Andrew didn't care if Mr. Richter got him in trouble or even beat him. Andrew only prayed the fire would continue burning. Its life was much more important than his.

"You son of a bitch, look what you've done," Mr. Richter cried as he arrived at Andrew's position. He raised his fist as if he were going to strike Andrew but hesitated—despite what Andrew had done, he was still a frail thirteen-year-old boy.

"You're coming with me, you little firebug psycho. We're taking you right to the police station and—" Mr. Richter was cut off by a strange hissing sound, one neither he nor Andrew had ever heard before.

Although the noise was foreign to Andrew, it didn't disturb him in the least. Rather, he felt it complemented the crackling and popping of his fiery mistress. Mr. Richter, on the other hand, was mortified by the sound and sensations he felt. Andrew saw that he suddenly wanted to flee.

"What the hell was that?" Mr. Richter asked, turning around to face the source of the noise.

Andrew didn't make much of the thing. It was tall and in a black robe with long, strange fingers. It sliced into Mr. Richter with those clawed fingers, sending blood flying everywhere. Some of it covered Andrew, but he didn't mind. He had no affinity for the particular set of clothes he wore.

Andrew was not fearful or fascinated, merely interested as to what was going on. Mr. Richter screamed out to Andrew for help but Andrew had no reason to help him. Mr. Richter was trying to make him *stop* setting fires—why in the world would he have use for such a person?

Mr. Richter screamed louder as the thing pinned him to the ground, using its deadly claws to strip his body of flesh. It was not digging in or impaling him—it was simply scraping his skin and muscle off the bone. It took this meat and brought it under its hood, stuffing its face as if it were a hungry child.

Andrew saw the fear, pain, and desperation in Mr. Richter's eyes—but this too had no effect on him. Mr. Richter didn't matter because Mr. Richter didn't make Andrew feel good. Mr. Richter really didn't make Andrew feel anything, so Andrew was indifferent to his suffering. Andrew watched the scene with growing curiosity. The creature had its way with Mr. Richter without much of a fight and after a few minutes of torturing him and sampling his flesh, it delivered the finishing blow. It used one hand to grab hold of his face and palm it, wrapping each of its fingers around his head in the process. Mr. Richter let out a muffled cry before the thing ripped his head clean off of his shoulders.

The Harbinger held Mr. Richter's head in its hand, then proceeded to pull it up and under its hood to eat. Andrew heard each of the crunching noises made as the creature feasted on Mr. Richter's skull. Its teeth sank into the head, and in between each voracious chomp, bone and brain matter fell from the thing's mouth onto the ground.

After it had gobbled up the last bits of skull, it looked over to Andrew and their stares met.

Andrew wasn't afraid—Andrew didn't know what fear was. He felt nothing as he stared into the darkness that held the being's eyes. Andrew simply waited for it to react; to say or *do* something.

It stared at him in the same fashion, seeming to have no real opinion of his existence. After a brief moment it disregarded him and continued feeding on the rest of Mr. Richter.

Andrew shrugged and got back to work. He picked up the gasoline container and continued to spread the flame. The thing tore at Mr. Richter's body for a few minutes before it went off to do whatever exactly it did.

Andrew had no thoughts about what it was or what the

encounter meant, but he was grateful the thing had prevented Mr. Richter from stopping him. After him, there had been nothing to stand in Andrew's way. The glorious fire would burn on.

The entire town is going to burn, Andrew thought as he snapped back to the present, his sadistic grin too broad for his face. He reached down into his pants and grasped his member once more, delighted to feel that his penis was erect again. He stood in the middle of Evergreen, just out of reach of the flames but close enough to feel their effect and breathe in the scent of his mistress.

"I love you," Andrew said as he started masturbating. He still didn't know the meaning of the word, but to Andrew the uncontrollable desire and obsession were the closest things to love he knew.

The fire danced and sang for him with motions and sounds so powerful and majestic not even the fog could conceal them. The fire danced wildly and unabated. With his help the fire would overtake everything—the world itself would burn to the ground.

"Yes, yes!" he shouted as he furiously tugged his penis. He closed his eyes and let his body feel the warmth of the flame while the fire within him burned brightly. He felt the pleasure rising up quickly; soon he would climax and experience that addicting sensation once more.

All thanks to fire. Glorious, glorious fire.

Caught up in thoughts of pleasure and flame, Andrew's ears did not pick up the sound of the siren steadily coming his way. The fog muffled the noise, and as the vehicle drew closer, the unmistakable blare of the siren could be heard and should have been detected.

All Andrew heard was burning—the crackle and whip of his lover's song as she claimed Evergreen Street.

"Yes! Yes! Yes! I love yo—" Just as Andrew was about to climax, his thoughts and actions were halted when Engine 1 of the Rowley Volunteer Fire Department slammed into him at twenty-five miles per hour.

Andrew's small body was no match for the raging metal machine. His back snapped upon impact and he was jolted forward, slamming to the ground. His face smashed to the pavement first and his teeth tore through his lips before shattering on the hard street below. He barely had time to register the fact that his mouth had become a mangled mess of blood and gums before the rest of the truck was upon him like a predator.

It drove over him and he was forced under. He was too big to simply be cruised over, though. The undercarriage of the engine caught him and cut into his skin, wedging him against the ground.

The fire truck kept on driving and Andrew's flesh was stripped to the bone as his body violently scraped against the ground. It dragged him over the pavement while simultaneously crushing his bones. Inside he was broken, while outside his skin was peeled from his body like he was a piece of fruit.

The excruciating experience seemed to last forever. The fire truck was too long and, unfortunately for Andrew, he was conscious the entire time the behemoth pulled his ragged body across the pavement. The friction was hot and unbearable. His skin and muscle were ripped away, the road-burn causing what was left to burn and blacken, sending even more agonizing sensations through Andrew's nervous system.

He exited from beneath the vehicle as it roared twenty feet farther before halting. Andrew's body was a mangled heap. His shoulder was dislocated, his femur was shattered, breaking through his skin at four points, and most of his face had been ground away and was left as a friction-burned, black and red mess. A flap of his forehead was swinging back and forth, held onto his skull only by a few strands of sinewy tissue. Only one of his eyes was functional, his spleen and appendix had ruptured, his sternum was broken and one of his lungs had collapsed. Both his wrists were shattered and his nose was nonexistent.

Andrew Murphy was a bloody mess.

In his last moments however, none of that mattered. Even as he lay suffering and dying, Andrew only paid mind to what his one good eye could see as his head tilted to the left, staring at the homes on Evergreen Street.

Fire. Glorious, glorious fire. He would not die in vain.

Andrew burned with desire as he stared at his mistress for the last time, and felt a single tear come to his eye.

Then he started to convulse violently, spitting up blood and teeth from between his mashed lips and wiggling violently on the ground like an insect that had been stomped on.

Andrew Murphy on Evergreen Street, convinced he had lived his life to its full potential as the fire burned brilliantly into the afternoon sky.

Tim Dolan was so preoccupied with getting to his destination and so blinded by the gray haze, he didn't even notice he had run over Andrew Murphy. There was no visual confirmation, only a light thunk and a barely audible scraping sound—the weight of the child had done nothing to affect the progress of the massive, speeding fire truck. Andrew's body had as much impact as a common bump in the road. In the back of his mind Tim briefly thought he may have struck something. There was certainly plenty that could be cast out in the road during a time of such disorganization, but that something could have been absolutely anything. It was most likely some garbage or debris scattered in the road. He was too focused on getting to the raging flames to consider he may have run over a person.

He stopped the fire truck and hopped out, pausing for a moment to take in the damage before shouting out orders. During that pause he became well aware of the futility of their efforts. They had one engine and four men, and more than a block was up in flames—they had no chance. This was especially true because Tim was the only actual firefighter on the scene.

Regardless, it was his duty to try. He shouted out various orders to the other men, who obeyed them to the very best of their ability. They were just preparing to tackle the wild flames when Tim heard a scream followed by strange noise that had no place amongst the hustle and bustle of his men and the crackle of the deadly fire.

Tssskkknnnnntchhhkknnhhhh.

Tim felt a thud against his leg and looked down to see the

object that had hit him. Even in the fog he had no trouble identifying the terrible sight. It was the severed arm of Jeff Hossler, ripped from his body halfway past the elbow. The broken bone jutted out of the shredded flesh and the arm twitched, causing the fingers to curl up and out, grasping into the air.

Tim looked up at what was before him.

Tskknktnknknntkchhhhhhhh

Doom had arrived.

Twenty-Four

As Tim Dolan was slowly torn apart limb by limb, his son Travis, age twenty-three, flew down Washington Street in his Dodge Neon, intent on getting out of town as fast as he could.

Travis didn't know exactly what was going on but he knew the town had descended into anarchy. Evergreen Street was up in flames, there were bands of vandals with guns claiming to be the law, and there had been looting, gun fights, and murder.

It was all too much for Travis to handle. He was a small town kid. He wasn't ready for any chaos. The worst part of it was no one seemed to understand *why* any of this was happening. The fog had rolled in and changed everything. The town lost communication and all remnants of sense and logic. So quickly the streets had gone from peaceful to barbaric—the town had transformed in mere hours.

He heard there was no way out of town and this in itself was reason for intense worry. The concept was one Travis couldn't accept. There was no way someone could be prevented from leaving a town—there was always a way out and Travis was intent on finding it. He wasn't going to stick around and become victim to one of those gun-wielding maniacs. They had claimed they were police officers because of Martial law, but Travis knew a majority of the fools who were patrolling the town. Half of them couldn't wipe their own asses and yet they were claiming to be in control. It was lunacy, and Travis had to get away before he fell victim to the erupting violence.

He cruised past Joiner's Hardware and saw it had been broken into and looted. Within the last two hours since the inception of Martial law, locals had gone out to gather supplies and weapons to defend themselves against the crazy groups of gunmen running the streets. A good half of them weren't even pretending to be police officers—they simply were victimizing people they didn't like and settling their scores from behind the barrel of a gun.

It was madness, absolute madness.

Travis had gathered a few things, including his switchblade for protection, and exited his house in an attempt to leave when he saw his neighbor, fifteen-year-old Naomi Pascal, sitting on the edge of the sidewalk. Her leg was mutilated from the shin down. It was twisted and bloody with bits of bone breaking through the skin, which itself looked mashed and stripped, but Naomi sat passively, staring into the fog like she didn't have a care in the world.

Travis didn't want to talk to her. He wanted to get in his car and get the hell out of town, but his concern and curiosity could not be repressed.

"Oh my God, Naomi," he called. "What happened?"

She turned, staring at him with apathetic eyes. "A car ran me over."

"Ran you over? What? How? Let's get you help!"

Her tone matched her facial expression. It was too calm and straightforward. "I was running through the street. Away from the thing that's out there in the fog and a car ran over my leg. The guy was speeding and kept going. My brother's dead too. The supermarket's been destroyed." She delivered these words with no emotion. "There's no help for me, Travis. There's no help for any of us." The once bright, cheerful girl had become a messenger of death.

"Your brother? The thing that's out there?" Travis' voice dropped and his left arm was shaking.

"It's hungry." She turned her head and blankly stared into the fog once more, seeming to accept her fate and that of the town.

Travis' thoughts were panicked. *She doesn't even care about her leg! I have to get away, from her, from the crazy people here, and from whatever is creeping in the fog! This is a sick nightmare! I just wish I could wake up and everything would be all right. I could have a nice breakfast and talk to Dad about how ridiculous the dream was and . . .*

But it wasn't a nightmare. There was no waking up; there was only an opportunity to flee. Travis' conscience shrieked in protest but its cries fell upon deaf ears as he said not another word to Naomi and climbed into his car. He drove away from the little girl who he had always been fond of and focused his thoughts on his own safety. Travis had already gone through the process to justify leaving without any of his family—it would be too dangerous to seek them all out.

He relaxed some as he rationalized his actions, but his knuckles remained white on the steering wheel. There was no visibility and staying on the road was a trial. Driving the four-fifths of a mile it would take to get out of town was no longer an easy task.

Travis turned onto Church and began cruising toward the intersection at Main where he could take the left onto 6 and get out of town. His hope was rising when a figure appeared out of the fog directly in front of him.

He had no time to react. Despite slamming on his brakes, Travis smashed into the figure. The body launched onto his hood and careened into the windshield, causing a long, jagged crack to splinter right in front of Travis' face. The body went up and over the car effortlessly, carried on by the momentous force of the Buick. It thudded over the roof before falling onto the trunk, rolling off of it and onto the street.

Travis sat in his car, stunned and mortified, trying to comprehend what he had just done.

As Travis was driving toward Main to get out of town, so was Harold Ferguson. He had seen a band of men with guns outside of his house subduing a young girl, who couldn't have even been seventeen, and to Harold it appeared they were planning to rape her. This disturbed Harold, not so much because he was worried about the girl, but because he was worried about *himself.* When there's rape in the street, it's clear things are getting bad. This, among other things, told Harold it was time to get out while he still could.

Harold did nothing to stop the men as they dragged the screaming girl behind a neighbor's empty home. Instead, he grabbed his keys and went to his car. He had heard some crazy things in the last few hours, but didn't care what was true or not. He just cared about getting away from the violence.

Harold Ferguson had only one real fear in life and that was the most basic fear of all: death. Harold wasn't one who cared about family, friends, or anybody else. Deep down, Harold only cared about himself and he was outwardly proud of the fact. Such was the rise of a popular saying among those who knew him and criticized him behind his back: "When the going gets tough, Harold gets the fuck out."

That's exactly what he did in his current situation. It was justified. After all, it was the natural instinct of preservation. That was what the human being was supposed to do over all else, survive, and Harold was going to make sure he fulfilled his purpose.

Harold grew even more concerned with his survival when he turned onto Washington en-route to connecting with Church. He saw another group of men, three of them, toting rifles as they walked in the middle of the street. He swerved around them, but they noticed him and began pointing and shouting, the leader raising his gun.

Harold took off, slamming the accelerator down in a panicked frenzy. This was exactly what he had feared. They were after him—those gun-wielding madmen were after him and sought to *kill* him. His precious life could be taken by some low-life looters looking for some money and entertainment.

Harold raced down Washington Street and, without stopping or looking, hastily made the right onto Church. Blowing through the stop sign and blinded by the fog, Harold failed to avoid the small compact car already traveling down Church toward Main.

Harold sideswiped the car. The appearance of the vehicle out of the fog paired with the sudden impact caused Harold to grossly overcorrect his driving. He veered to the right as hard as he could and went off the road onto the sidewalk. The frantic journey came to a screeching halt when he collided with a parking meter, bashing in the front of his car.

Heart racing, Harold sat at the wheel, amazed he had survived the incident without a scratch.

I could have been killed. Right then and there, I could have lost my life because some asshole was speeding down Church in the fog. And now look at things! My car is wrecked and those lunatics could still be following me! What if they catch up, then I'm fucked, aren't I? Now I have to try to walk through all of this danger just to get out of town! And all because of some jerk-off rushing down Church! How could they?! How DARE they?

Harold's survival instinct triggered a response mechanism. This response was violence. He stormed out of his car and walked toward the vehicle he had sideswiped. The driver had slammed on their brakes after being hit. It was a silver Toyota Corolla, probably early 2000s, and it had been in fine shape until Harold hit it—now the door was dented and long scratches in the paint stretched the entire length of the vehicle.

As Harold approached, his anger rising, the driver of the vehicle stepped out to confront him.

It was Kelly Handlan.

"Oh God, are you all right?" Kelly asked with legitimate concern.

Harold harbored no concern for Kelly. She was the reason his car was wrecked and she was the reason he was vulnerable to those rifle-wielding crazies. It didn't matter to Harold he was at fault for the accident. All that mattered was Kelly Handlan had gotten in the way of him escaping. It was the straw that broke the camel's back.

Harold Ferguson already had a temper problem, and this had only been exasperated by the strenuous situation at hand. When he saw it was Jack Handlan's bimbo wife who caused him to crash his car, he completely lost it.

That stupid cunt, the one Jack beats the shit out of? She's the reason I'm fucked? That stupid little bitch! I guess Jack isn't hitting her hard enough! Maybe I'll have to make up for it!

"You fuckin' bitch, look what you've done! Can't you even fuckin' drive?" Harold shouted, his blubbery face shaking and turning as red as an apple.

Kelly Handlan recoiled and took a step backward. She was all too familiar with this type of rage. "Hey, calm down. It was your fault, you know."

This really pissed Harold off. "My fault? Fuck you, you whore. Don't you know what you've done?" He stormed toward her, letting the evil fog cloud his mind.

Kelly Handlan, fresh bruises decorating her face, stumbled backward then tripped and fell, sprawling out onto the concrete. Just as she was able to scramble up and regain her feet, the portly man was upon her, making sure he landed her good.

BAM! Kelly saw stars as Harold punched her in the nose. Blood instantly gushed out. The fresh black eye was still tender and the shock from her nose caused sharp pain to radiate throughout her face. She wobbled but did not fall—years of taking punches from Jack had given her the chin of a seasoned boxer.

"You want more, you dirty cunt? Is that it?" Harold's hate was fueled by his own desperation to escape the horrible situation. Logic was gone from his mind as he picked a source for the release of his frustration. He couldn't accept responsibility for his own part in getting into the mess so he had to blame Kelly. By blaming her, by *beating* her, Harold could release the frustration and fear in a justified way. She deserved it. She had hindered his progress and had to pay the price.

"Don't do this." Kelly was able to keep a calm demeanor despite using her shirt sleeve to dam the river of blood running from her nose.

"Jack's gone soft on you, I bet! A woman as dumb as you needs some sense smacked into her!" Harold lunged forward again, but this time his punch did not connect—it was never given the chance.

WHAP! Harold took a jab in the mouth and his lip busted open. The sudden pop and taste of his own blood stunned him. Kelly Handlan stood defiantly, hands raised and ready to brawl. She had taken more than enough abuse from her chauvinist husband, she wasn't going to take it anymore.

"Back off, fat ass." There was no fear in her voice. Kelly had reached her breaking point.

Harold wiped his lip and shook off the disbelief. "You little bitch. Now I'm going to beat you into a fucking pulp." Harold took another step forward, but once again was hit before he could strike Kelly.

This time the hit wasn't from a punch. Harold was struck from behind by a much more powerful force.

Harold flew back onto the windshield of Travis Dolan's car as the hood struck him in the posterior. He hit the windshield with a force strong enough to push all the air from his lungs. His legs were thrown upward due to the centrifugal force, going over his head and sending him careening onto the roof of the car. He bounced off and onto the trunk, then bounced a final time before landing on the street with a thud.

Travis Dolan immediately stepped out of his car to check on the person he hit. When he closed his car door, he noticed another vehicle stopped not far from his. Just as he got a glance at it, the car sped off with a woman in the driver's seat. Travis hoped her quick departure wasn't because he had just killed a man.

He turned around again and peaked behind his car. He tried to get a look at the figure he struck. "A-are you okay? Hey, are you okay?"

There was a grunt of a response and Harold Ferguson pushed off of his knees to get himself to his feet. He let out a displeased growl as he felt the aching pain in his lower back.

"I'm so sorry!" Travis sputtered. Harold didn't hear his words—he only saw red.

Harold looked at Travis with evil, hateful eyes. He was no

longer concerned about safety but only with enacting vengeance. He heard a voice in his head—no, a voice all around him—screaming at him to kill Travis. It was the only thing he could do to make the situation right. It was the only way after all of his embarrassment he could come out on top.

"I'm going to fucking kill you," he breathed between gritted teeth while taking a purposeful step toward Travis, who saw he meant it.

"Hey, calm down, buddy. I'm sorry I hit ya but you were standing right in the road and—"

"Going to fucking kill you," Harold repeated.

Travis reached into his pocket and grabbed hold of his switchblade. He felt the handle and gripped it tightly. This was a weapon Travis had hoped he would never have to use but the moment was before him. He had gotten it as a novelty, something cool and badass he could play around with to impress friends, but now it might actually have to act as a weapon.

"BRRRAHHG!" Harold roared like a wild animal as he charged at Travis, hands extended and pointed to his throat.

Travis reacted without thinking, pulling the knife out of his pocket and pressing the button to release the blade. In one fluid motion, the knife was thrust into the doughy stomach of Harold Ferguson.

Harold's face showed his surprise as he felt the stainless steel penetrate his body. He stumbled back and away from Travis before falling down, hands cupped around the blood-spurting wound in the center of his stomach. His belly button had been pierced, replaced by a deep slit spilling blood into his hands. The wound was sizable, perhaps even fatal, and Harold was too stunned to even realize the initial damage done to his body.

Travis stood watching the scene, knowing the battle was won but still somehow feeling unsatisfied. Something in his head was urging him to continue the fight. The situation simply could not be put to rest.

"Kill him, Travis. You kill him before he gets up and tries to hurt you again. He's a madman! He was probably attacking that poor woman! Kill him, kill him good and put that switchblade to real use!"

Part of Travis hated his thoughts but another sizable portion of him *loved* them. The man was a threat. Travis would be justified in slicing his attacker into bits and pieces. He probably would be a hero for doing such a deed. Travis, who never experienced much excitement in his life, was seduced by the notion of being a powerful action hero.

He looked over and saw the man's eyes had reverted back to evil, shedding their temporary glaze of surprise in the process.

"Fuck you," the downed man spat. Travis knew that if the man could, he would murder Travis or anyone who crossed his path. The man was no longer a standing threat, but there was ground for the assault to continue. There was no reason such a man should ever be allowed to pose a threat again.

The debate was settled and Travis was on him in an instant.

Travis lunged and the man kicked and punched, so Travis brought his knee slamming into the man's groin, causing a groan of pain and a whoosh of air to escape the man's lungs.

There was little resistance after that. Travis plunged the

blade into the man's chest, then his sternum, then his stomach, stabbing him over and over again. Each time, the blade did its job, cutting into his flesh like it was butter. Warm blood shot up, splattering Travis' hands, each spurt an affirmation that the knife was doing its due diligence. The adrenaline surging through Travis' body was like sweet nectar. The release of all of his pent up, primal urges was intoxicating. He couldn't help but laugh as he sliced into Harold, his weapon more effective than he could have imagined.

The man screamed and squirmed, but Travis pinned him down and drove the switchblade into his body countless times, loving the sound of the man's gurgled screams as the knife pierced his flesh. For once, Travis had complete power, and in that one instant he was like a god. He let loose his will on a whim and all of his life's rage was released in those brief moments as Travis mutilated Harold Ferguson. He stabbed with so much speed, force, and passion, he didn't even realize he had killed the man until he paused to take a breather.

He looked down and surveyed the damage with pride. He had stabbed Harold a good forty times, giving his midsection the appearance of Swiss cheese. He didn't even remember doing so, but in his brief fit of rage Travis saw he had stabbed the man in the eye socket, destroying his hazel eye and delivering the finishing blow.

Travis stood and regained his composure. He looked down at his clothes and saw they were doused in blood. The fabric of his shirt was soaked through and droplets of blood ran down his arm like beads of sweat.

He let out a laugh. Mild-mannered Travis Dolan had never felt such a rush in his entire life. Finally he had lived out a scene straight from a Hollywood movie and experienced the thrill of fighting for his life. It was fantastic, it was new, and some dark part of him craved *more.* In one barbaric moment, a reserved, affable son of a firefighter had become a bloodthirsty savage.

He began to contemplate the meaning of what just happened when he heard the voice.

"Hey, you there—just what the fuck have you done?" The voice of Nathan Wright was neither shocked nor horrified, but instead held an air of amusement. It was as if he was belittling a child who had done wrong.

Travis turned toward Nathan and his two followers, who were standing far back from Nathan and looking at him with nearly as much apprehension as Travis. Suddenly Travis was hit with the magnitude of what he had *actually* done.

"He attacked me!" Travis blurted out, his fear rising at the sight of their guns. "I had to defend myself!"

"This is just the type of lawlessness Dan wants us to defend, boys." Nathan spoke as if he was captain of the football team. "And now we're going to stop it. Look at this guy here, thinking he can take the law into his own hands. Don't you know that privilege is only for a select *few* of us?" Nathan put on a sadistic smile at the end of his question. Despite all of the fear and panic whirling around in Travis' system, he could tell Nathan was out of his mind.

The madness was infectious. Just a moment prior, Travis had succumbed to the hatred. It was that which had dictated his murderous actions. Yet only a minute after the fact, here he was, struck by the psychotic, violent gleam shining out of another man's eyes. His stint had been brief, passing, fueled by one intense moment, but this man had long been over the edge. This man was a danger to *everyone.*

"This is a matter for the police. I'll turn myself in and they can investigate. I assure you this was in self-defense!" Travis put his hands up to appear less threatening, but Nathan Wright didn't give the impression he particularly cared about the procedure of law.

"I am the police. Sheriff McNair appointed me this morning. I'll deal with the situation here and now."

"But Tom Williams is the sheriff."

"Many things have changed in a short amount of time. All you need to know is right now I'm the law and I'm going to deal with this."

Travis saw Nathan's grip on the rifle tighten.

"Aren't you just a cook at the café?" Travis hoped to instill sense into the lunatic he recognized from his years of patronage at Rollie's Cafe. "How are you a cop?"

Nathan's hateful expression only intensified. "No, I *used* to just be a cook at Rollie's. Now I'm a lawman. Now I have the power and I'm going to use that power to protect our town from knife-wielding psychos like you. Now drop the knife and get to the ground!"

Travis didn't want to drop the knife. He had a strong feeling he would need it to save his life. "I don't trust you. You're going to kill me, aren't you?"

Nathan laughed. "Martial law. If I want to I can, but that all depends on how you act. Drop the knife and get on the ground or I'll pull the trigger."

Travis was sweating. He looked at the dead body of Harold Ferguson then back to the demented eyes of Nathan

Wright. He was stuck between a rock and a hard place. He had no intention of denying what he had done in his wild moment of insanity, but he also had no intention of complying with a psychopath.

"I'll go to the police station. You can follow me there. If I run you can gun me down. I'll turn myself into the sheriff and he can investigate."

"You tryin' to make the rules?" the unstable man shouted. "Didn't you hear that I'm in charge? That I'm the law?" The fog grew thicker with his shouts. Travis noticed the fear in the eyes of Nathan's compatriots, who stood behind him, looking on with diffidence.

"Hey, you two! Talk some sense into him. You guys aren't really cops. This has to be dealt with by the authorities. Help me out!"

Ryan Giordano and Matt Hawkins looked to Travis helplessly, letting their expressions show they too were prisoners of the madness.

Travis knew they were his only hope. "Hey, you guys, c'mon. Don't be afraid. That's all he has over you!"

"Hey, shut the fuck up!" Nathan bellowed, his face reddening and his veins bulging as he spat the words and aimed his Winchester.

Ryan and Matt looked to each other, both waiting for the other to offer guidance when Travis spoke again.

"Don't be irrational, this can all—" His words were cut off by the crack of a gun.

The bullet went through Travis' neck. As he opened his mouth to finish his sentence, blood dribbled out before he fell backward to the ground, choking to death on his own fluid.

As Travis fell, so did the final straw for Ryan Giordano. He raised his shotgun and pointed it at Nathan. Nathan turned around, the smug smile on his face quickly fading, replaced by an insulted grimace.

They were standing barely ten feet apart, guns pointed at each other's chest. Matt Hawkins stood as an onlooker, unsure of which side to take.

"Put the gun down, Ryan. Listen to your superior." Nathan's tone was icy.

"This has to stop, Nate. You're out of control!" Ryan was trembling but he held fast to the gun. There was a moment of silence as the scene became an old Western standoff. Matt opened his mouth to speak but his reasonable words were never heard.

They simultaneously pulled the triggers.

Nathan's chest was ripped apart as buckshot tore into him. One of the pellets soared high enough to tear into his cheekbone, lodging itself there. The rest blasted their way into his lungs and his heart, killing him as his chest exploded in a gory mess spraying into the air and raining onto the street.

Ryan was left with a crater for an eye socket when the Winchester round slammed into his left eye, turning it into a pulpy mess of chipped bone and torn brain matter. In cinematic fashion, their bodies both fell backward and slammed to the pavement at almost the exact same moment, both unmoving and utterly dead.

Matthew Hawkins stood, mouth agape, an unwilling witness to the carnage that unfolded before him. He had seen enough earlier when Nathan had shot and killed two innocent people—this was too much. Before him lay four dead bodies, one stabbed and brutalized, the others shot dead in a matter of seconds.

And Matt had stood by and done nothing. He let the killings happen as he sat back and worried about his own safety.

"I'm just as at fault as Nathan," Matt said to no one, tears streaming down his face. His own cowardice was responsible for the deaths of Eddie Rader, Derrick Laurel, Ryan Giordano, and the man with the knife who Nathan gunned down. Matt had *believed* the man when he said he stabbed the other person in self-defense—people in the town were going absolutely *insane.* But still Matt stood by and let Nathan shoot the man dead as a dog without raising a finger or peeping a word to stop him. Then when Ryan had gained the courage to do something about it, Matt let him die by not standing up along with him.

Matthew Hawkins wanted no more part of the sickness infecting his town. He wanted no more of the guilt surrounding him, thicker and more suffocating than the awful fog.

Matthew Hawkins had to get away from it all.

And so he did.

He slipped off his boot and put his rifle to the ground, pointing the barrel toward himself. Without hesitation, he leaned forward and opened his mouth, carefully holding the rifle barrel and guiding it inside. Matt didn't care to consider the ramifications of his actions. On the contrary, what he considered were the consequences of living on in his town as it fell to anarchy. He had seen enough carnage and he needed no more guilt on his conscience. Like the coward he was, Matt Hawkins needed an escape and he was going to get it.

He slid his shoeless foot next to the butt of the gun and lifted it, positioning his big toe over the trigger. It was an awkward position but one Matthew achieved with surprising ease. With the difficult part of his mission already accomplished, all it took was one light push down with his toe to end the suffering.

No one heard the gunshot that killed Matthew Hawkins. He was just another corpse amongst a grizzly scene of a town gone mad.

Twenty-Four

Tom Williams finally had enough. Tom tried to avoid conflict, but he had to challenge Dan's supremacy if any normalcy was to return to the town. Tom was fearful, but for the first time in years he felt a true obligation to his town and people. Even though he had willingly given up his badge, he was still sheriff—the things Dan had done were not in line with the actions of a true lawman.

He had heard the words of support and encouragement Dan had given to the "police officers" despite their gross neglect. There would be no repercussions for the men going out and slaughtering people—there were only consequences for the poor victims.

It was then Tom decided he had to step up and do something. For the first time in years he grew a backbone and decided to get things done.

But Tom wouldn't be able to reason with Dan or any of the brainless cronies who he entitled. Tom needed *outside* help and with that in mind, he decided to take a drive out of town to the Rosedale Police Barracks.

Since he was still recognized by the people as a legitimate police officer he didn't have any problem getting around. Once out of Dan's sight, Dan forgot about him and everyone else had no issue with Officer Williams taking his car and going out on "patrol."

The effort, however, would prove to be futile. Tom Williams witnessed the truth of what Todd Miles and Tiffany Bent had been trying to convince him of earlier. Tom had heard other reports as well but still refused to believe there was no way out of town. But after three trips down Main Street in the same direction, Tom had no choice but to believe. Every time he drove past the light on Beecher's, he became engulfed by fog and was unable to see anything until he somehow appeared at the intersection of Main and Church on the other side of town. Every time it was the same, and every time Tom passed other motorists who appeared to be going through the same scenario.

Normally Tom would panic. Normally he would run and hide—but now something was different. Now Tom truly thought of himself as the sheriff and savior of his town. His obligation was there and if he didn't fulfill it, everyone, including himself, would fall victim to the chaos McNair had created.

Tom continued driving down Main until a man flagged him down. At first he was nothing more than a silhouette behind the mist but as Tom's car drew nearer he was able to recognize the man who beckoned him.

It was Henry Yeltz, one of Tom's close friends. Tom pulled his car to the side of the road and rolled down the window to address his frantic friend. "What's the matter, Henry?"

Instead of answering, Henry slammed against the side of the vehicle and pulled at the door handle, desperate to get in the car. "Let me in, Tom! Let me in! They're after me!"

Without a moment's hesitation Tom unlocked the door and let his friend inside. He sped away from the area, figuring whoever was pursuing Henry was near. "Who's after you? What happened?"

"Those crazies! The ones with the guns who think they're cops. What in God's name is going on? You didn't tell them that they were cops, did you? These people are crazy—they were going to shoot me just for being outside."

Tom sighed, looking away in shame. "I didn't authorize this, Dan did."

"McNair? Who the hell gave him the power to do that?" Henry demanded. Tom paused before answering.

"Long story short, I did, but it was a mistake."

"Well, what the hell are we going to do, Sheriff?" Henry asked.

When Henry looked to Tom, hoping for leadership and support, Tom was compelled by his own growing sense of duty. Henry, as a friend and citizen, needed the help of the law as did so many out there who were being senselessly victimized. Dan's mobile militia solution was doing nothing but justifying the actions of the corrupt. Tom could not let it continue and he knew what his next course of action had to be.

"We mobilize," Tom responded. "We get every rational person together and march on the station. We can't sit back and become victims to this madness."

In only a half hour's time, Tom was able to scour the streets and round up a group of concerned citizens who had been victims of the bedlam or were simply out looking for solutions. There was Dominick Sculli, Roger Bell, Lisa Carter, Keith Harper, and so many more. They had seen the effects of arming men who were short on brains but high on inferiority complexes. It hadn't taken much to convince them to join Tom, and soon he had twenty-five volunteers meeting with him in the Presbyterian Church.

"So what do we do, Tom?" shouted Bobby Koloski, holding a pistol he had been using for self-defense.

"I don't think violence is the answer, friends. Violence is what put us in this situation!" Tom declared, pleased to see everyone listening attentively. "Now, we may need some weapons for protection but we shouldn't go out there looking for a fight. We should march on the police station and show Dan and the men the effects of their actions. They need to see the concern of real citizens!"

"Will that be enough?" Jill Donovan asked.

"They're all on one big head trip but they want to save our town. If we show up as an organized unit voicing our concerns they will have to listen. Dan is stubborn but there's no way he's going to ignore our collective pleas."

"I don't know, Tom," protested Dominick Sculli. "If we march on the station I think there's only going to be trouble."

Tom sighed. "There might be but it's better than sitting here doing nothing or going out there and starting a fight. We have to try to diffuse the situation."

"So you're saying we should bring all our guns then?" asked Roger Bell. Upon completion of his question the room broke out in a clamor. Tom's voice became drowned out by a multitude of heated arguments.

"Hey! Hey! Relax now. I think it's a good idea to bring some protection, but remember we aren't looking for a war."

"But we better be prepared if the war comes to us!" shouted Bobby Koloski, who was met with cheers of approval.

Tom shifted back and forth uncomfortably. The intentions of these people were good but it disturbed him to see they vehemently supported the use of violence. They almost seemed to *want* it, just like the men Dan had armed. It would be risky taking these people on a march right to the police station, but if Tom were to accomplish anything he had to work with what he was given.

He pushed his apprehensions to the back of his head and prepared to lead his people and town back to sanity.

Twenty-five

As the violence and mayhem unfolded in Rowley, Alyssa Perkins drove down 6 West heading toward Rosedale. She had some shopping to accomplish and always found the extra twenty minutes to Rosedale worth it. The prices at Braylon's Market were simply exorbitant.

Alyssa lived in Willow Park, a small forested community not too far from the shores of Lake Wiladongun. The closest areas to buy groceries for her family were up 6, and she found herself making the trip often.

This time it would be unlike any other.

As she drove down the decline leading to the

valley town of Rowley, she was surprised to see a wall of gray fog. It had been a gorgeous day when she had left her home and the lake looked like a sparkling paradise.

That paradise was lost when she saw the dreary weather she was driving into.

Alyssa didn't think much of it however; the weather in northeastern Pennsylvania is some of the most fickle in the country. It could be eighty one day and forty the next. It could be bright and sunny for an hour and then dark and stormy for the rest of the day. The fog she was driving into was thick and slightly foreboding, but she didn't think of it as anything unusual.

She drove through the fog and reduced her speed to a turtle's pace. Visibility quickly became limited and Alyssa took care to stay on the road.

She began to get nervous when she could barely make out the road in front of her—but thankfully there was no other traffic. Driving at her sluggish pace she handled each turn in the road with ease.

Then something peculiar happened.

After only about thirty seconds of driving through the fog, Alyssa emerged from it without warning two miles past Rowley on 6 West and halfway to White Hills.

Well that's strange, she thought, puzzled. *It usually takes a good two minutes to cruise through Rowley and that's going at a normal pace. I shouldn't even be at the intersection of Main and Church at the speed I was going.*

It was like Alyssa had hit a wall of fog, and then bypassed the town of Rowley completely. In her brief drive she had not seen a single building or car, or anything showing she had been in Rowley.

But that's just silly, whole towns just can't disappear. Maybe I focused so much on the road that my perception of time went a little off-kilter.

It was the only rational explanation Alyssa could come up with so it was the one she accepted. On her way back she would investigate further and take note of how long it took her to drive through town.

Although her explanation was reasonable, it was outright untrue. Alyssa Perkins, mother of four, had not been in Rowley at all. She had gone in and out of the fog and missed the town completely.

Rowley was isolated from the world, with no way in, and certainly no way out.

Rowley was trapped.

It was feeding time.

Twenty-six

The Harbinger wasn't a beast that preexisted mankind. It was no ancient demon that waited for man to come along to be a source of nourishment. On the contrary, man was actually responsible for the *creation* of The Harbinger.

The Harbinger was quite old by this point, older than any one individual man could dream of becoming, but it did not have a sense of its own age or even time itself. It had no cognizance of the workings of the world or any opinion on its own existence. It was a beast that lacked rationality and self-awareness—at least in the ways humans understood these concepts.

The Harbinger was an intelligent creature in the sense it could solve problems and deal with situations accordingly, but it lacked the dimensions of intelligence that most humans value: emotional understanding and long term planning. In many facets the creature was similar to Andrew Murphy—an acting body that did what felt good and avoided what felt bad.

What felt good for The Harbinger was hatred, pure unadulterated hatred. The beast was created out of sadness, fear, regret, and all of the ill-will mankind harbored. It existed in a spiritual and emotional realm more than it did in a physical realm. It was the culmination of all of the evil aspects of humanity—it only existed and thrived due to all of the strife and problems of the world. It was created from the darkest emotions, the most hidden fears and secret, hateful impulses, and those same things would provide its nourishment. From the darkest bowels of our souls came forth The Harbinger, cursed to live an eternal life consisting of hunting down and consuming humanity.

The Harbinger therefore did what felt good, and what felt good was *feeding.* The Harbinger consumed the flesh and souls of its victims, eating away at them slowly and deliberately. Their fear and hatred would be consumed and the victim became a part of The Harbinger, converting into the dark impulses that composed the hell-beast. With each victim claimed, the creature became more powerful and with each soul consumed The Harbinger ensured its continued existence. But The Harbinger did not merely eat just to survive—it reveled in the pleasure that came with each kill.

Since it was a beast of fear and hatred, drawing these

emotions out of its prey was essential in saturating the meat and sullying the soul enough to give The Harbinger optimal nourishment. By torturing its victims both physically and psychologically, The Harbinger was able to draw out the most corrupted parts of its victims souls.

Other than eating, the beast had no long term plans and "lived" day to day. It did not think very far beyond the moment and felt no emotion besides impulses of pleasure and, to a lesser degree, pain. It was keen to the emotions and feelings of others, but purely in a cold, logical sense. It ate to continue existing and it continued existing in order to eat. Its life was a cycle fueled by the repressed bitterness, fear, and hatred of humanity.

Physically speaking, The Harbinger could take on many forms and manipulate itself as it pleased. To most it took the form of a Grim Reaper-like figure simply because of the association of death that came with it. Their minds had a conception of death, and The Harbinger took this form in order to bring out feelings of impending doom and hopelessness. These feelings in turn would bring out a slew of related emotions and bad memories that marinated the meat of its victims.

It was composed of negative energy and emotion and therefore had no one true form. If gazed upon in its most pure state it would take on a different appearance to every viewer, depending on exactly what perversions emanated from their souls. The true image of the beast was incomprehensible to mankind and any who set eyes on it would only see the product of their darkest fears and nightmares. The longer one stared at the uncloaked beast the quicker they would descend into insanity.

The Harbinger was the sign of things to come. It was the bringer of death and the consumer of hatred.

The fog was its tool, but it, as a part of The Harbinger, also was fueled by mankind. If one were being poetic they would describe the fog as the clouding of the human mind and spirit. It was the blindness that occurs when hatred and fear overtake love and bravery. The more fear and hatred in an area, the more The Harbinger had to work with to trap its prey. The fog's power truly was dependant on the area The Harbinger was visiting. Each individual had a different reaction to the fog based on their mental and emotional states—some were much more susceptible to its effects than others.

The Harbinger did not actively control the fog—it was more so a product of its own existence. Every effect the mist had was not by design but by nature. In fact, any voices heard from the fog did not come from The Harbinger at all—they were just an effect that drew out the innermost unresolved turmoil of its prey. The more damaged and corrupted the person, the more easily they would be swayed and poisoned by the haze. Once they became infected with the malevolence there was no turning back and they were prime for killing. Ironically, everyone's downfall was their own doing—the fog only widened the preexisting cracks in their psyches.

If there was one thing The Harbinger desired most it was *drawing* fear and hatred out of an area that kept it pent up and growing. There were plenty of places The Harbinger could go to feed on strife and misery but the pleasure was never greater for the creature than when it was able to pull brewing hateful feelings to the surface and make them explode. The results were usually more violent since pent-up rage releases itself in wild and out-of-control ways. The amount of delicious hatred in the air would then spread like wild-fire. In the chaos The Harbinger could feed as it pleased, picking off people and tasting their own individual forms of fear and bitterness. Humans were a wonderful source of food simply because everyone was different. Their anger and phobias were always so unique—thus no meal was ever the same. The flavor of each kill varied and was succulent and refreshing in its own way.

The Harbinger loved hatred but hated love. The concept was rather simple: the antithesis of hatred is love and pure love is the only thing that can quell hatred. Love threatened The Harbinger's very existence. Without hatred to feed off of, The Harbinger would cease to be. Its ability to cause fright and bring out negative emotion was exactly what gave it strength, but when these tactics failed The Harbinger was left without power.

That is why it so quickly fled the garage where it had made its dwelling. The creature had become more human-like over the years as more and more souls added to the composition of its being. With the consumption of more individuals, The Harbinger had been unknowingly taking on the habits and customs of its victims. It now enjoyed having a home wherever it went—a place where it could eat slowly and savor the pleasure that came with mutilating the flesh of its prey. It had known when Ben and Elise had intruded into its den.

The Harbinger did not consider the true extent of any of its abilities, but it had the ability to sense fear and apprehension with a natural radar. Since it was a being of emotions it could pluck them out of the very air around it, a tactic it often used in selecting the best victims. When it felt this particular bit of fear it knew exactly where and from whom it was coming.

The Harbinger did not want its sanctuary threatened or destroyed so it had rushed through the streets to defend its temporary homestead.

When it had gotten there, however, things had gone horribly wrong.

Although the two had a fair amount of fear within them, their supply of hatred was lacking. The amount of fear The Harbinger was able to pull from them was sizable but it was squashed by the sudden rush of passion and love they felt for each other.

This was like a toxic poison to The Harbinger. Their kiss and the pure love they felt in that moment sliced through The Harbinger as searing, intolerable pain. The pain was so immense The Harbinger had no choice but to get as far away from the love as possible.

The Harbinger did not fear anyone or anything, but it did avoid everything that felt bad. True love was the most crippling sensation it could sense and although the two people were no threat to The Harbinger in terms of killing it, it still wanted nothing to do with them or the powerful love they felt.

Love was the only thing that could drive The Harbinger away.

So The Harbinger had left and returned to the streets to find prey that had already fallen victim to their own blind hatred and confusion. They could not muster love or passion in the current situation, only selfishness and fear. Those at the supermarket were wrought with worry, fear, and frustration; they had been tasty morsels. When it had come upon the firefighters, it sensed no love in any of them—a sense of duty yes, but happiness or true love, no.

This was premium, this was delicious. The fear it was able to inspire in them on top of their discontent with their lives and town had made them prime meals. It had torn each of the four men to pieces before it ate them, consuming their organs first little by little before crunching into their savory bones. It was exactly the rebound The Harbinger needed after encountering all of that toxic love.

The problem was that love was more powerful than hatred. When it was true and pure even one instance of love could ruin the flavor and condition of an area prime for feeding.

This troubled The Harbinger. Even after it enjoyed its meals it could still sense the love lurking in the town. It sensed the overwhelming sense of commitment and friendship within the two people and this was enough to make it want to go far, far away.

But it wouldn't. There was something happening in the town, something brewing up and boiling over, something too delicious to turn away from. In everyone else the hatred was reaching its peak, and soon a luxurious malice-filled chaos would ensue. There would be anger and violence and hopelessness. It was going to be a feeding ground, the most delicious buffet The Harbinger had ever encountered.

It had to take its chances. It could already sense the event beginning. If the monster was capable of happiness beyond basic impulsive pleasure, it would have felt it as it charged toward the chaotic scene brewing in the center of town.

The disdain for love was still fresh in the beast's mind but it wasn't enough to deter the monster from pursuing the succulent feast ahead.

The hatred, oh how it was so mouthwatering and irresistible.

Twenty-seven

Outside of the Rowley Police Department, Ernie Stevens played peacekeeper to a rowdy group of armed men, drunk from the strange mix of power and helplessness that came with the lawless situation. Each of them had a weapon and the power to kill. They had all been reduced to a Hobbesian State of Nature where anyone could easily kill anyone on a whim. With arms come rash decisions and those types of decisions were exactly what Ernie Stevens was trying to deter.

"Calm down, boys, just calm down! Leave those people alone, come on. They're scared out of their minds! We don't gotta make it worse!" Ernie shouted at a group of three men brandishing their weapons toward the growing crowd of citizens on the lawn of the police station.

Ernie wasn't fearful of these worried citizens, he was fearful *for* them. The vagabonds Dan had so casually armed had proven to be very trigger happy. They had taken his decree of martial law and ran with it. The last thing the town needed, on top of all the chaos, was a massacre right at the steps of the police department.

"Everyone, relax, calm down! Sheriff McNair will be out with our plan of action shortly." Ernie pushed past the small group threatening the citizens, positioning himself in between and doing his best to placate. "We all have concerns, but right now the real authority is Sheriff McNair. Let's not make hasty decisions."

"He isn't even the Sheriff! What right does he have to take over the town and arm dangerous people?" A man screamed at him from the ever-growing crowd confronting the pseudo-police force.

The size of the crowd was unknown. The fog obscured them, and their numbers could have been anywhere from the dozen or so visible to many times greater. Dan had originally scattered the crowd but then had ordered to let them re-gather. There were more pressing matters at hand than the few citizens who wanted to whine and protest.

"Hey, fuck you. We need a leader in a time like this. Why don't you fuckin' go home with your crying?" The boy who yelled at the crowd was a "police force" member. The kid could barely pass for sixteen and was holding a loaded crossbow.

Ernie stepped in front of the boy as he moved to raise the weapon. The shouts coming from the crowd grew quickly and the tension on the faces of all the men escalated at the same rate. Then, at the worst possible time, the small group expanded as Tom Williams and his band of freedom fighters arrived on the scene.

The "police squadron" around Ernie raised their weapons and stepped forward. It was clear this new force was holding weapons and conflict was imminent. If Ernie Stevens hadn't recognized the round figure of Tom Williams at the front of the pack, gunshots would have preceded words.

"Tom? Is that you? What's going on?" Itchy trigger fingers hesitated as everyone waited to see what would come from the exchange of dialogue.

"Yeah, it's me, Ernie. I just rounded up a few more concerned citizens." He walked closer so he could be seen through the thick fog.

"For the force?" Ernie asked naively.

"No, not for the force you got here. This craziness has to stop. The violence is out of control. We can't just arm citizens and expect them to be the law." Tom's words were met with shouts of support from behind him and cries of defiance from the front. Ernie Stevens shouted at his front line, waving his arms to prevent some of his men from firing on the spot.

"Hey! Hey! Relax now! We don't need bloodshed on the lawn of the police station! Relax and let the man speak!" Ernie's pleas were accepted begrudgingly. Even though the police force had blood-lust they still had some recognition for the chain of command.

Ernie turned back to Tom. "You aren't the Sheriff anymore, Tom. That's not your call."

"He was always the Sheriff!" yelled Dominick Sculli, and people on both sides broke out in shouts.

Tom and Ernie did their best to prevent their people from starting a meleé but their efforts looked to be in vain. Just as it appeared shots would be fired, everyone was silenced by a voice seamlessly piercing the fog.

"Attention!" Dan McNair's voice sounded as if it was coming from a megaphone. Not everyone could see him due to the haze, but they all paused and turned toward the sound of his voice, recognizing his oratory presence.

The armed vigilantes looked to him like he was some sort of savior. Whatever Dan had to say, they wanted to accept it. Whatever he said they wanted to believe—they *needed* him to legitimize their power and individual actions. Their sins were a product of his orders rather than their own choices. Whatever they decided to do was given a pass in their own minds. The guidance Dan offered was better than facing the situation alone. Anything was better than the disorganized bedlam they were in. Anything was better than the *truth.*

Dan spoke with an eloquence that he had never before possessed. As a man void of social skill or general tact he had never utilized words with dexterity, but now he spoke with a presence that came to him as if he were a well-seasoned politician.

"It has come to my attention that the stipulations put in place have not been working. We have people acting out in the streets, some of whom include the very men we have trusted to temporarily guard our safety. With this in mind, I am assuming direct control of all units of the provisional police force and assembling them into one mobile unit, big and powerful enough to deal with any criminals on the streets. This is effective immediately. We shall gather here and move out at once. All on the lawn are welcome to join the effort of preserving peace and security but let it be known that all who protest or stand in the way of order will be treated as criminals under martial law and will face harsh punishment." He believed he was succinct in his words and he saw no reason for anyone to object, however a voice from the crowd called out and caused him to cringe.

"You have to stop this, Dan. This police force business is doing more harm than good. I have thirty people here who can testify to that." Tom's claims were supported by a rallying cheer drifting out of the fog from an unknown amount of residents.

"Martial law has been enacted. I am the Sheriff. I do not have to stop anything. All of this is within my power and judgment." Dan was cool and collected despite the developing tension.

"Fuck you! Stop the killing. We need order not violence," a voice behind Tom cried and the crowd amongst the fog rustled with excitement.

"Quiet! Quiet!" Tom declared. "Dan, as you can see here your own people don't want this police squad. This method has caused corruption on the streets, violence, and rape! You have to be sensible—just listen to the testimony of these people. The things happening out there are horrible, and we need real help. We can't just arm amateurs and consider them cops."

The sound arguments Tom Williams spoke were not heard by Dan McNair. All Dan heard was the sneering voice of his uncle, calling out from behind the fog as he hid with Tom and the rest of the cowardly protestors.

"You're a pussy boy, just a regular stinkin' pussy! You can't control any of us, you can't do shit! Look, fat ass Tom has rallied up people against you! You're going to lose your title on the first day of the job! And you're going to lose it to him! You're no better than that blubbery sack of shit. He's got the upper hand on you now! You might as well just lie down and take it. Do ya get it, boy? Take it. You've already done plenty of that!"

"I will not stand here and be insulted, Tom. You willingly gave away your right to rule over this situation and now you stand before me in defiance. You have gathered a rebellious group and you're looking to undermine and usurp my power. Our town is gripped by pandemonium and your actions only serve to further divide us. We don't need division but unity under the law."

"Dan," Tom desperately pleaded, "that's exactly what—" He was cut off mid-sentence.

"Do we stand for the spineless who wish to get nothing done?" Dan asked his men and was met with a resounding "No!" from the crowd. He turned back to Tom and addressed him and his followers.

"You have one minute to disburse. Then we will start firing. Leave now with your lives and return to your homes." Dan's voice was bellowing but flat in tone, lacking any inkling of sympathy.

There was a collective gasp from people on both sides of the line in the sand, then a response from the demonstrators.

They pleaded to the men Dan had brainwashed.

"He's a tyrant! A monster! Don't listen to him, people. We're all in this together! He's using you all!" Both sides readied their arms and the fight Tom so desperately wished to avoid was upon him. He opened his mouth and shouted protests but he was drowned out and lost amongst the noise.

Dan's countdown sped up. He didn't respond to the clamoring, instead waited silently for what was to come.

The fog grew thicker than ever and neither side could see a single member of the other. People standing directly next to each other saw only dark outlines of their allies. The shouts were masked by the fog and came through as barely audible whispers.

Ernie Stevens stood next to Dan and looked to him with nervousness. "Sheriff, you're not really going to . . ."

"FIRE!" Suddenly there was raw emotion in his voice. His cry echoed outward and there was only a split second of hesitation before all of the armed police squad lined up, aimed their weapons, and fired. Without seeing a target they squeezed the triggers and sent a volley of rounds spiraling into the unknown. The only indication any of them had hit their targets was a few distant shrieks coming together to form a single, sickly sound. Pain and death radiated through the fog more loudly than anything else and the spirits of the Rowley Police Force rose as they heard the anguish of their victims.

"AGAIN!" McNair cried this time with unadulterated glee, and some of the men complied before the second syllable even left his mouth. More screams of terror and pain followed, most becoming distant as the crowd fled for their lives, some of them limping away severely wounded.

It wasn't completely one sided, however. A few members of Tom's renegade faction returned the fire and to the shock of the Rowley Police Force, some of their members fell wounded or dead. This didn't serve to deter the spirit of the newly crowned lawmen—it actually spurred them to go into a charge. Weapons raised, they ran forward onto the lawn and the battle began.

As his men advanced on the enemy, Dan McNair smiled broadly. He was showing his uncle and those stubborn residents who was in charge. It was *his* town through and through and he wouldn't let the position of power slip from his fingers. For the first time in his life, Dan McNair was in *control* and the feeling was addictive.

He stood back to be out of the general line of fire. He couldn't see exactly what was going on but knew his men would be victorious. He was positive they outnumbered the growing resistance on the lawn and even if they didn't, not all of the rebels came touting weapons.

Dan was right. Amongst the skirmish his force was winning, driving back Tom's make-shift team and slaughtering a large number of them. Whereas death discouraged Tom's crowd, the blood and gore incited Dan's rowdy mass of madmen, fueling their drive for victory.

On the other side, Tom ran around trying to stop his men from participating in the battle. Even as the first bullets starting flying he thought he could end the insanity. Tom finally realized he was in over his head when he heard a blood curdling scream pierce through the air only feet from where he stood. Tom turned and saw the gruesome fate that had befallen his dear friend, Henry Yeltz.

It was a gut-wrenching sight. Henry had been shot, but not by a bullet—he had been hit by an *arrow.* Not only had Henry had the misfortune of being shot with arrow, he had been shot in the *head.* By some miracle (or curse), the shot had not killed Henry. Instead, the arrow had lodged itself in his skull, only a fraction of an inch above his eye. It pierced through his right eyebrow and came to a stop somewhere within his brain.

Henry fell to his knees, letting out hysterical cries of pain. He threw his arms outward and shrieked as loudly as he could. His head whipped back and forth in violent motions, perhaps a natural reaction to attempt to dislodge the arrow. Despite his hysteria, Henry was conscious and cognizant of what had happened to him. He could do nothing to stop the pain or remedy the horrific situation. He thrashed like an animal caught in a trap, one succumbing to a mortal wound. Tom saw the excruciation in his friend's eyes and knew there was only one thing he could do. Tom pulled his gun from its holster and pointed it at Henry. It was the merciful course of action—no one deserved to suffer in such a way.

Tom put his friend to rest with a shot to the side of the head. It would be the only time he shot someone in his entire life, as well as the only time he would kill. He did it to let his friend rest in peace but his insides churned at the thought of what he had done.

Tom wouldn't have time to consider his actions. There were still men trying to kill him. They were the very men he had helped on various occasions, who had trusted him as their sheriff, and now those people wanted his head on platter.

Tom turned and fled with many of his men—already they had been defeated. The few who had stood and fought were being picked off and overwhelmed. Everyone else knew to scatter. Tom's effort had solved nothing—he simply led a few poor souls to a massacre. He thought about this as he leaped over his fallen comrades, each sight nearly causing a mental breakdown. Tom was soon out of the sight of his pursuers, but fate again turned against him when he was tagged in the stomach by a bullet.

Tom stumbled but did not fall as he felt the metal pierce his belly. He had been hit not by the men chasing him, but by one of his own companions as they ran and blindly shot backward toward the police force. Tom put one hand over the bleeding wound and kept hobbling on, attempting to get away from *everyone.* Madness had stricken every person in the town and he knew no one could help him or Rowley anymore.

Sputtering and spitting up blood, Tom ran for as fast and as long as he could.

Some of the Rowley Police Force chased the fleeing protestors as they ran down Main Street in the direction of Church. Most, however, fell back when victory was assured in order to receive praise and new orders from their vaunted captain, Sheriff McNair.

Dan reveled in his glory, standing amongst his troops as if he was a victorious general ready to lead his men on the final charge.

"What do we do? What next? Orders, Sheriff? I shot three

of 'em dead myself, Sheriff!" Dan took a moment to breath in the intoxicating smell of prestige before he responded with confidence.

"Continue down Main and slaughter anyone in your path. We have to kill off every last one of these dissenters. They want anarchy. They want an end to law. Only once we are free from their meddling can we bring this town back to order and safety!"

Men jumped, celebrated, and cheered upon his words, mobilizing to enact Dan's will. Some were covered in blood and already murderers, others were eager for the opportunity to get their hands wet—despite what they had done, each was infected with delusions of grandeur and violence. They wanted blood, and if they were to get it they would want even more.

The sickness was spreading.

TWENTY-EIGHT

"It's even thicker," Elise commented as she and Ben walked down Church Street toward Main, noticing how the fog had somehow become even more prevalent. "What are we going to do anyway, get some people together for some group smooching? I don't think a kiss is going to be able to stop this thing for good." Elise tried her best to throw a joke in the moment but her voice lacked humor.

"I don't know what's going to stop it. We figured out that it doesn't like love so maybe if we get some people together to stand up and support each other we can get the thing to leave. It likes hate and darkness so we need to have the people of Rowley stand together as a beacon of hope," Ben replied, now clad in a bed sheet bandage that stretched diagonally across his body.

"Easier said than done," noted Elise.

Ben sighed. "Yeah, I don't know if we're going to find anyone willing to stand up against that thing. Who knows what other horrors it's committed out there. It's probably killed more people than just those stored back in the garage . . ."

"Don't bring that up again. I'm going to have nightmares for the rest of my life."

Ben held firmly to her hand as they walked. "We're going to put that nightmare to rest today, Elise. Together."

"Together." She smiled and then let it fade as she continued speaking. "No matter what we do, people have died. People we know and maybe even some people we love."

Ben nodded. "I know. All the more reason to stop this thing."

"You're so calm, yet you said before you were afraid."

"More than I've ever been in my life."

"You don't seem it."

Ben smiled assuredly at her. "Courage is being scared to death and saddling up anyway."

"Is that John Wayne?" Elise asked, and Ben nodded. "Ha, I knew I'd hear you quote Poe, Twain, and Shakespeare but I didn't ever think you'd quote John Wayne. You're cheesy and I love you."

The last three words rolled smoothly off of Elise's tongue as if she had been casually saying them for years. The feelings had always been there for them both but never had they chosen to explore them. Now in their greatest moment of peril, all they had to carry them was the strength of their love—and neither one of them wanted to restrict it.

"Not to ruin the tender moment," Ben began tentatively, "but like you said before we may be walking to our deaths."

Elise nodded. "If we're in a situation where we are about to die, go and plant another kiss on me—I want to go out in romantic fashion."

"I'm serious."

"So am I."

They continued walking, both taking a few moments to let the sentimental feelings of their love sink in and wash away the bone-chilling cold of the fog. Ben broke the temporary silence. "This really was our last carefree summer together, wasn't it? This more than anything is making us step into adulthood."

"That's not a bad thing." Elise took a consolatory tone. "You've grown up more in the last day than you have in your entire life. Even I never would have imagined you would be leading me out to face the devil straight on. I guess I always knew you had it in you, but never thought I'd see it."

"You're beautiful," Ben commented, finding those words the only ones appropriate to describe his sentiment for her. They were not isolated in the fog, they were *together* in the fog, and with purpose in mind they were going to recruit others to save their town.

Just as they began to get overly optimistic they walked upon a scene that made both of their hearts drop.

The body of Matthew Hawkins was mostly headless—mostly, because his head had been blown apart and severed above his mouth, with his lower jaw and neck still attached to his corpse. Brain matter and blood splattered the ground around his body, and gory chunks of flesh encrusted his flannel shirt.

Elise clung to Ben upon seeing the horrible sight. Unfortunately, there was much more to see. Both gasped again as they peered through the fog and saw the full truth of the terrible scene.

Not far off to the left of the first body was Ryan Giordano's, his head cocked to the side as he lay motionless on the street, gazing at them both with a single-eyed stare. His left eye was gone, replaced by a pulpy mess of a crater which was stock-full of torn gray and red brain matter.

They saw Nathan Wright lying on his back and staring up toward the sky with holes in his chest. He was near the corpse of Travis Dolan. Travis had blood caked in between his lips and dark stains of it flowed in trails down the corners of his mouth and onto his chin, giving the appearance of an eternal bloody frown.

Behind his corpse was the stabbed body of Harold Ferguson. The scene was a blood-bath. The violence that occurred must have been immense, and it frightened Ben to realize all of the wounds on the victims had been done by people.

This wasn't the monster. This was people killing people. Is everyone starting to lose their minds? Has it really gotten that bad?

"Ben," Elise said shakily, "they were killed by guns and knives. I don't know if being out here is the safest thing."

Ben agreed but hiding was no longer an option. "I don't think we have a choice."

"I don't think it's going to be that easy to find help."

"I agree. But we don't have a choice."

Elise sobbed. "Dead, all of them dead. This is horrible! There's been too much blood, too much murder! We have to stop this but I don't know if we really can . . . I don't know . . ."

"Elise," Ben said firmly. "Together."

She sniffled and wiped a welling tear. "Together."

Hand in hand, they walked past the carnage, hoping it was the last terror they had to encounter. Barely over the first jolt, both were blindsided and sent reeling by the next terrible sight.

Ben saw the figure first, lying as a heap in the middle of the road and writhing in pain. The man held his bleeding stomach, clinging to life. As Ben and Elise rushed closer, they recognized the injured man as the one they thought would be their beacon of hope: Tom Williams.

"Oh no, Sheriff Williams, what happened?" Ben shouted, running over and kneeling at Tom's side. He had a bullet wound in his lower stomach and it was bleeding profusely. He had lost a great deal of blood and it was a miracle he was still conscious.

"They've lost it, Ben. They've lost their minds."

"Who?"

"Everyone. Dan McNair has helped this town regress into savagery. There's no turning back." He coughed, spitting up blood as he concluded his sentence.

"Dan McNair, your deputy?" Elise asked, stunned.

Tom nodded and his breaths became more belabored. "Senseless murders. They're shooting each other in the streets. There's no hope left." He let out a whooping cough and Ben thought the statement would be his last.

"No hope? That can't be! We have to stop the thing in the

fog! People can't be fighting each other," Ben pleaded to the dying man.

Tom grabbed hold of Ben's wrist firmly with his bloody hand and stared into his eyes. He spoke with a strained voice, each utterance taking nearly all the energy he had left. "You listen to me, Ben. You and the girl get out of town. Get as far away as you can. I tried to help . . . I really did . . . but . . ."

Tom's head slumped sideways as his chest rose and fell one final time. His hand went lax and dropped away from Ben's wrist, leaving a bloody smear of an imprint on his skin. For the first time since The Harbinger's arrival, Tom Williams was at peace.

Ben and Elise were at first too shocked to do or say anything; the only man they had ever known as Sheriff had died right before their eyes. On top of his terrible demise there was his *message,* which spelled out doom for the town of Rowley. Was there anything Ben and Elise could do? Was there any chance of stopping the beast?

Ben reached over, closed Tom's eyes, and recited a silent prayer. Elise put her hand on his shoulder and waited a somber moment before she spoke.

"Ben, you heard what he said. We saw the corpses back there. It's not just that thing that's dangerous anymore. People are losing their minds. Maybe we shouldn't do this."

Ben stood up, still facing away from Elise as he spoke. "Then what do we do? Go and hide and wait for those people or that nightmare to get us? What good will that do? We have to do something, even if we die trying."

"There's no guarantee we can stop it, and even if we do, people still may be acting crazy."

"No, if we stop it the chaos will stop."

"How do you know that?" Elise wanted to believe him and wanted to go through with their plan, but her feelings for Ben made her fearful of losing him.

"None of this was going on before that thing came here. The fog and everything that it's doing is driving people mad and pitting them against each other. If we get it out of town, all the strife will go with it." Ben spoke with more confidence than he had.

"And if we fail?" Elise asked, already knowing the awful answer.

"If we fail it's no different than if we don't try. Our town and everyone in it will die. The only way out is fighting that thing."

"I'm going to follow your lead here," Elise said. "I've always trusted you, but I haven't always taken your advice. I think now is the time to listen. Let's stop this thing, for Sheriff Williams, for those people in the garage, and for all of the victims of this terrible nightmare."

Elise wiped away her remaining tears and Ben placed his clean hand in her own. "Let's do this," he said calmly as they gave one last respectful glance to Tom before walking toward the intersection and the final battle ahead.

Twenty-nine

Dan McNair led his troops down Main toward the same location after his scouts had reported a sizable gathering of people there. After the massacre on the lawn of the police station, Dan was steadfast in his commitment to maintain proper order and balance. He was going to show his scumbag uncle his ability by wiping out every maggot that stood in his way. Then no one could question his leadership.

The resistance had not made his conviction falter in the slightest. What the town didn't need was dissension; it needed a singular, cohesive power structure. Under his command there would be no stragglers or naysayers, only strident purpose and achievement.

"What do we do when we get there, Sheriff?" A nameless man to his right asked.

"We give them a warning in order to maintain appearance. Then we fire. Once they are all dealt with we move onto handling whatever is in this fog."

"Yes, sir," the man replied with glee, offering Dan a salute he did not acknowledge. Dan was past the point of caring about the people of the town or even the sake of the town itself. Dan was in this for himself, for his own pride and perpetually damaged ego.

He would prove to his uncle and to the world that he was a real man. It didn't matter that he was molested and forced to lie down like a woman years earlier—he was still a man. With that sentiment in mind and heart he led his troops toward the intersection, letting them kill any wounded they found along the way. As long as they looked up to him and respected him, Dan was more than willing to let them fulfill their burgeoning blood-lust.

The crowd gathered at the intersection of Church and Main was sizable—there were about sixty people standing there for a multitude of reasons—some for no reason at all. Some had left their homes to find hope, or to find friends and family members or someone who could save them. Many of the new arrivals on the scene were survivors from the Police Station Massacre, but most of those had long abandoned any thoughts of fighting the law. There was still a select few that wished to unite the stragglers against McNair, but with the disorganization that characterized the entire scene their efforts were fruitless. The rest were there surveying the damage and the mood amongst the mayhem—they just wanted to have somewhere to be. They were the star-struck observers, like those who stand by the scene of a car accident or some disaster. They were the shell-shocked onlookers of the insanity that had ravaged their town.

Even those who had not been at the police station were armed. Some with guns, others with knives or gardening tools. By this point, every citizen in Rowley knew not to be on the streets without a weapon, but they lacked any real idea of what to do.

There were mutterings and conversations, disjointed thoughts and fears both rational and irrational. There were tensions, newly formed friendships, and overall clutter. They were like nomadic travelers with no other place to settle, all joined together for their own reasons amidst this tragedy.

Soon they would all be locked in a conflict for their lives.

Dan led his thirty men on a march to the enemy. When he reached his goal, he surveyed the situation the best his eyes would allow him. He barely was able to see anything except shadows and outlines, but he could make out small scattered groups of people sitting and standing. That was evidence enough for him. He would make his announcement then commence the killing. It didn't matter to him whether people complied or not. Dan McNair was going to assert his authority.

"Attention! You are gathered in the streets illegally. Return to your homes now or you will be fired upon."

Some people in his general vicinity heard Dan, but most

had no clue thirty something others had walked upon the scene. The fog was thick but not only in a visual sense—it set up a wall keeping people isolated from each other. They could not see Dan and he could not feel compassion for them, so without even giving time for a proper response Dan called out:

"Fire at will!"

Rifles, shotguns, pistols, and even a crossbow were fired in the general direction of the citizens. It was a firing frenzy. With each round shot, the fog grew thicker around them and they continued moving forward to spy their targets. Like the massacre at the police station, many of the fearful folks initially retreated but those who had not been at the scene regrouped and began to fight back.

It was a blind skirmish. Bullets whizzed by people without them even noticing, allies fell down dead or wounded without their partners being privy to it. The fog grew thicker and thicker as the hate and violence escalated and the battle continued. The gunshots were barely heard and the screams of the wounded were lost within the haze.

Dan fired indiscriminately. He didn't realize he had capped one of his own volunteers in the back of the head. As he walked over the man's body, he failed to recognize he had delivered the coup de grâce, and even if he had it wouldn't have mattered.

The situation devolved, fueled by senseless hatred and violence, and as the visibility became the lowest it had been in the last thirty-six hours, people began killing their own teammates. There was no rhyme or reason to their actions—they simply embraced murder.

No one had an identity in the fog. There was no thought or recognition, simply raw passion. That emotion was telling everyone to kill for the sake of killing and the glory of the adrenaline rush. Their minds, clouded by the haze, complied and they began to fire on or swing at whatever shape in the fog was closest to them.

Herman Daugherty struck a figure in the mist over the head with a lead pipe. The body fell to the ground without struggle and Herman was upon the man in an instant, wrapping his strong hands around the scrawny neck of his victim, wringing it with everything he had. He felt the windpipe of the victim collapse and he laughed at the man's weak attempts to pry his hands off. The victim pushed, slapped, and squirmed like a child, and when Herman heard the belabored choking of his victim, he was hit with a rush of joy.

It wasn't until his victim was nearly dead that he was able to recognize who it was. It was his own cousin, Mel Daugherty, who he had come to the town square and teamed up with for protection during the dire time.

Herman was surprised by the identity of his victim, and he took only a moment to contemplate the situation while staring at the frightened eyes of his cousin. His face was a deep shade of purple strewn with the thick lines of bulging veins looking ready to burst through the skin.

For a split second he considered letting his cousin go, but his primal instinct told him he was too far along to stop. He squeezed with all he had and fully crushed the neck of his beloved cousin, laughing like a madman as Mel's eyes rolled up into the back of his head and he took his final breaths.

Herman Daugherty was a man possessed.

Elsewhere in the fog, Molly Carpenter sought out Rachael Ludlow. This was her opportunity to teach that loudmouth bitch a lesson. This was her chance to get the revenge she so desperately sought.

Molly pushed past a figure. It was a man who appeared to have an ax lodged between his shoulder and neck. As she pushed her way past the staggering, screaming man, a hot spray of blood hit her in the face, covering her cheek—but Molly did not react. That man had nothing to do with her goal of revenge. Her only purpose in that fog was to find and kill Rachael Ludlow.

"Oh that stupid bitch Molly Carpenter, shacking up with a co-worker right in the office! Didn't she know she would be caught?" Molly heard Rachael laughing as she told Molly's story to yet another person.

That bitch! she thought. *She's out here in this fight and she's still gabbing away! I'm going to show her!* Molly clutched the handle of her carving knife tightly, more ready than ever to carve.

Then she saw the figure of a female, stumbling around in the fog.

Molly did not know if it was Rachael Ludlow or not, but something inside of her was incited by the sight of flowing blonde hair. Her mind wanted it to be Rachael—her mind *wanted* someone on which to take out all of her pent up frustration.

So the injured woman in the fog became Rachael Ludlow.

Molly was upon her before the woman had any time to react. She jumped on the woman's back and drove the carving knife down into her shoulder. It pierced the skin with such force that it scraped off of the bone, tearing into the woman's muscle.

The woman let out an agonized scream and Molly began shouting. "You want to talk now, Rachael? Still have things to say about me? Let's hear what you have to say now, you stupid bitch!" She brought the knife up and slashed across the woman's back, making sure to not penetrate too deeply this time—she wanted her to suffer.

Screaming, the woman fought desperately as Molly hacked away at her, lopping off folds of flesh with ease. Flaps of skin fell away from the victim's body and landed on the pavement with wet *thwaps*.

"Do you have any jokes to tell the rest of the office? Oh I know you do, please share them!" Molly laughed and hacked, then laughed some more. Revenge was sweet heaven and nothing could stop her now. When "Rachael" fell to the ground, Molly was on top of her in a split second, making sure she couldn't escape her punishment.

She forced the butchered woman to turn over and held her down while she pushed the blade near her face. "Let's see you talk when you don't have any lips or tongue! Let's see you tell stories then!" Molly Carpenter was possessed by the devil as she carved into the innocent woman's mouth, shoving the blade under the skin of her chin and popping it up through her lip. She cut and sliced, hacking away as much of the woman's mouth and lips as she could. The knife did not do the job cleanly. It slid and bounced off of the struggling woman's teeth and sliced into her gums, mangling them as

Molly yanked the knife up and down, mutilating the woman's mouth. Rubbery bits of gum and lip found their way into the victim's throat and she sputtered and spat in an effort not to choke on her own flesh. Blood flew up and combined with the blood of the axed man on Molly's face but none of this slowed her.

She cut and carved and loved the gurgled, choking screams of "Rachael." The fear in her eyes was entrancing and her scream when Molly cut half her tongue off was utterly decadent. Molly took the wet, bloody lump in her hand and forced it down to the woman's face, roughly rubbing it against her skin and pushing it into her eyes to taunt her. She then viciously stabbed away at "Rachael's" face without method, each thrust unguided and penetrating right to the bone.

Molly Carpenter raised her hands to the sky and let out a cry of pleasure as "Rachael" lay there and died miserably, her face not recognizable as anything but a ragged palate of red.

"Talk now! Talk about me and my affair now, you dirty whore." Molly threw her head back and laughed. Her moment of ultimate victory ended prematurely, however, when her hearty laughter was cut short by a stray bullet traveling through the fog. It was aimed at another, but had missed its target and soared through the mist until it found a place to stay.

That place was Molly's temple.

Molly fell forward and landed on top of the recently deceased woman she had so brutally murdered. Her body was left in an embrace with the slain form of "Rachael Ludlow."

~

Unlike Molly Carpenter, Zachary Sherman was fortunate enough to find the *real* Ernie Stevens, just as Ernie had fired off the last of his ammunition into Tiffany Bent.

Ernie turned in time to see Zachary and raised his gun to fire—but it was too late.

Zachary swung his shovel and hit Ernie Stevens squarely on the side of the head. The thunk that came was satisfying, and Zachary hoped he hadn't already broken Ernie's skull. He wanted to experience the pleasure of bashing Ernie's brains in while he struggled for his life.

Ernie fell to the ground, knocked into another world. The side of his head swelled up and before he had time to gain his bearings, the hard, metal head of the shovel struck him again, hitting him twice upon the forehead.

"You fucking prick! How could you take her from me? You knew I loved her, you knew it and you stole her! You fucking asshole!" Zachary struck Ernie without rhyme or reason, raining down heavy blows with his shovel. He smacked Ernie's arms and legs as he tried to defend himself. With each strike they retracted, enabling Zachary to zone in on Ernie's midsection and face.

"She shouldn't be yours! She should be mine! I love her, you bastard! I love her with all of my heart! Die, you fucker!" Zachary swung and smacked Ernie numerous more times, immobilizing him to the point where he was able to choreograph the final blow.

As Ernie lay, bloody, beaten, and battered, Zachary moved over him and positioned the tip of the shovel into Ernie's mouth. Ernie stared up at him dully, his broken face barely recognizable. All fight had been beaten out of him.

Zachary forced the head of the shovel as far as he could into Ernie's mouth and then put his foot to the back of it. He smiled down at the defeated face of Ernie Stevens and reveled in the moment before he killed his nemesis.

"Look who wins in the end. This is justice." Zachary smiled, then brought his foot down onto the back of the head of the shovel, forcing it into Ernie's mouth. The skin on the side of his mouth was ripped away when the metal found its way to the back of his throat, where it partially severed his head and hit his spine with sudden, blunt force.

Ernie Stevens did not die from the initial blow. He lived long enough to feel the pain of his grotesque injury and choke on his own blood. The skin below his cheeks flapped as he gurgled, spat, and shook, trying to breathe to no avail.

As he sputtered and died, Zachary Sherman looked on with sadistic amusement, loving the writhing motions of pain and gagging noises. He stared directly into the suffering man's eyes and waited for the moment in which he died. When that moment came, Zachary spit on Ernie's body and gave him a hard kick in the side.

"Good riddance, you bastard," Zachary shouted. He had only that moment to bask in his glory before he heard a cry that signaled his own fate.

Tsssskknnntchhhhhhh. Even before his mind could process what he heard, his heart knew it was pure evil. All of the happiness gained by bashing Ernie's face in disappeared in an instant.

Zachary Sherman turned around and saw the transformation of a nightmare.

The Harbinger stood behind him, swaying back and forth

gently, finding pleasure in his hateful act of violence. Zachary hadn't seen the beast before, but somehow he knew its form. As he studied it he wasn't surprised by its existence, simply scared beyond his being.

It raised its head up to the sky and let out its cry, only this time it was more guttural—more deafening. This time it was not a hiss, but a beastly roar rising from the core of its darkness.

Pop! Crunch! Snap! As it cried out into the air it began to transform. The changes happened right before Zachary's eyes and he was left petrified, unable to avert his stare from the magnificent disaster.

Its dead white hands transformed into long, sharp, piercing black claws—but that was far from the end of it. Its arms snapped under the robe and Zachary saw the thing's arms breaking at four points and continuing to move and shift. The sound of broken bones and mashing flesh was a hellish symphony, every sound and motion perfectly coordinated despite the spontaneous appearance.

Then the arms grew to unnatural proportions. They went rigid and snapped together. They shot out from under the robe at an incredible speed, each growing out to a length of five feet before supplanting themselves onto the ground as if they were clawed feet.

More popping and cracking sounds were heard, followed by ripping as the fabric on the back of the being's robe tore, revealing appendages springing forth. They were four incredibly long, leg-like appendages, black as night, fitting the form and composition of its awful arms.

These appendages resembled spider legs and they were

at least three times the length of the being's elongated arms. They shot out of its back from near each shoulder and hip. The upper two rose and waved toward the sky as if they had experienced emancipation from their prison while the lower two legs dug themselves into the ground. These lower two legs lifted the rest of the monster into the air, bending to support the weight but still leaving the creature standing twice its original height.

In a flash, the nightmare had become some type of twisted spider creature and Zachary could tell it wanted him.

He could feel that it was *hungry.*

Zachary freed himself from the bonds of paralysis and ran. It cried out behind him in a tone more wretched and horrifying than ever.

TSSSSRRRNNNNNNNNTCHHHH! The sound was piercing and powerful. Zachary turned to look back at his pursuer and saw it go into action.

It moved with speed it shouldn't have possessed. It spring-loaded its body on its back spider legs and launched forward through the air. Just as Zachary's mind began to make sense of the action, the beast was on his heels, spanning the distance between them in no time.

It landed behind him, and raised one of its upper spider legs. Then like a scorpion's tail, raised the appendage, thrusting it into Zachary's shoulder.

The pain was excruciating. In one terrible instant Zachary was thrown to the ground as the sharp appendage stabbed through the flesh and bone of his shoulder, lodging itself within.

The leg held him to the ground for a brief moment before

lifting him. The motion caused Zachary debilitating pain. The leg was the width of a Wiffle ball bat and its diameter destroyed Zachary's shoulder as it supported his full weight.

He screamed as he felt the pain and saw the monster pulling his body closer to its own. Zachary wiggled and struggled, the physical pain secondary to his rampant fear. He kicked and swung with his one capable arm. He didn't care if he broke free and fell ten feet to the ground—anything would be better than getting close to that awful *thing.*

His shoulder started to go numb and Zachary felt a coldness spreading from his wound throughout his body. It was as if his very essence was freezing from contact with the beast.

Tssnnnkkknnntcchhhh. It hissed as it brought Zachary close enough to grab with its two long, clawed arms. Its massive hands wrapped around his midsection and held him firmly in place while it brutally dislodged its appendage from his shoulder.

Rippppppp. Cracckk! It pulled its arm upward and tore through his flesh and bone. The appendage exited through his upper shoulder, leaving it mangled and hanging from the socket. Zachary didn't even try to move it—the sound, combined with the rush of terrible pain, told him his shoulder was irreparably destroyed.

The creature brought him closer. As had everyone who had been close to the beast, Zachary did not want to see its face—he knew it was a nightmare.

But Zachary didn't have a choice in the matter. The beast revealed itself. With a strong flick of its neck, it launched its hood back. Before Zachary could turn away, the creature's face saw the light of day.

Zachary started losing his mind when he saw a sight that couldn't exist. It was a sight that couldn't have been real, yet was staring him straight in the eye.

The face under the hood was that of Ernie Stevens. It was the Ernie Stevens who had been a scourge to his life and murdered moments earlier. There were some startling new developments to his features, however, that told Zachary this wasn't the same Ernie Stevens he knew.

It had the basic semblance of Ernie Stevens' face. There was his brown mustache and wavy hair along with his straight nose and slightly raised cheekbones. The face could be identified as being Ernie Stevens-like, but the similarities stopped there.

There were no eyes. That was the first thing Zachary noticed. There *were* eyes, this thing was seeing him—yet there were *no* eyes.

Two deep, dark craters sat where Ernie Stevens' hazel eyes were supposed to be. They were holes as big as baseballs, cracked and jagged around the edges as if they were slowly expanding and shattering the rest of Ernie's face in the process. They were deep chasms with no sign of eyes or anything but utter darkness. It was like someone had taken a China doll and carved the eyes out completely, leaving awful craters surrounded by cracked, dead flesh.

But these holes were *looking* at Zachary. They were peering into his soul and analyzing every thought, feeling, and memory he had ever had. The eyes were *raping* his soul and he felt disgust and agony as he was sized up by the creature.

It was then Zachary noticed the flesh was dead. There was

a greenish hue to it he had not noticed while transfixed upon the eyes. Chunks of flesh were missing here and there, and within the wounds were puss-filled growths that looked like swollen pimples ready to burst.

Its mouth was smiling, but the mouth was no longer normal. Since the thing had revealed its face the mouth had grown exponentially, stretching across the cheeks in an unnatural smile. A bloated tongue hung listlessly out of the side of Ernie's mouth, looking as malformed and puss-filled as the putrid lumps within the wounds. His gums were shiny and black as night with chunky, rotten, black blood seeping from them. There were no teeth. As Zachary stared at the monstrosity, he lost all sense of reality.

Those eyes were the gateway to Hell. Zachary was staring at not a face, but a representation of everything wrong with existence.

Then the sight changed again. The face of Ernie Stevens peeled away and morphed into something even more horrifying.

His scream devolved into a wet cry as his face was ripped away from his skull. The pain was the most immense that could be experienced, as Zachary's flesh and soul were consumed in hefty, savage bites.

The Harbinger then stopped playing with its food and proceeded to eat him. It crunched into his skull and feasted on his succulent brain. It took a few more hearty bites before discarding the corpse without a second thought. There were many other courses to move on to.

Zachary was but an appetizer.

THIRTY

Ben and Elise arrived hand-in-hand to the scene of mass violence, but like the participants they could see nothing but a wall of gray haze.

Ben noticed the fog had grown thicker and stopped walking, drawing a breath as he did. “I think it’s close.”

She nodded. “I can sense it, too. Are we going to have to face it alone?”

“Together.”

“You know, I was scared just a minute ago, but standing here with you I don’t think I’m afraid of anything.”

"I know how you feel." The moment was tender and Ben had enough bravado to move in for another kiss. Just as he was contemplating it, he saw a shadowy figure lunging at him from the corner of his eye.

Ben pushed Elise away and turned to face the attacker. It had appeared out of nowhere, hidden and lurking behind the thick mist.

Swipe! Ben felt the air in front of his face move as something sliced through it. He stumbled back a step, and then was able to get an eye on his attacker, who stood only an arm's length away.

It was Tony Ristori, Ben's own next door neighbor. The middle-aged man was equipped with a baseball bat that had come mere inches from smashing Ben's face.

Ben looked to him with disbelief. "Tony?" he asked dumbfounded.

Tony didn't respond. He lunged like a warrior confronting his enemy. Suddenly the man didn't appear to be Tony Ristori at all but a horrible, zombified version of him. Those eyes weren't the relaxed, gentle eyes of Tony Ristori. They were dead and blank, as alienating and disturbing as the fog itself. He let out a battle cry and swung the bat again. Ben jumped backward to dodge the swing. "Tony, what's the matter with you?"

"I'll fucking kill you!" Tony roared as he rushed forward. One misstep from Ben was all it took for Tony to catch up to him and connect with a frenzied swing.

THWAP! The baseball bat struck Ben's hip and he felt a rich wave of pain. He doubled over and fell to his knees. Tony had hit him on the point of the bone and the painful daggers that came as a result forced Ben to submit.

The man Ben had always thought of as quiet and amiable now stood before him a crazed psychopath, looking to Ben with merciless eyes as he raised the bat to deliver the killing blow.

And just before Tony was about to strike, Ben saw it. Looking into those malevolent eyes, Ben saw the creature, the essence of the monster terrorizing his town. In Tony's savagery he saw hatred as pure and unadulterated as what he felt in the presence of The Harbinger.

It had poisoned him. Perhaps it had directly poisoned the whole town. Ben remained stricken by this concept as Tony swung the bat toward the crown of his skull.

THUD! Another being came out of the fog, and this one stopped Tony Ristori dead in his tracks. The look on his face went from crazed to pained as all air was forced from his lungs with the powerful blow.

Ben blinked and shook his head. He then saw what had come out of the mist and saved his life.

Elise stood between Ben and Tony, her foot deeply embedded in Tony's crotch. She had delivered a solid strike to his testicles. Tony stood for a moment before falling over onto his side, gasping and wheezing in pain.

Elise scrambled over to Ben and helped him to his feet.

"Are you okay? Can you walk?" The fear in her eyes was a far cry from the serenity that had been there in the tender moment prior.

Ben winced and grabbed his hip. "I took a shot but I should be fine." He did his best to force a smile through his grimace. "You saved my ass."

"I'd say I saved your head."

"You're a wise-ass."

"You love it." There was a pause and somehow the sweet moment began to develop again before the groan of the rising Tony Ristori snapped them back to reality.

"Let's get the hell outta here before he gets more fight in him," Elise said. They darted off through the fog. They barely made it ten feet when they encountered another person in the haze, this one too far away to identify but close enough to see he was holding a revolver and pointing it their way.

Ben and Elise ducked and dodged, running as far from the assailant as they could. It almost wasn't enough. Ben felt the force of a bullet whiz by his right ear, coming within inches of slamming into his skull. The sound of the shot was drowned out by the fog. There could have been an innumerable amount of bullets flying through the air while Ben and Elise were none the wiser.

"What's happened to Rowley?" Elise shouted as they ran aimlessly through the chaos.

"Everyone's falling apart. They let the thing poison them," Ben replied, nearly tripping over a corpse.

"They're killing each other! But *it's* here, too. That thing is here and they're fighting each other." Elise became desperate as she finally realized they were getting no help. "What do we do?" She pleaded for answers—in those trying moments Ben had been emerging as saint and savior.

All he could do was provide an honest answer as they dipped and dodged the obstacles in the skirmish.

"I don't know."

Dan McNair didn't know either. He knew nothing besides insanity and hatred. Finally pushed over the edge, Dan released his years of bottled frustration by firing his 9mm at random people in the fog. His only semblance of a purpose was to prove his power and manhood to a figure that did not exist.

Dan McNair's uncle had been dead for years and Dan was well aware of this. However, the fog had been able to pull out the unresolved memories that became his undoing. He had been teetering on the edge of sanity and those conceptions were what finally pushed him over the edge.

The only thing that mattered was proving his dead uncle wrong. Dan McNair was a *man* and he was a man in *charge.*

He smiled. "A man in charge," he said to himself as he squeezed the trigger of his handgun and put a round into the forehead of Bobby Koloski. He was aware he had killed six people in the skirmish (unbeknownst to him he had killed an additional two with stray bullets) and he hoped he could kill many more.

I'll show every one of them!

He raised his gun and moved in circular motions, aware he could be hit from any angle in the free-for-all. He searched for someone else to kill, but in the process stumbled upon his ultimate goal. He nearly walked into the figure—he stopped only a few feet from where it stood.

He saw the hooded beast described to him by witnesses, only this thing was much more formidable than what had been portrayed. It had giant, bug-like legs coming out of its back and supporting it. They were monstrous and twitched and lurched even as the figure stood completely still.

Its regular arms held a victim within their grasp. The powerful claws locked around the man's arms just above the elbows. The helpless victim kicked and struggled but all efforts were in vain as the beast pulled in either direction. With a sickening rip the man's arms were torn out of their sockets.

A speck of blood landed on Dan McNair's cheek as he stood unblinking, captivated not by the gruesome sight of the man's body falling to the ground or the creature's carefree tossing aside of the man's limbs, but by the sight of the thing's face.

Its hood was pulled back and Dan saw something he had been seeing in his nightmares for twenty-three years.

The face of the creature was that of his dead uncle, Chad Weiss. It had his pudgy face and raised cheekbones, his small, upwardly-turned nose resembling that of a pig, his stringy blonde going on gray hair, and his fat lips, complete with yellowing, cigarette-stained teeth.

The only thing different were the eyes. Instead of his icy blue eyes, there were two deep holes, each seeming to be crudely dug into the area where his eye sockets should have been. They were dark and empty as if the inside of his uncle's head was hollow. They were also oddly proportioned, with each of them taking up too much of his face. The outsides of the holes were cracked and worn and the flesh around them gray and dead.

Dan didn't hear the victim letting out his last cries as he bled out on the ground only feet from him. He didn't take time to consider that the being before him was not his uncle but an unholy monstrosity—to Dan all that mattered was his uncle was there.

Now was his opportunity to prove his manhood.

"You bastard! I'll kill you once and for all!" Dan pointed his pistol at Uncle Chad and fired right into his body. As he shouted, Uncle Chad looked up from his victim and walked toward Dan, using all four of his spider-legs to quickly traverse the area.

Uncle Chad stopped when round after round ripped through the soft fabric of his robe and lodged into his chest. To Dan's surprise, Uncle Chad did not grimace in pain or fall backward and die—instead he put on a smile—an impossibly *large* smile. It was as if his lips had conquered more of his face, growing so fast Dan had not even been able to observe the change.

His normally puffy lips were now thick and fat. Uncle Chad smiled at Dan, and a bloated tongue fell from the side of his mouth. It was infected and held a blackish, purple hue. There were yellowing boles on his tongue, which flapped and wiggled with every one of his motions. Every time a bullet found its way into Uncle Chad's body, the smile became broader, and as it did Dan saw the black, infected gums barely holding his uncle's teeth into place.

His uncle's mouth finally stopped growing. It became frozen in its disgusting smile. Uncle Chad tilted his head to the side, cocking it like a bird would. His head turned and turned until it was nearly sideways, his swollen tongue loosely hanging out of the side of his mouth.

And though the lips did not move, Uncle Chad spoke to him. "*You think you're tough, you faggot? You think 'cause you got a gun that makes you a big man? Hahahahahah! I'm going to show you what a real man is! I'm going to show you a real man's cock just like I did when you were a boy!"*

"You shut up," Dan shouted. "You shut the fuck up now, you stupid bastard! You took my childhood! You took my fucking childhood!" Dan's scream now merged with a sorrow-filled cry as he aimed his gun and fired the last remaining round into the skull of his uncle, the bullet striking him squarely between the eyes.

There was no blood. There was no recoil. Uncle Chad's face remained frozen in its sickening smile. The only difference was now he had a small, dark hole in between his eyebrows, a hole that seemed to reveal a hollow, empty skull.

"What are you?" Dan asked The Harbinger, lowering his gun and staring in horrified awe.

It did not respond. Instead, using its powerful back legs it leaped through the air, tongue waving around wildly as it came crashing down on its prey.

Its top two appendages pierced through Dan's shoulders and slammed him to the ground, pinning him while the beast arched itself over his body. Just as Uncle Chad had pinned Dan down and had his way with him twenty-three years earlier, he did so again.

Dan couldn't breathe. He was wrought with physical pain and the wrenching memories of what had corrupted his childhood. He couldn't avoid or fight them now—Uncle Chad was upon him and forced Dan to relive it all.

"Why? Why?" Dan sobbed the same words he had as a child.

Twenty-three years earlier, Uncle Chad had answered by kissing his neck and beginning the molestation. Now, Uncle Chad did something much worse.

Six deep cuts sprang from Uncle Chad's nose, all of them straight lines running across the entirety of his rubbery face. They bled lightly, in the way a wound would if a scab had broken, and despite his child-like fear and confusion, Dan knew something awful was about to happen.

Somehow he knew what was coming.

With a sticky ripping sound the beast began to feed.

Uncle Chad's face peeled back, each section defined by the bloody lines lifting up and pulling back like the blossoming petal of a flower. As the face peeled away, Dan saw the atrocity that lay beneath.

Teeth. Countless teeth.

The thing's head had opened up and Dan was mere inches from the inside of its face flaps, each lined with bloody muscle and covered in row after row of tiny, razor-sharp teeth. They lined each petal of its mouth, leading straight back to the throat.

It was a black, dark hole, a gateway to the hellish existence that came with being consumed by this beast. It was only the size of a plate, but it was darker and denser than anything Dan's mind could understand.

It was a portal to an existence no soul deserved to suffer.

Dan couldn't comprehend the nature of the beast about to consume him. He continued attempting to wrap his mind around it when the flower-mouth closed over his face and the countless razor-sharp teeth slowly started grinding away at him.

The teeth dug into and tore away at his skin, running up and down and grating away at his flesh. Each tooth moved independently and seemed to have a goal of its own. No inch of his face was spared and his wounds were bitten into time and time again. The teeth dealt with his skin first, stripping Dan's face of it before diving into the muscle and tissue below. The process was agonizingly slow and Dan felt every bit of anguish. He let out low whimpers as the beast sunk a few of its teeth into his eyeballs, consuming the eyelids before popping his eyes and devouring them.

Tkksnknnntchhkkknntchh, the beast cried out in pleasure.

Next Dan's cheeks, flesh and bone together, were torn away from his face. He heard the crunching sound as his nose was ground up and eaten, and continued to hear all the noises until the flaps of the monster's mouth reached around the side of his head and bit his ears off.

Even as Dan's ears were ripped away he still heard something. Up until the very moment in which he died, Dan heard a noise that had haunted his dreams for most of his life.

The last thing Dan McNair heard was Uncle Chad's raucous laughter, heartily chortling away as Dan's body was eaten and his soul eternally consumed.

The Harbinger took its time eating Dan McNair. The amount of strife and hatred within his being made him a delicacy. The rest of its courses could surely wait until The Harbinger was done enjoying this particularly tasty morsel. It had prepared Dan incredibly well. It had drawn out the most twisted and delicious parts of his psyche. This made its conquest of him pure ecstasy.

After The Harbinger had eaten every bit of Dan's flesh (and even the bone, which was rare for the creature) it continued to do the two things it knew how to do.

Kill and eat.

It flew through the fog at impressive speeds, using its newly-formed appendages to strike out and impale unsuspecting victims. It pulled in two here, three there, toying with them for a short time before tearing their bodies completely apart. Even the ones who were beyond hatred, the few people in the meleé who wanted out, couldn't escape now. The fog had surrounded them all. It was The Harbinger's trap and as long they were in proximity, they could not escape.

It was like shooting fish in a barrel.

Everything was going wonderfully for the hell-beast, but when it ripped out the throat of Jill Donovan it realized what was close.

Love. The feeling of it burned The Harbinger. The two lovers were approaching.

The Harbinger tossed Jill Donovan's ragged body aside and moved to take care of business. It would free itself from all bothers, then continue to consume.

Kill and eat. Eat and kill.

It dashed off into the mist in the direction of Ben Dowling and Elise Sutter.

Thirty-one

“Do you feel that?” Elise stopped them.

“What?” Ben asked gasping, hoping another maniac wasn’t coming their way.

“Cold. It just got colder, it’s *still* getting colder.”

Ben felt the tips of his fingers protest as chilly air surrounded them. His heart rate increased yet his blood cooled.

“It’s coming,” he said, and Elise nodded with certainty.

“This is it.” She was calmer than he had anticipated. In the time they had been taking on this task her emotions had fluctuated greatly, but now she was steadfast in her demeanor.

Ben kept his hand in hers and turned to the right, Elise following his every motion. It was coming from that way. Ben could feel it, and the one thing Ben knew he could trust was his feelings.

They were perhaps his only hope.

"What are we going to do?" If there was nervousness in Elise's voice, Ben missed it.

"We're not going to let it win. We're going to tell that thing this is our town. We're not going to let it scare us. We're not going to let it poison our minds. We're not going to give into its games. That thing is only as strong as we make it. We are going to reclaim our town."

"I think everyone else has made it very strong."

"Then we're going to have to be stronger." Ben turned his head, looked at Elise and kissed her softly. She met his lips with her own and they danced together only for a brief moment before the kiss was interrupted by the terrible sound.

Tsskknnntchhknktsschhh.

Both turned and saw the beast appear out of the fog. It had changed greatly since they first saw it. They noticed the deep black appendages protruding from its back and acting as legs. They also noticed how long its arms and deadly claws had become. The hatred of the town had obviously fueled the monster's transformation.

But when they saw the creature's face, both of them saw something very different but equally as debilitating. The sight was enough to rattle them to the point where The Harbinger was able to draw out sweet fear from their bodies.

Ben saw a face similar to what the others had seen. It was

an apparition's face, complete with distorted features including a hanging tongue. It was, however, a much closer representation of the real thing than the others had been. The identity of this face brought a crippling sense of panic to Ben's heart.

It was Elise's face—the face of the angel he loved so dearly. Her skin was as soft and flawless as it had always been. Her delicate lips were trembling slightly as she stared at Ben, facial features forlorn. The representation was uncanny: her wavy blonde hair was the same color, texture, and length as always, her nose was identical, her cheekbones flawless, but there was one major difference in this Elise.

Instead of her beautiful, emerald green eyes there were two dark holes roughly cut into her head. Ben's mind struggled to make sense of this. He was so drawn in by the resemblance to Elise that he tried to explain their existence rather than reject what he was seeing.

Then suddenly she spoke to him.

"Ben, how could you? How could you let me die? How could you let me be brought right into the arms of the monster? Didn't you love me, Ben? Didn't you want to keep me safe?"

"I do want to keep you safe," Ben replied, playing into the beast's game. Elise's lips were not moving, yet she was speaking to him. Her voice came out of the fog.

His logic failed him as the haze brought out his fear of losing Elise, emotions so powerful they made him temporarily irrational. Despite the fact she stood right next to him he was transfixed.

Her soft skin began to change, slowly at first, then more rapidly. It peeled away from her face, small wounds tearing themselves open and revealing bloody infections below. Her skin was ripped away by an unknown force and her mouth opened in a desperate, silent scream. Bloody tears spurted out of her eye-holes and ran down her face. His beautiful angel was becoming the picture of a nightmare, and still she called out into his mind.

"You've killed me. This is what I shall become and it is all your fault. Why, Ben? How could you let me down? I thought you loved me." The voice was truly that of Elise and the sound of her disappointment and heartbreak was almost too much for Ben to bear.

Ben's eyes began to water. "I-I do, Elise . . ."

She titled her head and walked toward Ben, her arms extending as if she was preparing to embrace him. Her skin was still peeling away, rotting and falling off the bone in chunks.

Then she began to twitch.

Elise saw a similar sight to the one Ben had seen, however, for her, the face on The Harbinger was Ben's. It was a perfect match to his own save for those terrible dark holes. Like Ben, Elise was stricken by this ghastly apparition of her lover mourning and pleading.

"Save me now! Grab me and run before I end up like this. It's going to eat my soul. It's going to rip out my eyes! It wants to eat us both! Run, save me! Save us both! I don't want to become part of the fog!" His skin peeled away and blood gushed from his eyes—both Ben and Elise were seeing the same horrifying picture of each other approaching and both were rattled to their cores.

The Harbinger started twitching, spinning its head to the

side at an impossible angle while reaching out for them. It drew closer and closer and couldn't wait to sink its teeth into the pair.

Their moment of weakness gave it power over them. Their fearful state readied their bodies for consumption, and The Harbinger prepared to strike.

Then Ben felt Elise's hand grasp his more firmly, and the touch of her warm skin to his own jolted him free of the illusion. He stepped forward, positioning himself in front of her as a guardian.

"You're not Elise! I love Elise! I'll protect her until my last breath and even if that's coming now I'll die loving her. That's more powerful than fear, hatred, or anything else you're going to throw at me. You can kill me but you're never going to stop my love!" Ben proclaimed fiercely, standing firm in between the creature and Elise without an ounce of fear. The spark of his love and will to protect Elise wiped all worry away.

The Harbinger halted its approach. It looked to him with questions in its mind—it had a moment of *hesitation.*

"And I love Ben." Elise stepped forward and stood defiantly beside him. It was barely ten feet from them but they stood together unwavering. "Kill me, I don't care. I'm in love."

It was like a quote from a movie and Ben was hit with another surge of warmth at the words. This was no façade. He wasn't *using* his love as a weapon—he was feeling it and its power because it was true, and because of that, he didn't fear a thing.

The Harbinger was enraged by this. A moment prior it had a delicious meal, and now it was being faced with the awful feelings of bravery and love. These were as toxic to it as fear and hatred were to its victims—it didn't even want to be *near* such feelings, let alone eat them.

It showed its anger, waving its appendages around violently, swinging them with force toward Ben and Elise. It slashed its claws through the air and let out its terrible hiss. One slash would kill them both, one strike and their faces would be obliterated—but still they stood unblinking and unwavering, hands tightly clasped together.

"I love her, and I love my town!" Ben shouted. "You can kill and cause destruction and do whatever you please but I'll still love my town. This is where I grew up. This is where my friends and family are from. I love them all and you can't stop that!" Ben let his heart spill forth memories of the past—memories of enjoying sports with friends in Rowley Park, memories of riding his bike all across town in the cool autumn air, memories of celebrations with his family and special moments with Elise. He felt it all unabated. Nothing the creature could do could take away his love or his memories. It held nothing over him.

"Kill me and I'll still love forever."

TSSSKKKNNTSSSTCHHHSSNNTCKKK, it responded, spitting its bloated tongue from its mouth. It was falling apart, losing its composure, and in desperation it lunged forward. Using its back spider legs, it jumped and landed in front of the pair, towering over them with claws and appendages raised and ready to strike.

Elise looked up at the nightmare, and then slowly and carefully turned to Ben. If this was her last moment it would be a romantic one. Their eyes met and there was nothing else in the world. There was no fog, no monster, no tragedy in their town They looked into each other's eyes and saw years of happiness and care, years of a love carefully cultivated until that one special moment.

It was beautiful, and in an odd way neither would have preferred it to turn out in any other fashion. Their lips met and it was love in its purest form. They embraced and waited for the inevitable.

But it never came.

They held the embrace and the kiss, ready to accept their fates. It was then they heard the sound of the beast's shriek.

It was the same hissing noise as always, but they could hear *pain* once more. They turned and looked to see the beast staggering backward, wildly flailing its claws and appendages. It gathered its bearings but still continued to go backward.

It was *retreating.*

For Ben, it made perfect sense. Hate is as powerful as one lets it be. Yes, the town had allowed the beast to become powerful but there was one thing that could stop hatred right in its tracks and that was love.

Love doesn't allow the spread of malice or strife. Love puts an end to the bitter, festering emotions of cowardice and hatred.

The big, bad shadowy nightmare was afraid of love and it ran away from Ben and Elise.

Ben wouldn't let it escape that easily. "Elise, we have to get it!" he declared as their kiss ended.

She nodded, staring at him a woman won over. "Together."

Both ran toward the monster—something that had never happened to The Harbinger.

"I love her! I love this town! I love the people here! I'm going to live here and love here and rebuild! It's wonderful. I'll get to enjoy the fall festival and the winter concert and every play at the theater. I love it all!" Ben shouted at the creature as he pursued it, the beast stumbling backward and whipping its arms at Ben to keep him back.

"I'll die for this town! I'll die because I love it! Either you love it or you get out! There's no place for hatred here! I'm going to embrace every innocent survivor of your evil!"

TSSKKKNNTCHHH! TSSKKKKKKKCCH-HHTNNNKKK! It was obviously in pain, and its own emotional sensitivity had gone from its strength to its downfall. The Harbinger couldn't ignore the emotions in the air, and the powerful nature of the love radiating from Ben and Elise was too much to handle. It burned through the monster's core and began destroying the evil giving it power.

It had to get away. It had to escape. Killing them would only result in absorbing the pure love it so desperately wanted to avoid. Despite all of the hatred it had caused and harvested, this one case of love was more powerful than all else combined.

The Harbinger had to go through with one last-ditch effort. It had to strike fear into their hearts if it was to have any chance of consuming their souls. It couldn't give up on this town so easily. With disregard for its own safety, it stopped its retreat and charged.

Ben stood in front of Elise, waiting patiently for whatever was to come. He was no longer afraid of death or whatever the thing could do to him. If he had to die to save his town, then so be it.

The Harbinger got to Ben and rose to full height in front of him. It raised one appendage, violently striking Ben with great force and sending him sprawling through the air.

Ben flew through the fog before slamming down to earth. He landed harshly on his side, then bounced and tumbled over the pavement for fifteen feet, acquiring various scrapes, bruises, and a sprained wrist along the way.

The Harbinger hissed in agony as it felt its appendage burn from contact with the love-filled being. Its spider leg twitched and shook before suddenly retreating back into The Harbinger's body, popping as it snapped itself back into place and slid under the robe.

Elise was hit with a sudden rush of fear. She hurried over to where Ben lay, nearly hysterical, fearing she had lost the man she loved.

"Ben, oh my God. Ben, are you okay?" she asked.

The Harbinger felt her fear return and let out a mighty cry. It could get her now—and once it got her, it would be easy to get him. Their love could be used against them to bring out fear and suffering.

It charged Elise.

Ben reached up and grabbed Elise's arm as she knelt before him. "I'm fine. I'm better than I've ever been. Don't be afraid, that's how it can hurt us. Be strong and face it. It has your face when I look at it and I think you see mine. Look at my face on that monster and see me—don't see that nightmare, see me. And love me Elise. Love me and this town and it can't hurt either of us."

"But—"

"Elise," Ben gasped, "trust me." His eyes won her over like they never had before. She turned and stood, awaiting the beast with a newfound confidence.

It came upon her and arched itself up, raising its three appendages and two sets of claws high into the air while it paused to determine whether it really should strike. As it opened itself up, Elise stared at the destroyed face of Ben with its torn, bleeding tissue and hollow eyes, and forced herself to see his real face.

She felt love for Ben and before her eyes the face healed. It went from a bloody nightmare to a normal representation of Ben's face—save for the eyes which remained as cold and dead as ever.

"I love you, Ben Dowling, and I always will," Elise said calmly as she felt her heart flutter at thoughts of a future with Ben. She reached forward and gave the beast something it had never before received:

An act of love.

Elise wrapped her arms around the hooded figure and put her face into its chest without any concern for her own safety. She imagined she actually was holding Ben in her arms and she hugged with all the strength and love she could muster. "I love you," she said, Ben the only one on her mind.

The Harbinger froze, and for ten seconds there was nothing but stillness and silence. After that pause, Elise heard a weak, defeated cry. It was a hiss much feebler than anything the creature had ever before uttered.

It was a dying cry.

It squirmed and struggled, trying to wiggle free of Elise's

grasp without touching her. Soon its motions became stronger and more panicked. It thrashed with ferocity but still Elise held firm.

Then it had no choice. With all the power it could muster, it pushed its hands down and shoved Elise, barely able to gather the strength to dislodge her from its body. The almighty Harbinger was able only to knock Elise backward with enough force to break her grasp and cause her to temporarily lose her balance.

It stood back from Elise and raised its head to the sky, waving its arms and appendages around as it suffered defeat. It cried out, *Tskknnkknnntchhhh! Tsssknkntchhhhh!* But these cries were of sadness, pain, and loss. No longer were they sounds that drove fear into the soul. They were cries to be *pitied.*

Then came the fog.

It was like they were at the center of a vacuum. All around them air whirled and pulled itself toward The Harbinger. The fog was returning to its source, entering the robe of The Harbinger at every opening, causing the dark cloak to flap violently in the new wind.

It threw its body around while it took back its essence, its cries drowned out by the deafening sound of the fog as it whipped, swirled, and came back into place.

Ben forced his way to his feet and embraced Elise. He held onto her so neither of them would be pulled into the beast by the force of the winds. They saw bodies flying through the whirlwind along with the haze. They were the dead bodies of those who had been poisoned by The Harbinger's hatred. All the evils The Harbinger had brought and created were returning to their source.

The bodies of the dead careened through the air, merging with the mist and becoming sucked up into the void that was The Harbinger. The dead were consumed for good, taken away with the awful fog that had corrupted them. When all had returned, The Harbinger swelled up, its robe expanded to ridiculous proportions, and exploded.

With a force equal to that which had just sucked in all of the hatred, The Harbinger sent itself and the fog outward in a single, mighty shock wave. Ben and Elise were able to stand firmly with arms wrapped around each other. Every other person in the vicinity was floored by the sudden blast and extreme force, but Ben and Elise stood tall.

Together.

The shockwave lasted only a moment, and when it was gone so were The Harbinger, the fog, and all the madness they had caused.

The intersection of Church and Main was suddenly illuminated with bright sunshine bearing down from a cloudless blue sky. The surviving townspeople, most of whom were still armed and in combat mode, looked around dazed and bewildered. Confusion swept over them as the constant fog suddenly vanished. The sunshine then began to not only illuminate in a physical sense, but enlighten their minds and break them free of the fog's trance.

People awoke. They saw the nature of the madness they had partaken in and realized the destruction they had wrought. Some broke down and sobbed, others waited for the dream to end, and a few more embraced, grateful the ordeal was over.

Ben and Elise stood in an embrace. Around them the blood of the fallen stained the streets and served as evidence the nightmare had been all too real. Citizens wept, the injured staggered, and the smell of three blocks worth of burning homes permeated through the air as fire raged. Despite all of the chaos around them, in that special moment, Ben and Elise only knew the reality of each other and their love.

Even as their town lay in shambles around them, Ben and Elise held each other and kissed. They continued that kiss as they felt hope, love, and sanity return to a town that had become desperately lost.

The fog had cleared, and for Rowley there would be a new tomorrow.

Epilogue

Larry Eckman sat on a park bench in Clarton, Vermont, and thought about how the town had changed in his forty-three years of living there. He had moved to the sleepy, rural town of Clarton from Boston when he was just thirteen years old. His family liked it there because, unlike the city, it was quiet and peaceful. It was an idyllic getaway from the hustle and bustle of Boston.

Larry never really liked it in Clarton. He always missed Boston; there was always so much to do and fun to be had. Clarton was a place for old people to rot as they sat around feeding birds in the park.

Larry came to prove his own theory. As he sat

on the bench and threw birdseed to the pigeons, he thought about how living in Clarton had drained him of his ambitions over the years. He had settled into the easy, peaceful life the town offered but he had also given up all ambition for leisure. Forty-three years after moving from Boston he was still in Clarton, but unlike then he had no real future ahead of him.

People just come here to die, he thought bitterly as he tossed a large handful of seed toward one particularly bloated pigeon. It was harassing the others and pushing them out of the way, so Larry decided to give it its own little pile. Hopefully it would leave the others alone.

The pigeons brought him peace. They took him into a calm realm where he didn't have to think about the past, present, or future. All that mattered was what was at hand and that was feeding the pigeons, who like Larry, never really seemed to leave the town.

C'mon, it can't be that bad of a place, his thoughts tried to reason with him.

No, it is that bad. Clarton's caught up in the petty small town mentality. It's filled with small town politics, liars, and hypocrites. Everyone here pretends they're happy when deep down they're absolutely miserable.

Larry failed to note the hypocrisy in his own thoughts. He failed to take notice of how when he generalized the population of the town, he actually was giving a spot-on description of himself.

Larry hadn't placed any blame on himself over the years. No, it wasn't his fault he was stuck in the dead-end town. It was Bucky Meyers' fault—he was the one who cost Larry that baseball scholarship when . . .

The birds suddenly flew away, taking off as one flock and flying through the summer air with a speed and desperation Larry had never seen from his avian friends.

They left mounds of feed behind as they took off into the sky and so quickly began fading into the horizon. They left as if something spooked them, like that one time when a child hopped on the sidewalk near them.

This time was different though. This time there was no pesky kid or immediate danger—there wasn't anyone else in the entire park. There was just Larry, sitting on the bench feeding the birds and getting lost in morose thoughts about his life.

Then he noticed this wasn't the case. There was fog slowly creeping in from across the stream that defined the back boundary of the park. Where did it come from?

Larry stood up and let the bag of birdseed spill from his lap onto the ground. He was mesmerized by the rolling haze as it came across the open green field of Langley Park. It was so different, unlike anything Larry had seen before. He was captivated, but also somewhere deep down he was petrified.

I ain't never seen a fog like that, not here in Clarton.

Clarton, Vermont was in for a great many surprises.

David James Bright is an author of horror and transgressive fiction. His debut novel, Harbinger, has received acclaim from such authors as New York Times Best Seller Jonathan Maberry. He is currently a graduate student at the University of Scranton and resides in northeastern Pennsylvania.

HOBBES END PUBLISHING

For the latest news about our authors and events, or to learn more about upcoming releases and other projects from Hobbes End Publishing, visit:

www.HobbesEndPublishing.com

10819927R00214

Made in the USA
San Bernardino, CA
26 April 2014

an apparition's face, complete with distorted features including a hanging tongue. It was, however, a much closer representation of the real thing than the others had been. The identity of this face brought a crippling sense of panic to Ben's heart.

It was Elise's face—the face of the angel he loved so dearly. Her skin was as soft and flawless as it had always been. Her delicate lips were trembling slightly as she stared at Ben, facial features forlorn. The representation was uncanny: her wavy blonde hair was the same color, texture, and length as always, her nose was identical, her cheekbones flawless, but there was one major difference in this Elise.

Instead of her beautiful, emerald green eyes there were two dark holes roughly cut into her head. Ben's mind struggled to make sense of this. He was so drawn in by the resemblance to Elise that he tried to explain their existence rather than reject what he was seeing.

Then suddenly she spoke to him.

"Ben, how could you? How could you let me die? How could you let me be brought right into the arms of the monster? Didn't you love me, Ben? Didn't you want to keep me safe?"

"I do want to keep you safe," Ben replied, playing into the beast's game. Elise's lips were not moving, yet she was speaking to him. Her voice came out of the fog.

His logic failed him as the haze brought out his fear of losing Elise, emotions so powerful they made him temporarily irrational. Despite the fact she stood right next to him he was transfixed.

Her soft skin began to change, slowly at first, then more rapidly. It peeled away from her face, small wounds tearing steadfast in her demeanor.

Ben kept his hand in hers and turned to the right, Elise following his every motion. It was coming from that way. Ben could feel it, and the one thing Ben knew he could trust was his feelings.

They were perhaps his only hope.

"What are we going to do?" If there was nervousness in Elise's voice, Ben missed it.

"We're not going to let it win. We're going to tell that thing this is our town. We're not going to let it scare us. We're not going to let it poison our minds. We're not going to give into its games. That thing is only as strong as we make it. We are going to reclaim our town."

"I think everyone else has made it very strong."

"Then we're going to have to be stronger." Ben turned his head, looked at Elise and kissed her softly. She met his lips with her own and they danced together only for a brief moment before the kiss was interrupted by the terrible sound.

Tsskknnntchhknktsschhh.

Both turned and saw the beast appear out of the fog. It had changed greatly since they first saw it. They noticed the deep black appendages protruding from its back and acting as legs. They also noticed how long its arms and deadly claws had become. The hatred of the town had obviously fueled the monster's transformation.

But when they saw the creature's face, both of them saw something very different but equally as debilitating. The sight was enough to rattle them to the point where The Harbinger was able to draw out sweet fear from their bodies.

Ben saw a face similar to what the others had seen. It was

Its regular arms held a victim within their grasp. The powerful claws locked around the man's arms just above the elbows. The helpless victim kicked and struggled but all efforts were in vain as the beast pulled in either direction. With a sickening rip the man's arms were torn out of their sockets.

A speck of blood landed on Dan McNair's cheek as he stood unblinking, captivated not by the gruesome sight of the man's body falling to the ground or the creature's carefree tossing aside of the man's limbs, but by the sight of the thing's face.

Its hood was pulled back and Dan saw something he had been seeing in his nightmares for twenty-three years.

The face of the creature was that of his dead uncle, Chad Weiss. It had his pudgy face and raised cheekbones, his small, upwardly-turned nose resembling that of a pig, his stringy blonde going on gray hair, and his fat lips, complete with yellowing, cigarette-stained teeth.

The only thing different were the eyes. Instead of his icy blue eyes, there were two deep holes, each seeming to be crudely dug into the area where his eye sockets should have been. They were dark and empty as if the inside of his uncle's head was hollow. They were also oddly proportioned, with each of them taking up too much of his face. The outsides of the holes were cracked and worn and the flesh around them gray and dead.

Dan didn't hear the victim letting out his last cries as he bled out on the ground only feet from him. He didn't take time to consider that the being before him was not his uncle but an unholy monstrosity—to Dan all that mattered was his uncle was there.

Dan McNair didn't know either. He knew nothing besides insanity and hatred. Finally pushed over the edge, Dan released his years of bottled frustration by firing his 9mm at random people in the fog. His only semblance of a purpose was to prove his power and manhood to a figure that did not exist.

Dan McNair's uncle had been dead for years and Dan was well aware of this. However, the fog had been able to pull out the unresolved memories that became his undoing. He had been teetering on the edge of sanity and those conceptions were what finally pushed him over the edge.

The only thing that mattered was proving his dead uncle wrong. Dan McNair was a *man* and he was a man in *charge.*

He smiled. "A man in charge," he said to himself as he squeezed the trigger of his handgun and put a round into the forehead of Bobby Koloski. He was aware he had killed six people in the skirmish (unbeknownst to him he had killed an additional two with stray bullets) and he hoped he could kill many more.

I'll show every one of them!

He raised his gun and moved in circular motions, aware he could be hit from any angle in the free-for-all. He searched for someone else to kill, but in the process stumbled upon his ultimate goal. He nearly walked into the figure—he stopped only a few feet from where it stood.

He saw the hooded beast described to him by witnesses, only this thing was much more formidable than what had been portrayed. It had giant, bug-like legs coming out of its back and supporting it. They were monstrous and twitched and lurched even as the figure stood completely still.